the best of cosmopolitan fiction

the best of cosmopolitan fiction

edited by Kate Figes

British Library Cataloguing-in-Publication Data

The best of Cosmopolitan fiction.
  I. Figes, Kate
  823 (F)

  ISBN 1-85242-226-2

First published 1991 by
Serpent's Tail, 4 Blackstock Mews, London N4

Typeset in 10½/12½pt Plantin by
AKM Associates (UK) Ltd., London

Printed in Finland by Werner Söderström Oy

contents

introduction

For many years now, *Cosmopolitan* magazine has published fiction of the highest quality from writers as talented and diverse as Margaret Atwood, John le Carré, Penelope Lively and Salman Rushdie. We are immensely proud of our track record; we devote more pages to fiction than any other glossy women's monthly magazine. We read manuscripts and proofs of hundreds of books months before they are published in order to select extracts from the finest and most controversial novels around, so that our readers see them first, often before publication.

We also read thousands of short stories from published and unpublished writers to find the very best for publication. I have made the final choice of twenty-four of these for inclusion in this selection of *Cosmopolitan* fiction. They reflect the range of talent published in *Cosmopolitan* over the years, with marvellous stories by many well known names – Maeve Binchy, Primo Levi, David Lodge, Alison Lurie, Edna O'Brien, Ruth Rendell and Alice Walker, as well as wonderful stories by writers who are less well known but no less talented: Rose Tremain, Tobias Wolff, Lorrie Moore, Lucy Ellmann and Alice Adams. All of these stories have had their first British publication in *Cosmopolitan* magazine, but the majority have not subsequently been published in anthologies. They have therefore disappeared in a sense and demand to be made really available again to a wider audience.

I have not included extracts from any novels because I feel that an extract from, say, Ian McEwan's *The Innocent* or Angela Carter's *Wise Children* (both of which have featured in the magazine) is less interesting months or even years after publication of the book itself. But I have included two winners from our annual short story award, Christine Harrison and

Janice Galloway. This award, co-sponsored by Perrier, is open to both published and unpublished writers and offers £6,000 in prize money.

I hope that regular readers of *Cosmopolitan* will find plenty of their favourite authors in this selection. I hope too that those not familiar with the wealth of fiction that can be found there will now turn to *Cosmopolitan* for a feast of fine writing in the future.

Kate Figes

the best of
cosmopolitan
fiction

maeve binchy

Picnic at St Paul's

Once, a long time ago, ten years ago, Catherine had spent a week in Suzi's smart Washington apartment. About four times a year for ten years she had reason to regret this, even though it had been pleasant enough at the time. But every three months or so, she got phone calls from Americans sent to torment her by Suzi.

"Hi, Catherine, I'm Mitzi Bernbach. I'm a friend of Suzi's. She said that I mustn't come to London without calling to say 'Hi'. Suzi's sent you a little gift. When can we meet so I can give it to you?"

Suzi's little gifts ranged from totally unusable, absurd toys like an elephant that held a pencil in his trunk to a map of some walk that Catherine had taken by the Potomac River in the distant past. She had to put on a show of enthusiasm for whoever had transported the gift, but always ended up feeling resentful, buying some ridiculous souvenir of London in return, and feeling under an ungracious obligation to entertain whatever wandering American had landed friendless in London. More than once she considered changing her address, but it seemed ridiculous to be hunted out of where she was happy by a vague threat from across the Atlantic.

Through all these penniless Mitzis and Jerrys and Chucks she had learned the course of Suzi's life. Suzi was still an ambitious young Washington hostess, for the younger set. She gathered people who were not yet successful but who had potential. She no longer ran her flower shop; instead she ran a contract flower hire service. Apparently, she visited the homes of rich people and advised them on what flowers to buy or rent for occasions: she then got commission from various florists for the orders that were put in. Only Suzi could have seen the potential in using the same set of expensive cut flowers for three separate occasions in a single day. She had been known to arrive in her van after a christening at one house to collect the flowers and rearrange them for someone else's bar mitzvah party, and take them on to a twenty-first all on the same day. Everybody paid slightly less for their flowers; everybody was happy.

But Catherine, though she admired Suzi's well-organised mind from afar, did wish that one day Suzi would lose her address where Catherine was filed under "Contact, useful, Britain". The last visitor had been a real pain. He had telephoned from the airport with some terrible tale about his friends not being there to meet him and Suzi having said that he must call Catherine if he was in any trouble. He had slept on Catherine's sofa for four nights. He never seemed to change his socks, her house smelled of feet for a week after he left, he had no money, no interests and no charm. He had even eaten the thoughtful gift of a jar of ginger which Suzi had sent Catherine this time.

So it was with a heavy heart that she greeted the voice on the phone, which told her yet again that Suzi had asked it to call. It called at midnight, just after she had gone to sleep. She thought it was morning, and was bitterly disappointed to find that it wasn't. Catherine hadn't been sleeping well, and she now regarded getting off to sleep as a kind of achievement. This new Suzi person had committed a great crime.

"I think I ought to tell you," Catherine said with tears in her voice, "I really don't know Suzi Dane at all well. Ten years ago, yes, ten whole years ago, I spent six nights in her apartment in Washington, while you were still at school. I knew her only because of a complete accident. I found her purse in a telephone kiosk and returned it to her. She invited me to stay for a week. I am not, as she claims, a lifelong friend. I have no room for anyone to stay. I have no time to take you to the Changing of the Guard, or to the Tower of London. I do not want to hear what Suzi is doing now, and how rich and successful she has become. I'm sorry, I know I'm taking it out on you, but really I've had quite enough of Suzi's friends, and I think it's better to tell you that straight out. Besides, I'd just got to sleep, and I haven't slept properly for weeks. Now I'll never get back to sleep."

To her horror she burst into tears.

There was a kind of silence interrupted by a few soothing noises at the other end of the phone. Catherine could hear them as she put down the receiver and went to hunt for some tissues. Twice, as she blew her nose hard, she made a move to hang up—she had been so rude, there was no saving the conversation now. Twice she didn't in case she thought of some way of rescuing it.

After a final blow, she picked up the receiver cautiously.

"Are you still there?" she asked.

"Yeah, I'm still here," said the voice, which didn't sound hurt, sulky or even surprised.

"Well, as you can gather you caught me at rather a bad time," she said. "Perhaps I should ask you to ring again. Tomorrow lunchtime maybe? I'll be fine by then. I'm very sorry for getting upset. I must have still been half asleep."

"That's OK. I shouldn't have called so late."

He didn't sound like Suzi's usual friends. He hadn't said yet how broke he was, how he had nowhere to stay, how he had carried over this little gift. Also to his credit, he didn't sound apologetic. Catherine couldn't have borne him to be sorry; it was in fact her fault, five past midnight wasn't too late to call someone.

"What was your name again? I'll telephone you when I'm awake," she said, trying to be cheerful.

"It's no use trying to go back to sleep if you've got insomnia," he said calmly. "The damage is done now. You must get up, have a shower, get dressed, and pretend it's day. Do whatever you'd do during the day. Vacuum the house, write letters, cook a meal, go for a walk, listen to the radio, read a book, but don't go back to bed, no matter how tired you feel."

"And how will I feel tomorrow?" she asked.

"Rotten, but you'll feel rotten anyway so why not get something done instead of lying there trying to go to sleep?"

"But we need sleep," said Catherine with interest.

"Not nearly as much as we think. In two or three days, you'll just drop off somewhere and sleep soundly. Listen, I'll leave you to get on with it all, and call in a few days."

"Get on with what?" asked Catherine in amazement.

"Whatever you're going to do," he said and hung up.

Startled at her own obedience, Catherine got up, washed and dressed. Then she made scrambled eggs and had a cigarette. She certainly felt more relaxed than she had at eleven o'clock when she had been worrying whether she would get to sleep that night. She took out all her old silver and polished it, she put on some Strauss waltzes which she liked but which Alec had said were impossible to listen to. She had pretended to Alec that she only kept them because they belonged to someone else.

When the silver was shining at her and reflecting her busy face bent over it, she decided that she'd put it out on a shelf rather than hide it in the back of the cupboard. Alec had thought it was vulgar to exhibit silver; the cottage mentality, he called it. He also said it was an invitation to burglars. Catherine put the silver on shelves around the room and stood back to admire it. Each piece had a story. The teapot was the first thing her parents had bought when they got married; they had hardly enough coal to light a fire but they thought you weren't properly married without a nice silver teapot. The silver rose vase was a gift from the office where she had worked happily for six years but which Alec said was a non-job. She had left it a year ago, and often wondered why she was no longer there. It had been happy, it had been cheerful going to work on Mondays. Most people didn't have that at work. She certainly didn't have that now.

The silver napkin ring had been a present from her sister Margie. Margie had saved for a year, putting a pound a week aside to get something in solid silver. Margie was innocent and simple. Alec thought she was very sweet and wondered whether she had had brain damage as a child. He thought that they should get her to see a specialist. Catherine knew that Margie was just slow and loved working in a hotel kitchen where they fed her, looked after her, and tucked her up at night in return for days scouring and scrubbing and washing up. Catherine thought that people should be left where they were if they were happy. She went to see Margie every week. It was two bus journeys and a taxi at the other end, and took up most of Sunday. Sometimes that irritated Alec if he wanted to spend the day with her. He only once went to the hotel. He had stayed an hour.

It was nearly three o'clock, Catherine realised, when she glanced at the digital watch which Alec had given her for Christmas. She had never got used to the way the figures changed on it; secretly she would have preferred a watch with hands. Where had the hours gone? No wonder she felt so tired, perhaps she should go to bed now, she would definitely sleep. But that odd Yank on the phone had sounded so certain that he was right in his plan, she didn't like to disobey him. She made more tea, found a programme on the World Service and started some knitting which she hadn't taken out for weeks. It was to be a big chunky sweater for Margie, red and white. It would make her look very fat, but it was the colour scheme she wanted. Several Sundays Margie had asked how it was getting on. Peacefully until dawn Catherine sat there knitting and then she had a stretch, took a walk down the quiet streets and back home to finish the sweater. She felt tired but, as the American had said, no more tired than she normally felt after a night of little snatches of sleep and long periods of looking at the patterns on the ceiling made by the light that came through the windows.

She began to wonder about this American, what she should do when he called. She half wished that he would ring now; she felt able to go out and wander around London in the sun on a Saturday morning. She wouldn't resent having to do her unpaid London guide act today. In fact, she would take him to the Albert Memorial. Tourists loved that, and they could walk around the park for a bit. Of course he would want to go to Harrods, even penniless Americans liked to tour the great store, which they seemed to regard as a sight to be seen rather than a shop where you bought things. Perhaps she would take him to St Paul's. Yes, she'd like that, and they could walk for a bit along the Embankment, they might even take a boat trip, but mainly they would walk around St Paul's. Catherine liked St Paul's, it wasn't as fussy as the Abbey, and it seemed to have a confident life of its own.

The flat was clean and shining after her work through the night; the sweater was wrapped up and ready to take tomorrow to Margie. Had Saturdays always been a bit empty since she and Alec had split up or was it just today? Outside the world was waking up, and she wanted to be a part of it. She would like to put on her nice leather jacket and her good tartan skirt and walk with someone who didn't know London. Why didn't this friend of Suzi's ring, she hadn't been that rude to him, had she? The morning dragged, she couldn't think of anyone she wanted to telephone or to meet. Three years of Alec had cut her off from a lot of friends, and Catherine was too proud or too something to ring everybody up and ask could she join the party again just because the affair was over.

In the afternoon she went to the cinema, and felt sleepy on the bus coming home. The phone was ringing as she let herself into the flat, but stopped before she got there. Tired as she was, she felt furious, because she was sure it had been the American.

He was beginning to assume quite extraordinary proportions in her mind. It had something to do with sounding cool and unruffled. Unlike any of Suzi's other friends, he appeared to be able to look after himself, and to give advice to hysterical strangers on the phone. Catherine planned a night programme for herself. She would stick all her photos into albums, she would make herself an autumn skirt in nice autumn colours, she would methodically remove from her vision anything that reminded her of Alec, and she would restore the things she had liked before he came along. The sight of the silver cheered her up. By four a.m. she was too exhausted to do any more, but she refused to go to bed. Out into the silent streets, and a long long walk, but not nervous. London was her city, she was never nervous here. Right up to the steps of St Paul's.

She wished they left churches open at night; many people might like to wander around them when they couldn't sleep. Of course many more who had nowhere to sleep might use the pews as beds. But would that matter? If it was meant to be the house of a loving God, then surely he would like that sort of thing? As she sat on the steps she remembered a day when she and Alec had come here. A military band was playing and the tourists had loved it. Alec had said it was a form of prostitution to change your city to make it appeal to tourists so that they would spend their money there.

She must clear her mind of Alec in the same way that she had cleared her flat of memories. He was no good for her, he had never loved her—he never loved anyone—he had made her feel inferior, he had brought little laughter into her life. Why had she loved him? Chemistry perhaps, if that wasn't too ridiculous an idea.

She walked home, tired, legs dragging, but her mind awake.

At eleven o'clock, when she was just leaving the flat on the first stage of her journey to Margie's, the phone rang.

"Am I talking with Catherine?" he asked.

"I'm glad you rang. You know, I didn't even get your name the other night," she said breathlessly.

"I'm Bob," he said. "Look. I was wondering, could I take you to lunch somewhere today? You must be feeling a bit too tired to fix yourself lunch, and you'll probably want to sleep tonight."

Catherine was surprised that he seemed to assume she had followed his advice. Today was bad, she explained. She had to go and see her sister miles away. Could they make it one evening during the week, when she'd be happy to cook him a meal? Maybe they could meet on Tuesday, she could leave work early, they might stroll up to St Paul's, if he hadn't already seen it and then she'd be happy, really happy, to make dinner for them.

"No," he said. "I'll be gone by Tuesday. Would your sister like it if I took you both to lunch?"

Catherine thought for a moment. Perhaps Margie wouldn't mind all that much if she didn't go to see her today. There was no hard and fast rule that she must turn up every Sunday. Margie was so easy to please, just a telephone call and some explanation, and she agreed to the visit being cancelled.

"It's nothing very concrete with my sister," she said, feeling a little treacherous. "No, nothing that can't keep. Let's meet for lunch."

"Are you sure your sister wouldn't like to come, too?" he asked.

"She's miles away, she'd hate to make the journey," said Catherine, and they fixed to meet in a pub.

"I know a nice place for lunch," he said, which was more than Catherine did. Nobody who lived in London knew where to go for Sunday lunch.

He said he was tall and would carry *The Sunday Times*, and she said she was small and dark and would carry the same thing. All giggles, over-excited and over-tired, she rang Margie at the hotel.

"Something's come up, love," she said. "I can't make it. I was just ready to leave, and I have your sweater finished. Next Sunday without fail."

"Right," said Margie glumly.

"You're not upset? I really have to meet this man from America, he's a friend of Suzi's and he has nowhere to go."

"I've nowhere to go," said Margie.

"I know, Margie, but you're there, and you have all your friends. He has nobody."

"I have nobody on a Sunday either," said Margie.

"Nobody has anybody on a Sunday," cried Catherine in exasperation. Why, oh why, of all days, could Margie not be sunny and cheerful today? Why must it be today that she was low?

"Could you bring him here for lunch?" asked Margie. "You could book a table and we could all have lunch in the dining-room. I'm allowed to do that you know . . . on Sundays, if there are guests."

"No, he has to stay in the centre of town," lied Catherine. "Listen, I'll give you a ring later tonight. OK?"

"OK," said Margie doubtfully.

Catherine changed her clothes, she put on the good leather coat and nice tartan skirt, she put on make-up, and splashed on her best perfume. She spent so long doing it that she had to take a taxi to the pub. She recognised him at once, tousle-haired, intense, reading *The Sunday Times*, young but sensitive.

"Bob?" she said confidently, disturbing him from his half-pint and his reading.

"No, but I wish I was," he said in a Geordie accent.

Annoyed, Catherine went to the bar and sat on a stool.

"A large vodka and ice," she said to the barman.

"On no sleep?" asked the elderly man beside her, a man whom she hadn't noticed before.

"I'm Bob Dane, Catherine," he said, like a family doctor who had been asked to take someone away quietly to the asylum without upsetting the neighbours. "I'm very pleased to know you. Shall we take our drinks to that corner over there?"

He was in his late sixties, at least. Damn him, damn him, why did he have to pretend to be young, and eligible, and some kind of Lancelot to her on the phone? He was an old, old man.

She hadn't even taken in his name.

"My little Suzi said that I mustn't leave London without seeing you and I'm very glad we're seeing each other," he said, carrying the drinks to the table he had pointed out.

His name registered.

"You're Suzi's . . .?" she asked.

"I'm Suzi's father," he said.

"I didn't even know she had one. I hardly know her, you know," gasped Catherine.

"We're not very close. Suzi lives her life, I live mine. Since Suzi's mother died, when she was eighteen, she's been very much her own person," said the man. "I'm not surprised you didn't know of me. In fact we've only got together recently. I was quite shy of approaching her. But now we meet like friends, and as you so rightly said, Suzi has a lot of friends, she likes them. She regards me as an interesting new addition to her collection."

Catherine drank most of her vodka neat.

"How about the sleeping?" he asked kindly.

"I did what you said. I've stayed out of bed since midnight Friday. My legs and back feel tired but the rest of me is awake."

"You'll sleep tonight," he said positively.

Catherine nodded. "I'm sure I will."

There was a silence.

"You said something about wanting to go to St Paul's, Catherine, so I took a little liberty. I packed a picnic, It's such a lovely day I thought we might eat it on the steps, or near by." He pointed at his carrier-bag. "It's all in there, the wine, the glasses, *pâté*, cheese, bread, and even some grapes! The hotel packed it all, and there's no problem if you'd prefer to eat somewhere more conventional. I can just give it back to them."

Catherine looked at him, a nice confident face, grey hair, light tan, heavy gold ring on his finger. He was a successful retired American businessman. There seemed no reason to hurt him, he didn't look like someone who would hurt her.

"A picnic would be lovely," said Catherine.

"You mustn't feel that you have to take back anything you said about Suzi to me on the phone," he said, just as Catherine was wondering how she might possibly do this. "I know only too well what a burden some of her lame dogs can be. I had a great hesitancy about calling you because of this. I felt sure you had been stuck with Chuck and Mitzi amongst others."

"Well, yes," agreed Catherine, laughing.

"Yet we mustn't be too hard on Suzi. She has this odd cosmic theory that the people of the world should all get to know each other, and that some of us are too timid to go up and say Hi, therefore an introduction helps."

"Oh, in theory she's right," agreed Catherine enthusiastically. "I suppose selfishly I feel it's all one-way traffic. You see, I don't know anyone going to the United States much, so I don't send my friends to *her*."

"I know. I understand that, but you must never underestimate Suzi. She may indeed be over-busy, over-successful, and very haphazard about whom she deposits on whom, yet she does care about people. It's not just a wish to be at the centre of some web, you know."

"Oh, I never thought that," cried Catherine insincerely.

"I'm sure you didn't," said Bob gravely. And Catherine knew he saw through her.

They walked in the autumn lunchtime sun to the steps of St Paul's; it had become autumn overnight. Catherine didn't need to do her guide-to-London act, because Bob had obviously been to Britain several times a year. It turned out that he was a doctor, but he had retired early and organised medical conferences instead. He was in Europe a great deal.

"Why didn't Suzi ever give you my address before?" asked Catherine.

"Well, as I said, we've only been close in the last couple of years."

"But since then?" she persisted.

"Oh, I don't think she thought the time was ripe," he said mysteriously.

They walked around the building, they chatted to each other amicably about Wren, and what he thought he was at, and what other people thought of him in his time. Bob told her about the cathedral at Rheims which was overpowering in its detail, and about temples in Salt Lake City which were equally startling. They both felt they could cope with St Paul's.

As they had their picnic he told her about a woman he had loved once. When Suzi's mother died, he had contacted her again and the woman had told him to get lost. He said it was hurtful to be told that at fifty you were finished and no use to anybody; he had been very lost in those days, but now at sixty-four somehow he felt more secure. He said he didn't feel old enough to have a daughter of thirty-two, and that when he heard of the older generation, he never included himself in that category at all.

Catherine told him how she had been in love for three years and only very recently had stopped. She said she tried hard not to feel bitter but this man had really hurt her a lot, and it was hard to take up the reins again.

The evening shadows came and they talked, and then they walked along the Embankment, and she told him more, about how she couldn't sleep because she kept wondering did other people manage relationships better than she did. She had worked out one day that she was happy twenty percent of the time with this man and decided that it wasn't enough so she had ended it. He had been surprised and annoyed. She had liked him feeling that way.

But sometimes as she was going to sleep alone, she wondered about the rest of the world. Perhaps twenty percent was average for happiness with another human being. Maybe she had wanted too much, and didn't know how to compromise. What did Bob think? How much happiness had he enjoyed with Suzi's mother, say?

"Oh, about ninety percent," he said. "You were right to finish with Alec. What we must do is make sure that the cure isn't worse than the disease."

"I didn't say his name, how did you know?" asked Catherine. She made a point of not mentioning Alec's name, ever. It made him seem like more of a person if his name was allowed to occur in conversation.

"Suzi told me," he said calmly.

"But how could Suzi possibly know? I send her a Christmas card once a year. I send her a note of three lines thanking her for whatever she has sent me by one of her ghastly friends. I never mentioned Alec to her, not once. I haven't seen Suzi for ten years. Nobody ever seems to believe that."

"Chuck told her," said Bob.

Chuck. Chuck. The man with the smelly socks and no money, the man who had eaten the jar of ginger, the man who met Alec twice. How dare Chuck mention Alec's name at the other side of the world. She was speechless with rage and shock.

"Chuck told Suzi that it was a bad scene, and Suzi asked me to see if I could help you straighten things out. I guess I arrived just in time. At least I'm able to fix your sleeping problems. That's better than talking you out of Alec."

"You couldn't have talked me out of Alec, nobody could," Catherine said, stunned by his intrusion and confidence. "I don't know what makes you and Suzi think you have any right to interfere in other people's affairs. People you don't even know. It's outrageous."

"Yeah, but you were agreeing earlier that we are all too buttoned up about getting to know people, the British particularly."

"But it's my business, nobody else's."

"Your friends care," said Bob simply.

"You're not my friend. Suzi's not my friend. I've no friends who care."

"Margie might care if you talked to her about it," said Bob.

Catherine felt weak at her thighs as if she were going to fall. She didn't know whether it was tiredness or the sense of unreality. How did this old, old American man know about Margie? She never told people about Margie, only Alec had known, for all the good he had been.

"Mitzi mentioned to Suzi that you had a mentally defective sister who was a problem to you. She said she was in a hotel somewhere and you felt ashamed to include her in your life. That's why I was so anxious we should meet her today and talk, all three of us."

Yes, Mitzi had been told about Margie. That's because Mitzi had stayed three weeks in Catherine's flat, and had asked where she went every Sunday. God damn Mitzi and Chuck and whatever other transatlantic spies she had harboured.

They were passing a seat, and Catherine sat down. Bob talked on in his calm voice.

"I have rented a car, we could ride out and see your sister. I could act as an intermediary, you and she could discuss how she could participate more in your life. You would feel the benefit, she would feel the benefit."

Catherine was able to speak and she did, slowly and carefully.

"I know you mean well. I know Suzi means well. I know Americans are thicker-skinned than we are; they are also more friendly and they risk insult more easily out of kindness. I also know it's foolish to make generalisations about my nationality. Now given all this, can I thank you for your interest, and walk back to a bus-stop with you, and part friends in some sort of way? I won't begin to tell you how impossible I would find it to thrash out my whole life and problems with a stranger, however kind."

"But you spoke very frankly about your relationship with Alec."

"Because I thought you were someone who hadn't much interest and whom I would never meet again," said Catherine desperately.

"You mean you'd prefer to talk to someone who could be of no help?" asked Bob. "Really, that seems very introverted. Why don't you talk to an animal or a doorpost then, if you want no reaction, no help?"

"I don't want help," she said, choked.

"You do, my dear Catherine, you do, you're afraid to admit it. This British reserve may have got you all through national crises but it's no good for a young girl all by herself."

"Please don't say any more," begged Catherine.

Bob opened his mouth to begin again a measured reasoned cliché of pop psychology. He seemed to regard her as someone who had to be talked down. A violent hatred of Suzi rose in Catherine.

On shaking legs she rose and ran haltingly down the Embankment towards a bus-stop. Behind her Bob was calling, "Catherine, Catherine, we must talk, you need to talk." Behind her St Paul's towered knowingly over it all.

edna o'brien

Startings

Anna's friends said that soon she would meet someone wonderful. It had to be. She worked as a costumier in a theatre and knew a lot of people. Yet she went to parties alone and said, "It's more of an adventure." But that was mere bluff. The truth was, she had no choice, and she was beginning to feel increasingly separate. She laughed when her friends foretold this new adventure. She did not believe it or disbelieve it. An Indian clairvoyant told her the man's initials and his occupation, and she felt it as a very pleasant certainty in the pit of her being. But she did not hurry towards it. She was learning.

When he came through her door, she did not see him as her promised one, but she did see him as someone vital, appealing, and very watchful. He sat on the floor, apart. He was called Bobby. Her friend Ken had brought him. Ken was a director, and she had often worked with him. They had been through many a scrape together and had nursed each other through many an emotional storm. So there they all were, friends, having a drink. Her teenage sons were in the room, and it was a question of chatter, music in the background, two young people playing a game of cards, and herself frequently jumping up to pass nuts, to pass olives, to refill the glasses. It was a beautiful spring evening and the sunlight poured, as if in heraldry, through the golden gauze-like curtains. Happiness prevailed. The double freesias in the vases were the colour of clotted cream, and when he put his face to them he smiled at the absence of perfume. Shop flowers, she had to say, do not have a perfume.

"Is that a fact?" He put the question to the air. Although apart, he seemed to be registering everything. He would focus and narrow his eyes, as if considering. He looked at the pictures on her coral walls and admitted that he never looked at pictures but that these were quite something. One picture dominated a whole wall. It was a wheat field and so convincing that the high golden stalks seemed to move occasionally to a breeze or the reaper's scythe. Then he asked who the singer was on the record and looked at the dust jacket to make a note of the label. It was the same with the wine. He repeated its name and the name of the French shippers.

She thought that perhaps he was complimenting her or perhaps he was making note of these things for his own particular advantage. Her impression was that he was at once sure and unsure. He had a beautiful physical poise but was canny about what he would say. We often ask strangers the bluntest questions. So she did. She asked him what he wanted in life, and he whistled and gave a sudden grin.

"Just to make you laugh, that's all," he said, and looked at her to see if he had made a conquest. It was as if he were drinking her in. The evening drifted on and on, and no one wished to leave, although they all had different appointments. They might have been placed under a spell. He and Ken were going to a play, and yet they refused to budge and refused to absorb directions on how to get there. In the end, they left.

When she next saw him, a couple of nights later at an after-theatre party, Bobby said how nervous she had been and she said that she was always nervous—nervous even when her cleaning woman brought her little boy for tea and they all made cinnamon toast and munched it and joked. He was an American working in England, and he had been in a hotel room for ten days and was beginning to feel cooped up. He mimed it. She saw him as a caged monkey and asked if he had been born in the Year of the Monkey according to the Chinese calendar. He did not know. His eyes were a cornflower blue and sometimes flashed like galvanised metal. The colour was arresting and it fluctuated, as if it were dye that deepened and became pale at intervals, depending on his mood.

They talked about strange cities, strange hotels, and the random excitement of being alone and knowing no one. They talked of the false ecstasy attached to ordering prawns and a cocktail brought to one's room. In her New York hotel, she said, what she remembered most was the single red rose on her breakfast tray each morning. He asked which hotel it was, and laughed because indeed they might have met. He mentioned other haunts of his and she knew them, too, because she had been taken there. They were both gypsies. When people talk, it is usually something else they are trying to say, and he said that on that first meeting he was asking her not to be nervous, to come out with them, and she said that she was saying not to get near, not to trespass.

But they met again and again, always with Ken, who was the butt of their jokes and the witness to their budding attraction. Bobby would take her hand as if it were the most natural thing in the world and whirl it clockwise and anti-clockwise, and they would look at each other as if trying to read faces. They were at once friendly and wary. She took Bobby and Ken for a walk in Hyde Park and showed them the difference between primroses and grape hyacinths. With regard to nature, they were barbarians. At the Serpentine, they all watched as the ducks squabbled over bread. Their attention was caught by two drakes who were having a hardy battle. One or the other of the combatants would disappear, only to re-emerge drenched and more pugnacious. It was the courting season.

"Terrific," he said, and flinched as if nature were a puzzle to him. The landscape where he lived was desert, and he described going out there on his motorcycle to work off his tension, and she saw a man with a coil inside his chest. Then she took them to where all the birds congregated and sang, some to woo, some to compete, some to plead, and some, as she said, to serenade the people.

"The birds at juke in the bushes," she said.

What did that mean?

She told him that she had learned that in Ireland, read it in a schoolbook long ago.

"I'll take you to Ireland," he said to her late one night. Ken had gone home, and she and he were in his hotel room, talking, talking. They sat close together, like children, with hands held, fingers locking and interlocking, telling each other snatches of things. Once, in a bar, he had broken twenty willow-pattern plates. Once, in a waiting room, he had acted Ionesco's *The Chairs*.

By then she knew that he was married, that he was estranged from his wife, that he was a little in love with Anna, a little in awe, and that he was not running to her, he was not doing that.

"Why take me to Ireland?" she said, again probably meaning something else, probably meaning don't.

" 'Cause you're always taking me somewhere," he said.

There was an obstacle. She did not really want to sleep with him, not because she did not want to sleep with him but because she was reluctant and she was afraid. What is more, she had lost the habit. She was in her late thirties, divorced, her children were grown, and though she was consumed with desire it had gone underground and moved in her like a wraith and sometimes spoke in dreams. It was there, but secretive.

He guessed what was running through her mind. "No way I would," he said, as if sleeping with someone was too strenuous and too much of a commitment. "It's probably very nice, but I like this." And he dangled their two hands in the air and seemed pleased with what he saw. So going to Ireland was simple, and he would arrange it all.

They arrived at the hotel in the evening. The avenue was miles long, with big redwood trees on either side. It curved round and round, and she was breathless to get a view. A sally hedge and cropped yews skirted the bounds of a beautiful formal garden. The rhododendrons were out. Like torches of deep red reaching higher and higher to the heavens. The cut stone was covered over with a thin cape of bronze lichen, and the corners of the building curved into little horseshoe gazebos. The lake beyond was the colour of dun earth. The trunks of the trees were reflected thinly, down, down into the water, thin and precarious as a flamingo's legs. She saw it all—the mooring place for the boat, the green-domed boathouse, and the steps that led to the front porch with two men or, rather, figures in armour—and she thought, Do I deserve this?

The season had just begun and the porters were full of affability, and their welcome seemed to say that it was nice to have donned their blazers and their black bow ties to greet new faces. The other new faces, as far as she could see, were somewhat tentative. It was as if people like her had just stepped in to a masked party and were unsure. Bobby made up for all that by scanning everything, by looking closely at the huge photographs that decked the lounge, by having a quick drink at the bar as they passed by. He juggled some nuts in the air before popping them into his mouth. He gave her a sip of his bourbon. She walked toward one of the huge, blown-up photographs and beheld a bleached sea road strewn with small bleached stones. It spoke of hardship, of poverty.

That was my childhood, she thought, and conceived of a bicycle or a workman or a dog—something to make it human. His childhood was New York, second-generation Irish—men with sombre personalities until the moment they drank. When they drank, they changed character, he said. He kissed her in front of the picture, in front of the other guests, in front of the curly-haired barman, and in front of her awkward self.

He was excited and like a schoolboy playing truant. Then he took her wrist and they went up in the tiny lift, speculating about the room. It was a suite. As they came through the door, the first thing she could see was another bar reflected in the window opposite, then all of a sudden the porter switched on the bar light and the bottles multiplied and were reflected in the rear mirrors. She could see how barmen might be proud of their wares and how they might keep their mirrors very clean and dust the necks of the bottles and never let the labels be soiled or smeared the way the pages of her cookery book were. The room was so huge that they walked round it and met and embraced and separated, and told each other more stories, or snippets of stories. It was like shorthand. It was their way of discovering each other. Her stories with the merest tincture of pain, like cochineal invading an icing, and his with a zaniness and a certain subversiveness.

Very soon, menus were brought and he lolled over her shoulder as he debated what they should have. They would have everything. They would get plump together, they would jog together in the beautiful grounds, they would go boating together to the island across the way, and they would swim at midnight. The waiter said a boat could be arranged but they would get their death of cold if they were to swim or even paddle.

When the waiter had gone, Bobby told her a story about a cat and an eagle, and she listened with all her attention. It was a fable, really. It involved danger and it involved dependence. The lamplight was very soft and so was their mood. The rooks were cawing in the trees outside and the time seemed to exhale its own passing, so perfect and unruffled it all was. He got up and stretched.

"I would have gone crazy if I hadn't met you," he said.

"Do I resemble someone else?" she asked.

"No one else, absolutely no one else," he said.

There was something she had to tell him, but she did not know how. She blurted it. How she saw a doctor.

"Oh, a shrink," he said, and dazzled her by totting up the amount that he, his wife, his eldest child, and his several girlfriends had spent in that department. She had to tell him then of a dream she had had that was shocking in its simplicity. She had dreamed of sleeping with her doctor, had supplied every detail of it—the folded sheet, the red herringbone stitching on the rim of the blanket, his breathing, the subtlety of their reach, the beauty of their closeness—and how then the doctor had merged into her father and then returned to being himself again, and how as they made love the doctor's face floated between being his own and being her father's and that no matter which face she kissed the other was behind it, like a shadow, floating, and the benefit of those two faces was totally and uncannily satisfying. It made one ask for nothing more.

She wanted him to know that, but she did not know why she wanted him to know it. She was by the window looking out. Night had fallen.

"I love when you move," he said.

"What race would you think I was?" she said.

"Russian," he said.

"Good," she said, and he laughed because he had been jesting with her. She was the race she was, every particle of it. Eyes, bones, hair, inflammability. They were alike. She felt that, too. Brother and sister. Kin.

Before dinner, they went outside to fetch a book he had left behind in the hired car. The place was a thicket of darkness. On the path, they stumbled and clung to each other and did not know which direction to take. There was the wonderful cleansing sound of rushing water, and they both said that they had not felt so well in years. They groped toward the car park. He put the key in the door and, upon opening it, an inner light came on. On the back seat was an attaché case, which he snapped open, and in it were a tin of boiled sweets, a lady's knickers, and a pair of black evening gloves.

"Come on!" he said, and accused her of being responsible for it. But it was not their car at all. Their key opened several car doors, and each time they laughed, because neither of them could remember the number of their car, its colour, or even where they had parked it. They had been so engrossed in each other that they had forgotten.

"What did you see as we drove here?" she said.

"You," he said, and then added, "Stone walls, small fields, and a lot of bog."

She said that she had seen a statue of a saint in the upstairs window of a pub and that its head had come off and was resting on its shoulder, and did he think it was kept on by glue or by persistence?

He said probably persistence and that she was a wonderful person and to hell with his car and his swanky book on Zen Buddhism. Some of the hotel windows were lit up, and soft red lights beckoned from the stone front.

The wine she most loved was on the table and there were five fluted daffodils set into a piece of green sponging that was too bulky for the small vase. The curtains and wall coverings were a sumptuous red, and in the recess where they sat they could see the garden outside and a fire at the end of the room glowing.

"You're smart," he said. "I have decided you're smart."

She looked at him and wondered. She thought, He thinks I am vivid, I think I am dull. He probably sleeps like a baby, I toss and turn. She thought she was not going to be able to carry it off, but there he was disarming her, telling her something else.

"What would you say is your biggest handicap?" she said.

"Thinking," he said. "I'm always thinking about thinking, and not doing much real thinking."

"What if I said that I didn't want to be here?"

"I'd think about it and I'd start thinking that you would think you wanted to be here."

"Could you?" she said, so imploringly.

"No, but I wish I could," he said, so sadly.

She thought. It will be all right, it will take a day or two, but I will adjust, I will get used to being with someone, I will bloom.

"Tell me about your kids," she said, realising that his language was infecting hers.

"They're not as good as yours," he said, " 'cause I'm not as good as you."

"You miss them?"

"No," he said. "They do racing and stuff like that . . . They're on their way . . . I wouldn't want them to be late starters like me." He gave a little smile that was almost rueful. She thought then of starting. Were he and she starting, and if so what? Would these three days bring them nearer or farther from one another? Where were the boulders, the thorns, the gorges—where were they, and when would they loom into view?

He asked what excited her. She said did he mean sexually.

He said any way.

She said the lifting of a skirt was more exciting than two bare bodies, more suggestive. Then they discussed films they loved, or moments of films that they loved, and they were almost obstreperous in pronouncing their own choices as best.

She asked if he knew what Keats said when he saw his beloved take off her glove. " 'Snared by the ungloving of thine hand.' "

"God!" he said, delighted, and then added that he would have to read Keats and a lot of other stuff to keep up with her! They were eating fresh poached salmon, and he said one thing he had never done was fishing. She said it made people very patient, and he twitched his nose at that.

"But you fish the brain," she said quietly.

"Right," he said, gladdened that she had noticed that trait in him.

Her fingernails dug into her left palm.

Always she had loved the first moments, weeks and months of an affair, but now it was different. She wanted these by-passed or saved for later, she wanted it as it was with her children, easy and silent, and with an immeasurable understanding. In the past, it might have been his wife, his children, his this, his that which sent her hurrying to isolation. But it was no longer those things, it was no longer the commencement, the enjoyment, the agony, or the conclusion of the affair. It was something else. She wanted a love ordained from within. Two sets of inner eyes knowing and comprehending.

"I don't think I can go through with this," she said. He sensed it just before she said it. He had been telling her a story, his fork held in mid air, and he dropped it and let out a volley of swear words.

"Why not?" he said, and she could see that it had shaken him. He still smiled, but the light behind the smile had gone grey, was quashed. It was hard to say why, except that she muttered how she was unused to being with someone and giving nothing. Her role was to give, not to take. Or she could tell him that she was on tenterhooks, that she was afraid. She could not tell him that she feared to be ugly for a moment, or to show signs of tiredness, or failure, or fatigue. By telling him these things she would make him believe them. Nor could she say that possibly her flesh was too white, her jokes were artifacts, her breasts sagged. Time had made its numerous erosions on her. To herself she was like a doll who smiles and flutters and is then put away in its box of chaff, and is taken out again, but only briefly.

"I've been away too long," she said, but that was to herself.

"I don't want to go on with this," she said, and she saw puzzlement come over his face and sensed that he felt he had just encountered an anomaly, a woman whom he did not know and would not be able to fathom.

"I'll tell you what I'll do," he said. "I'll take a walk. I'd like a walk. I'll take a long walk and give you time to think."

"I'd rather go," she said, and as she rose he gave her hand a little squeeze and it seemed to say, "You're a fool to by-pass this."

"See you," she said, but she could not see him through the prism of tears that blinded her to everything in the room, as she hurried to what was dark and impenetrable outside.

alice walker

To Hell with Dying

"To hell with dying," my father would say. "These children want Mr Sweet!"

Mr Sweet was a diabetic and an alcoholic and a guitar player and lived down the road from us on a neglected cotton farm. My older brothers and sisters got the most benefit from Mr Sweet, for when they were growing up he had quite a few years ahead of him and so was capable of being called back from the brink of death any number of times—whenever the voice of my father reached him as he lay expiring. "To hell with dying, man," my father would say, pushing the wife away from the bedside (in tears although she knew the death was not necessarily the last one unless Mr Sweet really wanted it to be). "These children want Mr Sweet!" And they did want him, for at a signal from Father they would come crowding around the bed and throw themselves on the covers, and whoever was the smallest at the time would kiss him all over his wrinkled brown face and begin to tickle him so that he would laugh all down in his stomach, and his moustache, which was long and sort of straggly, would shake like Spanish moss and was also that colour.

Mr Sweet had been ambitious as a boy, wanted to be a doctor or lawyer or sailor, only to find that black men fare better if they are not. Since he could become none of these things he turned to fishing as his only earnest career and playing the guitar as his only claim to doing anything extraordinarily well. His son, the only one that he and his wife, Miss Mary, had, was shiftless as the day is long and spent money as if he were trying to see the bottom of the mint, which Mr Sweet would tell him was the clean brown palm of his hand. Miss Mary loved her "baby", however, and worked hard to get him the "li'l necessaries" of life, which turned out mostly to be women.

Mr Sweet was a tall, thinnish man with thick, kinky hair going dead white. He was dark brown, his eyes were very squinty and sort of bluish, and he chewed Brown Mule tobacco. He was constantly on the verge of being blind drunk, for he brewed his own liquor and was not in the least a stingy sort of man, and was always very melancholy and sad, though frequently when he was "feelin' good" he'd dance around the yard with us, usually keeling over just as my mother came to see what the great commotion was all about.

Towards all of us children he was very kind, and had the grace to be shy with us, which is unusual in grown-ups. He had great respect for my mother for she never held his drunkenness against him and would let us play with him even when he was about to fall in the fireplace from drink. Although Mr Sweet would sometimes lose complete or nearly complete control of his head and neck so that he would loll in his chair, his mind remained strangely acute and his speech not too affected. His ability to be drunk and sober at the same time made him an ideal playmate, for it meant that he was as weak as we were and we could usually beat him in wrestling, all the while keeping a fairly coherent conversation going.

We never felt anything of Mr Sweet's age when we played with him. We loved his wrinkles and would draw some on our brows to be like him, and his white hair was my special treasure and he knew it and would never come to visit us just after he had had his hair cut off at the barbershop. Once he came to our house for something, probably to see my father about fertiliser for his crops because, although he never paid the slightest attention to his crops, he liked to know what things would be best to use on them if he ever did. Anyhow, he had not come with his hair since he had just had it shaved off at the barbershop. He wore a huge straw hat to keep off the sun and also keep his head away from me. But as soon as I saw him I ran up and demanded that he take me up and kiss me with his funny beard which smelled so strongly of tobacco. Looking forward to burying my small fingers into his woolly hair I threw away his hat only to find he had done something to his hair, that it was no longer there! I let out a squall which made my mother think that Mr Sweet had finally dropped me in the well or something and from that day I've been wary of men in hats. However, not long after, Mr Sweet showed up with his hair grown out and just as white and kinky and impenetrable as it ever was.

Mr Sweet used to call me his princess, and I believed it. He made me feel pretty at five and six, and simply outrageously devastating at the blazing age of eight and a half. When he came to our house with his guitar the whole family would stop whatever they were doing to sit around him and listen to him play. He liked to play *Sweet Georgia Brown*, that was what he called me sometimes, and also he liked to play *Caldonia* and all sorts of sweet, sad, wonderful songs which he sometimes made up. It was from one of these songs that I learned that he had had to marry Miss Mary when he had in fact loved somebody else (now living in Chica-go or De-stroy, Michigan). He was not sure that Joe Lee, her "baby", was also his baby. Sometimes he would cry and that was an indication that he was about to die again. And so we would all get prepared, for we were sure to be called upon.

I was seven the first time I remember actually participating in one of Mr Sweet's "revivals"—my parents told me I had participated before, I had been the one chosen to kiss him and tickle him long before I knew the rite of Mr Sweet's rehabilitation. He had come to our house, it was a few years after his wife's death, and was very sad, and also, typically, very drunk. He sat on the floor next to me and my elder brother, the rest of the children were grown up and lived elsewhere, and began to play his guitar and cry. I held his woolly head in my arms and wished I could have been old enough to have been the woman he loved so much and that I had not been lost years and years ago.

When he was leaving, my mother said to us that we'd better sleep light that night for we'd probably have to go over to

Mr Sweet's before daylight. And we did. For soon after we had gone to bed one of the neighbours knocked on our door and called my father and said that Mr Sweet was sinking fast and if he wanted to get in a word before the crossover he'd better shake a leg and get over to Mr Sweet's house. All the neighbours knew to come to our house if something was wrong with Mr Sweet, but they did not know how we always managed to make him well, or at least stop him from dying, when he was often so near death. As soon as we heard the cry we got up, my brother and I and my mother and father, and put on our clothes. We hurried out of the house and down the road for we were always afraid that we might someday be too late and Mr Sweet would get tired of all the dallying.

When we got to the house, a very poor shack really, we found the front room full of neighbours and relatives and someone met us at the door and said that it was all very sad that old Mr Sweet Little (for Little was his family name, although we mostly ignored it) was about to kick the bucket. My parents were advised not to take my brother and me into the "death room", seeing we were so young and all, but we were so much more accustomed to the death room than he that we ignored him and dashed in without giving his warning a second thought. I was almost in tears, for these deaths upset me fearfully, and the thought of how much depended on me and my brother (who was such a ham most of the time) made me very nervous.

The doctor was bending over the bed and turned back to tell us for at least the tenth time in the history of my family that, alas, old Mr Sweet Little was dying and that the children had best not see the face of implacable death (I didn't know what "implacable" was, but whatever it was, Mr Sweet was not). My father pushed him rather abruptly out of the way saying, as he always did and very loudly for he was saying it to Mr Sweet, "To hell with dying, man, these children want Mr Sweet"— which was my cue to throw myself upon the bed and kiss Mr Sweet all around the whiskers and under the eyes and around the collar of his nightshirt where he smelled so strongly of all sorts of things, mostly liniment.

I was very good at bringing him around, for as soon as I saw that he was struggling to open his eyes I knew he was going to be all right, and so could finish my revival sure of success. As soon as his eyes were open he would begin to smile and that way I knew that I had surely won. Once, though, I got a tremendous scare, for he would not open his eyes and later I learned that he had had a stroke and that one side of his face was stiff and hard to get in motion. When he began to smile I could tickle him in earnest because I was sure that nothing would get in the way of his laughter, although once he began to cough so hard that he almost threw me off his stomach, but that was when I was very small, little more than a baby, and my bushy hair had gotten in his nose.

When we were sure he would listen to us we would ask him why he was in bed and when he was coming to see us again and could we play with his guitar, which more than likely would be leaning against the bed. His eyes would get all misty and he would sometimes cry out loud, but we never let it embarrass us, for he knew that we loved him and that we sometimes cried too for no reason. My parents would leave the room to just the three of us; Mr Sweet, by that time, would be propped up in bed with a number of pillows behind his head and with me sitting and lying on his shoulder and along his chest. Even when he had trouble breathing he would not ask me to get down. Looking into my eyes he would shake his white head and run a scratchy old finger all around my hairline, which was rather low down, nearly to my eyebrows, and made some people say I looked just like a baby monkey.

My brother was very generous in all this, he let me do all the reviving—he had done it for years before I was born and so was glad to be able to pass it on to someone new. What he would do while I talked to Mr Sweet was pretend to play the guitar, in fact pretend that he was a young version of Mr Sweet, and it always made Mr Sweet glad to think that someone wanted to be like him—of course, we did not know this then, we played the thing by ear, and whatever he seemed to like, we did. We were desperately afraid that he was just going to take off one day and leave us.

It did not occur to us that we were doing anything special, we had not learned that death was final when it did come. We thought nothing of triumphing over it so many times, and in fact became a trifle contemptuous of people who let themselves be carried away. It did not occur to us that if our own father had been dying we could not have stopped it, that Mr Sweet was the only person over whom we had power.

When Mr Sweet was in his eighties I was studying in the university many miles from home. I saw him whenever I went home, but he was never on the verge of dying that I could tell and I began to feel that my anxiety for his health and psychological well-being was unnecessary. By this time he not only had a moustache but a long flowing snow-white beard, which I loved and combed and braided for hours. He was very peaceful, fragile, gentle, and the only jarring note about him was his old steel guitar, which he still played in the old sad, sweet, down-home blues way.

On Mr Sweet's ninetieth birthday I was finishing my doctorate in Massachusetts and had been making arrangements to go home for several weeks' rest. That morning I got a telegram telling me that Mr Sweet was dying again and could I please drop everything and come home. Of course I could. My dissertation could wait and my teachers would understand when I explained to them when I got back. I ran to the phone, called the airport, and within four hours I was speeding along the dusty road to Mr Sweet's.

The house was more dilapidated than when I was last there, barely a shack, but it was overgrown with yellow roses which my family had planted many years ago. The air was heavy and sweet and very peaceful. I felt strange walking through the gate and up the old rickety steps. But the strangeness left me as I caught sight of the long white beard I loved so well flowing down the thin body over the familiar quilt coverlet. Mr Sweet!

His eyes were closed tight and his hands, crossed over his stomach, were thin and delicate, no longer scratchy. I remembered how always before I had run and jumped up on him just anywhere; now I knew he would not be able to support my weight. I looked around at my parents, and was surprised to see that my father and mother also looked old and frail. My father, his own hair very grey, leaned over the quietly sleeping old man, who, incidentally, smelled still of wine and tobacco, and said, as he'd done so many times, "To hell with dying, man! My daughter is home to see Mr Sweet!" My brother had not been able to come as he was in the war in Asia. I bent down and gently stroked the closed eyes and gradually they began to open. The closed, wine-stained lips twitched a little, then parted in a warm, slightly embarrassed smile. Mr Sweet could see me and he recognised me and his eyes looked very spry and twinkly for a moment. I put my head down on the pillow next to his and we just looked at each other for a long time. Then he began to trace my peculiar hairline with a thin, smooth finger. I closed my eyes when his finger halted above my ear (he used to rejoice at the dirt in my ears when I was little), his hand stayed cupped around my cheek. When I opened my eyes, sure that I had reached him in time, his were closed.

Even at 24 how could I believe that I had failed? That Mr Sweet was really gone? He had never gone before. But when I looked up at my parents I saw that they were holding back tears. They had loved him dearly. He was like a piece of rare and delicate china which was always being saved from breaking and which finally fell. I looked long at the old face, the wrinkled forehead, the red lips, the hands that still reached out to me. Soon I felt my father pushing something cool into my hands. It was Mr Sweet's guitar. He had asked them months before to give it to me; he had known that even if I came next time he would not be able to respond in the old way. He did not want me to feel that my trip had been for nothing.

The old guitar! I plucked the strings, hummed *Sweet Georgia Brown*. The magic of Mr Sweet lingered still in the cool steel box. Through the window I could catch the fragrant delicate scent of tender yellow roses. The man lying there on the high old-fashioned bed with the quilt coverlet and the flowing white beard had been my first love.

deborah moggach

Smile

We had to wear these SMILE badges. It was one of the rules. And they'd nailed up a sign saying SMILE, just above the kitchen door, so we wouldn't forget. It's American, the hotel. Dennis, the chief receptionist, even says to the customers, "Have a nice day," but then he's paid more than I am, so I suppose he's willing.

I was on breakfasts when I was expecting. Through a fog of early-morning sickness I'd carry out the plates of scrambled eggs. The first time I noticed the man he pointed to the SMILE badge, pinned to my chest, then he pulled a face.

"Cheer up," he said. "It might never happen."

I thought, *it has.*

Looking back, I suppose he appeared every six weeks or so, and stayed a couple of nights. I wasn't counting, then, because I didn't know who he was. Besides, I was on the alert for somebody else, who never turned up and still hasn't, being married, and based in Huddersfield, and having forgotten about that night when he ordered a bottle of Southern Comfort with room service. At least I'm nearly sure it was him.

I was still on breakfasts when I saw the man again, and my apron was getting tight. Soon I'd be bursting out of the uniform.

He said, "You're looking bonny."

I held out the toast basket, and he took four. Munching, he nodded at my badge. "Or are you just obedient?"

It took me a moment to realise what he meant, I was so used to wearing it.

"Oh yes, I always do what I'm told."

He winked. "Sounds promising."

I gave him a pert look and flounced off. I was happy that day. The sickness had worn off; I was keeping the baby, I'd never let anybody else take it away from me. I'd have someone to love, who would be mine.

"You've put on weight," he said, six weeks later. "It suits you."

"Thanks" I said, smiling with my secret. "More coffee?"

He held out his cup. "And what do you call yourself?"

"Sandy."

I looked at him. He was a handsome bloke, broad and fleshy, with a fine head of hair. He had a tie printed with exclamation marks.

I've always gone for older men. They're bound to be married, of course. Not that it makes much difference while they're here.

When he finished his breakfast I saw him pocketing a couple of marmalade sachets. You can tell the married ones; they're nicking them for the kids.

When I got too fat they put me in the kitchens. You didn't have to wear your SMILE badge there. I was on salads. Arranging the radish roses, I day-dreamed about my baby.

I never knew it would feel like this. I felt heavy and warm and whole. The new chef kept pestering me, but he seemed like a midge—irksome but always out of sight. Nobody mattered. I walked through the steam, talking silently to my bulge. This baby meant the world to me. I suppose it came from not having much of a home myself, what with my Dad leaving, and Mum moving in and out of lodgings, and me being in and out of Care. Not that I blame her. Or him, not really.

I'd stand in the cooking smells, look at my tummy and think, *You're all mine, I'll never leave you.*

When she was born I called her Donna. I'd sit for hours, just breathing in her scent. I was always bathing her. It was a basement flat we had then, Mum and me and Mum's current love-of-her-life Eddie, and I'd put the pram in the area way so Donna could imbibe the sea breezes. Even in our part of Brighton, I told myself you could smell the sea.

I'd lean over to check she was still breathing. I longed for her to smile—properly, at me. In the next room Mum and Eddie would be giggling in an infantile way, they seemed the childish ones. Or else throwing things. It was always like this with Mum's blokes.

I'd gaze at my baby and tell her, *You won't miss out. You'll have me; I'll always be here.*

Behind me the window pane rattled as Mum flounced out, slamming the door behind her.

I went back to work, but in the evenings, so I could look after Donna during the day and leave her with Mum when she was sleeping. They put me in the Late Night Coffee Shop. It had been refurbished in Wild West style, like a saloon, with bullet holes printed on the wallpaper and fancy names for the burgers. The wood veneer was already peeling off the counter. Donna had changed my world; nothing seemed real any more, only her.

I had a new gingham uniform, with a flounced apron and my SMILE badge. I moved around in a dream.

One night somebody said, "Howdee, stranger."

It was the man I used to meet at breakfast.

He put on an American accent. "Just rolled into town, honey. Been missing you. You went away or something?"

I didn't say I'd had a baby; I liked to keep Donna separate.

He inspected the menu. "Can you fix me a Charcoal-Broiled Rangeburger?"

It was a quiet evening so we hadn't lit the charcoal. Back in the kitchen I popped the meat into the microwave and thought how once I would have fancied him, like I fancied the bloke from Huddersfield, like I almost fancied Dennis in Reception. But I felt this new responsibility now. Why hadn't my parents felt it when I was born? Or perhaps they had, but it had worn off early.

When I brought him his meal he pointed to my badge. "With you it comes naturally." He shook salt over his chips. "Honest, I'm not just saying it. You've got a beautiful smile."

"It's added on the bill."

He laughed. "She's witty too." He speared a gherkin. "Somebody's a lucky bloke."

"Somebody?"

"Go on, what's his name?"

I thought, *Donna*.

"There's nobody special," I said.

"Don't believe it, lovely girl like you."

I gave him my enigmatic look—practice makes perfect—and started wiping down the next table.

He said, "You mean I'm in with a chance?"

"You're too old."

"Ah," he grinned. "The cruel insolence of youth." He munched his chips. "You ought to try me. I'm matured in the cask."

Later, when he finished his meal, he came up to pay. He put his hand to his heart. "Tell me you'll be here tomorrow night. Give me something to live for."

I took his Access card. "I'll be here tomorrow night."

During breakfasts he'd paid the cashier; that's why I'd never seen his name.

I did now. I read it once, on the Access card.

Finally, I got my hands to work. I pulled the paper through the machine, fumbling it once. I did it again, then I passed it to him.

"What's up?" he said. "Seen a ghost?"

That night Donna woke twice. For the first time since she was born I shouted at her.

"Shut up!" I shook her. "You stupid little baby!"

Then I started to cry. I squeezed her against my nightie. She squirmed and I squeezed her harder, till her head was damp with my tears.

Even my Mum noticed. Next day at breakfast she said, "You didn't half make a racket." She stubbed her cigarette into her saucer. "Got a splitting headache."

I didn't answer. I wasn't telling that last night I'd met my father. I couldn't tell her yet. She'd probably come storming along to the hotel and lay in wait in his room.

Or maybe she'd be indifferent. She'd just light another fag and say, *Oh him. That bastard.*

I couldn't bear that.

The day seemed to drag on for ever. Overnight, Brighton had shrunk. It seemed a small town, with my father coming round each corner, so I stayed indoors.

On the other hand Eddie had grown larger. He loafed around the flat, getting in the way. I needed to talk, but nobody was the right person. Just once I said to him, raising my voice over the afternoon racing.

"Did you know I was called Alexandra?"

"What?"

"My Mum and Dad called me that, but when I was 12 I changed it to Sandy."

"Did you then?" He hadn't turned the volume down. Then he added vaguely, "Bully for you."

I didn't know how to face him. On the other hand, I would have died if he didn't turn up. I waited and waited. I nearly gave up hope. I had to wait until 10.30. I felt hot in my cowgirl frills.

He came in and sat down at the table nearest my counter. I walked over with the menu, calm as calm. I didn't think I could do it.

"I thought you weren't turning up," I said.

"Me?" His eyes twinkled. "You didn't trust me?" He took the menu. "Oh no, Sandy, you give me a chance and you'll find out."

"Find out what?"

"That I'm a man of my word."

I couldn't answer that. Finally I said, "Oh yeah?" with a drawling voice. "Tell us another."

"Honest to God, cross my heart."

I looked at him, directly. His eyes were blue, like mine. And his nose was small and blunt, a familiar little nose in his large, flushed face. I wanted to hide my face because it suddenly seemed so bare. He must be blind, not to recognise me. I was perspiring.

Then I thought: why should he recognise me? He last saw me when I was four. Has he ever thought of me, all these years?

Taking his order into the kitchen, my mind was busy. I stood in front of the dead charcoal range, working out all the places I'd lived since I was four . . . Shepperton, Isleworth, Crawley . . . There was nothing to connect me to Brighton.

SMILE, said the sign as I walked out.

"You travel a lot?" I said, putting his plate in front of him.

"A conversation at last!" He split the ketchup sachet and slopped it over his chips, like blood. He nodded. "For my sins. So what's my line of business, Sandy?"

"You're a rep."

"How did you guess?"

"Your hands."

He looked down with surprise and opened out his palms. There were yellowed calluses across his fingers.

"You're an observant lass. Do I dare to be flattered?" He put out his hand. "Here. Feel them."

I hesitated, and then I touched his fingers. The skin was hard and dry. I took away my hand.

"You've always been a salesman?" I asked.

"Well . . ." He winked. "Bit of this, bit of that."

"Bit of what?" I wanted to know.

"Now that would be telling."

"You've been all over the place?"

"It's the gypsy in my soul!" he said. "Can't tie me down."

There was a pause. Then I said, "Eat up your dinner."

He stared at me. "What's got into you?"

"Nothing."

There was a silence. I fiddled with my frills. Then I went back to the counter.

When he paid he said, "I know you don't like old men but it's Help The Aged Week."

"So?" I put on my pert face.

"You're off at half eleven?"

I nodded.

"Let me buy you a drink." He paused. "Go on. Say yes."

The bar had closed. Besides, it was against the rules for me to go there. You're only allowed to smile at the customers.

But who knows where a smile might lead? It had led me here.

He had a bottle of Scotch in his room, and he ordered me a fresh orange juice from Room Service. When it arrived I hid in the bathroom.

His things were laid out above the basin. I inspected them all: his toothbrush (red, splayed), his toothpaste (Colgate); electric shaver; aftershave (Brut, nearly finished). I wanted to take something home but that was all there was. The towels belonged to the hotel so there was no point. I wondered where he kept the marmalade sachets. But they weren't for me.

"Welcome to my abode," he said, pulling out a chair.

I sat down. "Where is your abode?"

"Pardon?"

"Where do you live?"

He paused. "You don't want to hear about my boring little life."

"Go on," I said, giving him a flirtatious smile. "Tell me."

He hesitated, then he said shortly, "Know Peterborough?"

"No."

"Well, there." His tone grew jaunty. Eyes twinkling, he passed me my glass. "A fresh drink for a fresh young face. How old are you, Sandy?"

"Nineteen."

"Nineteen." He sighed. "Sweet 19. Where have you been all my life?"

I tried to drink the orange juice; it was thick with bits. There was a silence. I couldn't think what to say.

He was sitting on the bed; the room was warm and he'd taken off his jacket. The hair was an illusion; he was thinning on top but he'd brushed his hair over the bald patch. Far away I heard a clock chiming.

I wasn't thirsty. I put down the glass and said, "What do you sell?"

He climbed to his feet and went over to his suitcase, which had a Merriworld sticker on it. He snapped it open.

"Let me introduce Loopy."

He passed me a rubbery creature dressed in a polka-dot frock. She had long, bendy arms and legs and a silly face. He fetched a pad of paper, knelt down on the floor and took her from me. Her arms ended in pencil points. Holding her, he wrote with her arms: TO SANDY WITH THE SMILE. Then he turned her upside down and said, "Hey presto." He started rubbing out the words with her head.

"Don't." I pulled his hand back. I took the paper, which still had TO SANDY WITH, and put it in my apron pocket.

He said, "Rubber and pencils all in one. Wonder where the sharpener ought to be . . ."

"What?"

"Just my vulgar mind."

"Where do you take these things?"

"Ramsdens. Smiths. That big shopping centre."

I knew all the places; I connected him with them. I'd bought Donna's layette at Ramsdens.

He took out a clockwork Fozzy Bear, a Snoopy purse and a magnetic colouring book.

"So you sell toys," I said.

"It's the child in me," he said. "I'm just a little boy at heart."

"Are you?"

"Happy-go-lucky, that's me."

"Anything for a laugh?"

"No use sitting and moaning." He took another drink. "Got to enjoy yourself."

I gazed at the scattered toys. "Just a game, is it?"

"Sandy, you've only got one life. You'll learn that, take it from me." He shifted closer to my legs.

"Anything else in there?" I pointed to the suitcase.

He leaned back and took out a box. "Recognise it?"

I shook my head.

"Ker-Plunk."

"What?

"You were probably still in nappies. It's a Sixties line, but we're giving it this big re-launch." He patted the floor. "Come on and I'll give you a game."

He took out a plastic tube, a box of marbles and some coloured sticks. "Come on." He patted the floor again.

I lowered myself down on the carpet, tucking my skirt in. This damn uniform was so short.

"Look—you slot these sticks in, like this." He pushed them into perforations in the tube, so they made a platform; then with a rattle he poured the marbles on top, so they rested on the sticks.

"Then we take it in turns to pull out a stick *without*," he wagged his finger at me, "without letting a marble drop through." We sat there, crouched on the floor. "If it does, you're a naughty girl."

I pulled out a stick. He pulled out one. I pulled out another.

"Whoops!" he said, as a marble clattered through the sticks.

"Bad luck!" he cried. "I'm winning!"

Sometimes his marbles fell through, sometimes mine. I won.

"Can't have this," he said. "Got to have another game."

He poured himself some more Scotch, and settled down on the floor again, with a grunt. We collected the sticks and pushed them into the holes, then poured the marbles on top.

I didn't want to play, but then I didn't want to leave, either. We pulled out the sticks; the marbles clattered down the tube.

He slapped his thigh. "Got you!"

Outside the window, the clock chimed again. Sitting there amongst the toys I thought, *Why did you never do this with me before? At the proper time?*

"Your turn," he said. "Stop daydreaming."

I pulled out a stick. My throat felt tight and there was an ache in my chest.

"Whoops!" he cried. "Bad luck!"

I felt a hand slide around my waist. The fingers squeezed me. He shifted himself nearer me, so our sides were touching.

"Silly game, isn't it?" he said.

I moved back, disentangling myself. "I must go."

"But we haven't finished!" He looked at me, his face pink from bending over the game.

I climbed to my feet. "Mum'll be worried."

"Come on, you're a big girl now." He held up his hand. "Come and sit down."

"No."

He winked. "Strict, is she?"

I shrugged. He climbed to his feet and stood beside me. We were the same height.

"What about a kiss then?"

I looked into his eyes. Then his face loomed closer. I moved my head; his lips brushed my cheek. I felt them, warm and wet. I bent down and picked up my handbag. My hands were shaking.

"Must go," I said, my voice light.

He saw me to the door, his hand resting on my hip. "Can I see you home?"

"No!" I paused. "I mean, no thanks."

He opened the door. "I'm leaving tomorrow, but I'll be back next month. Know what I'd love to do?"

"What?"

"Take you down to the pier. Never been to the pier. Eat ice-creams." He squeezed my waist, and kissed my cheek. "Know something?"

I whispered, "What?"

"You make me feel years younger." He paused. "Will you come?"

I nodded. "OK," I said.

He buttoned me into my coat, and smoothed down the collar. He stroked my hair.

"You're a lovely girl" he murmured. "Tell your Mum to keep you locked up. Say I said so."

I couldn't bear to wait at the lift, so I made for the stairs. As I went he called, "Tell her it's my fault you're late." His voice grew fainter. "Tell her I'm the one to blame."

Six weeks took an age to pass. I'd looked at the ledger in Reception; he was booked for 15th April.

Donna was sleeping better, but for the first time in my life I slept badly. I had such strong dreams they woke me up. I'd lie there, next to her calm face, and gaze at the orange light that filtered in from the street. I'd put his piece of paper under my pile of sweaters. That was all of him I had, so far. I said nothing to my Mum.

On 15th April Eddie knocked on the bathroom door.

"You're planning to stay there all day?"

I was washing my hair. "Go away!" I shouted.

At seven o'clock prompt I was on station in the Coffee Shop.

Time dragged. 8.00 . . . 8.13 . . . Each time I looked at my watch, only a minute had passed.

9.30. The doors swung open. It wasn't him. Business was slow that night, the place was nearly empty.

10.30 . . . 11.00 . . .

At 11.30 I closed up and took the cash to Dennis, in Reception.

"Not got a smile for me?"

I ignored him and went home.

When I got back, Mum was watching the midnight movie. I was going to my room but she called, "Had a flutter today."

I nodded, but she turned.

"Don't you want to see what I've bought?" She reached down and passed me a carrier bag. "Put it on Lucky Boy and he won, so I splashed out at Ramsdens."

I stared at her. "Ramsdens?"

"Go on. Look. It's for little Donna."

I went over, opened the carrier bag and drew out a huge blue teddy bear. "Cost a bomb," she said. "But what the hell."

Next day I made enquiries at Reception. He'd checked in, they said, during the afternoon as usual. But then he'd come back at six and checked out again.

Later I went to Ramsdens and asked if the Merriworld representative had visited the day before.

The girl thought for a moment, then nodded. "That's right. Jack." She paused to scratch her ear-lobe. "Jack-the-lad."

"So he came?"

She pursed her lips. "Came and went."

"What do you mean?"

She looked at me. "What's it to you?"

"Nothing."

She shrugged. "Dunno what got into him. Left in a hurry."

He'd seen Mum. He'd seen her buying the bloody teddy bear.

He didn't come back. Not once he knew she was in Brighton. At Ramsdens, six weeks later, there was a new rep called Terry. I checked up. Not that I had much hope. After all, he's scarpered once before.

But Donna smiled. It wasn't because of the teddy, she was too young to appreciate that, though Mum would like to believe it.

And it wasn't wind, I could tell. It was me. She smiled at me.

e l doctorow

The Writer in the Family

In 1955 my father died with his ancient mother still alive in a nursing home. The old lady was 90 and hadn't even known he was ill. Thinking the shock might kill her, my aunts told her that he had moved to Arizona for his bronchitis. To the immigrant generation of my grandmother, Arizona was the American equivalent of the Alps, it was where you went for your health. More accurately, it was where you went if you had the money. Since my father had failed in all the business enterprises of his life, this was the aspect of the news my grandmother dwelled on, that he had finally had some success. And so it came about that as we mourned him at home in our stockinged feet, my grandmother was bragging to her cronies about her son's new life in the dry air of the desert.

My aunts had decided on their course of action without consulting us. It meant neither my mother nor my brother nor I could visit Grandma because we were supposed to have moved west too; a family, after all. My brother Harold and I didn't mind—it was always a nightmare at the old people's home, where they all sat around staring at us while we tried to make conversation with Grandma. She looked terrible, had numbers of ailments, and her mind wandered. Not seeing her was no disappointment for my mother, who had never gotten along with the old woman and did not visit when she could have. But what was disturbing was that my aunts had acted in the manner of that side of the family of making government on everyone's behalf, the true citizens by blood and the lesser citizens by marriage. It was exactly this attitude that had tormented my mother all her married life. She claimed Jack's family had never accepted her. She had battled them for 25 years as an outsider.

A few weeks after the end of our ritual mourning my Aunt Frances phoned us from her home in Larchmont. Aunt Frances was the wealthier of my father's sisters. Her husband was a lawyer, and both her sons were at Amherst. She had called to say that Grandma was asking why she didn't hear from Jack. I had answered the phone. "You're the writer in the family," my aunt said. "Your father had so much faith in you. Would you mind making up something? Send it to me and I'll read it to her. She won't know the difference."

That evening, at the kitchen table, I pushed my homework aside and composed a letter. I tried to imagine my father's response to his new life. He had never been west. He had never travelled anywhere. In his generation the great journey was from the working class to the professional class. He hadn't managed that either. But he loved New York, where he had been born and lived his life, and he was always discovering new things about it. He specially loved the old parts of the city below Canal Street, where he would find ship's chandlers or firms that wholesaled in spices and teas. He was a salesman for an appliance jobber with accounts all over the city. He liked to bring home rare cheeses or exotic foreign vegetables that were sold only in certain neighbourhoods. Once he brought home a barometer, another time an antique ship's telescope in a wooden case with a brass snap.

"Dear Mama," I wrote. "Arizona is beautiful. The sun shines all day and the air is warm and I feel better than I have in years. The desert is not as barren as you would expect, but filled with wild flowers and cactus plants and peculiar crooked trees that look like men holding their arms out. You can see great distances in whatever direction you turn and to the west is a range of mountains maybe 50 miles from here, but in the morning with the sun on them you can see the snow on their crests."

My aunt called some days later and told me it was when she read this aloud to the old lady that the full effect of Jack's death came over her. She had to excuse herself and went in the parking lot to cry. "I wept so," she said. "I felt such terrible longing for him. You're so right, he loved to go places, he loved life, he loved everything."

We began trying to organise our lives. My father had borrowed money against his insurance and there was very little left. Some commissions were still due but it didn't look as if his firm would honour them. There was a couple of thousand dollars in a savings bank that had to be maintained there until the estate was settled. The lawyer involved was Aunt Frances' husband and he was very proper. "The estate!" my mother muttered, gesturing as if to pull out her hair. "The estate!" She applied for a job part-time in the admissions office of the hospital where my father's terminal illness had been diagnosed, and where he had spent some months until they had sent him home to die. She knew a lot of the doctors and staff and she had learned "from bitter experience" as she told them, about the hospital routine. She was hired.

I hated that hospital, it was dark and grim and full of tortured people. I thought it was masochistic of my mother to seek out a job there, but did not tell her so.

We lived in an apartment in the corner of 175th Street and the Grand Concourse, one flight up. Three rooms. I shared the bedroom with my brother. It was jammed with furniture because when my father had required a hospital bed in the last weeks of his illness we had moved some of the living-room pieces into the bedroom and made over the living room for him. We had to navigate bookcases, beds, a gateleg table, bureaus, a record player and radio console, stacks of 78 albums, my brother's trombone and music stand, and so on. My mother continued to sleep on the convertible sofa in the living room that had been their bed before his illness. The two rooms were connected by a narrow hall made even narrower by bookcases along the wall. Off the hall were a small kitchen and dinette and a bathroom. There were lots of appliances in the kitchen— broiler, toaster, pressure cooker, counter-top dishwasher, blender—that my father had gotten through his job, at cost. A treasured phrase in our house: *at cost*. But most of these figures went unused because my mother did not care for them. Chromium devices with timers or gauges that required the reading of elaborate instructions were not for her. They were in part responsible for the awful clutter of our lives and now she wanted to get rid of them. "We're being buried," she said. "Who needs them!"

So we agreed to throw out or sell anything inessential. While I found boxes for the appliances and my brother tied the boxes with twine, my mother opened my father's closet and took out his clothes. He had several suits; as a salesman he needed to look his best. My mother wanted us to try on his suits to see which of them could be altered and used. My brother refused to try them on. I tried on one jacket which was too large for me. The lining inside the sleeves chilled my arms and the vaguest scent of my father's being came to me.

"This is way too big," I said.

"Don't worry," my mother said. "I had it cleaned. Would I let you wear it if I hadn't?"

It was the evening, the end of winter, and snow was coming down on the windowsill and melting as it settled. The ceiling bulb glared on a pile of my father's suits and trousers on hangers flung across the bed in the shape of a dead man. We refused to try on anything more, and my mother began to cry.

"What are you crying for?" my brother shouted. "You wanted to get rid of things, didn't you?"

A few weeks later my aunt phoned again and said she thought it would be necessary to have another letter from Jack. Grandma had fallen out of her chair and bruised herself and was very depressed.

"How long does this go on?" my mother said.

"It's not so terrible," my aunt said, "for the little time left to make things easier for her."

My mother slammed down the phone. "He can't even die when he wants to!" she cried. "Even death comes second to Mama! What are they afraid of, the shock will kill her? Nothing can kill her. She's indestructible! A stake through her heart couldn't kill her!"

When I sat down in the kitchen to write the letter I found it more difficult than the first one. "Don't watch me," I said to my brother. "It's hard enough."

"You don't have to do something just because someone wants you to," Harold said. He was two years older than me and had started at City College; but when my father became ill he had switched to night school and gotten a job in a record store.

"Dear Mama," I wrote. "I hope you're feeling well. We're all fit as a fiddle. The life here is good and the people are very friendly and informal. Nobody wears suits and ties here. Just a pair of slacks and a short-sleeved shirt. Perhaps a sweater in the evening. I have bought into a very successful radio and record business and I'm doing very well. You remember Jack's Electric, my old place on Forty-third Street? Well, now it's Jack's Arizona Electric and we have a line of television sets as well."

I sent that letter off to my Aunt Frances, and as we all knew she would, she phoned soon after. My brother held his hand over the mouthpiece. "It's Frances with her latest review," he said.

"Jonathan? You're a very talented young man. I just wanted to tell you what a blessing your letter was. Her whole face lit up when I read the part about Jack's store. That would be an excellent way to continue."

"Well, I hope I don't have to do this anymore, Aunt Frances. It's not very honest."

Her tone changed. "Is your mother there? Let me talk to her."

"She's not here," I said.

"Tell her not to worry," my aunt said. "A poor old lady who has never wished anything but the best for her will soon die."

I did not repeat this to my mother, for whom it would have been one more in the family anthology of unforgivable remarks. But then I had to suffer it myself for the possible truth it might embody. Each side defended its position with rhetoric, but I, who wanted peace, rationalised the snubs and rebuffs each inflicted on the other, taking no stands, like my father himself.

Years ago his life had fallen into a pattern of business failures and missed opportunities. The great debate between his family on the one side, and my mother Ruth on the other, was this: who was responsible for the fact that he had not lived up to anyone's expectations?

As to the prophecies, when spring came, my mother's prevailed. Grandma was still alive.

One balmy Sunday my mother and brother and I took the bus to the Beth El cemetery in New Jersey to visit my father's grave. It was situated on a slight rise. We stood looking over rolling fields embedded with monuments. Here and there processions of black cars wound their way through the lanes, or clusters of people stood at open graves. My father's grave was planted with tiny shoots of evergreen but it lacked a headstone. We had chosen one and paid for it and then the stonecutters had gone on strike. Without a headstone my father did not seem to be honourably dead. He didn't seem to me properly buried.

My mother gazed at the plot beside his, reserved for her coffin. "They were always too fine for other people," she said. "Even in the old days on Stanton Street. They put on airs. Nobody was ever good enough for them. Finally Jack himself was not good enough for them. Except to get them things wholesale. Then he was good enough for them.

"Mom, please," my brother said.

"If I had known. Before I ever met him he was tied to his mama's apron stings. And Essie's apron strings were like chains, let me tell you. We had to live where we could be near them for the Sunday visits. Every Sunday, that was my life, a visit to mamaleh. Whatever she knew I wanted, a better apartment, a stick of furniture, a summer camp for the boys, she spoke against it. You know your father, every decision had to be considered and reconsidered. And nothing changed. Nothing ever changed."

She began to cry. We sat her down on a nearby bench. My

brother walked off and read the names on stones. I looked at my mother, who was crying, and I went off after my brother.

"Mom's still crying," I said. "Shouldn't we do something?"

"It's all right," he said. "It's what she came here for."

"Yes," I said, and then a sob escaped from my throat. "But I feel like crying, too."

My brother Harold put his arm around me. "Look at this old black stone here," he said. "The way it's carved. You can see the changing fashion in monuments—just like everything else."

Somewhere in this time I began dreaming of my father. Not the robust father of my childhood, the handsome man with healthy pink skin and brown eyes and a moustache and the thinning hair parted in the middle. My dead father. We were taking him home from the hospital. It was understood that he had come back from death. This was amazing and joyous. On the other hand, he was terribly mysteriously damaged or, more accurately, spoiled and unclean. He was very yellowed and debilitated by his death, and there were no guarantees that he wouldn't soon die again. He seemed aware of this and his entire personality was changed. He was angry and impatient with all of us. We were trying to help him in some way, struggling to get him home, but something prevented us, something we had to fix, a tattered suitcase that had sprung open, some mechanical thing: he had a car but it wouldn't start; or the car was made of wood; or his clothes, which had become too large for him, had caught in the door. In one version he was all bandaged and as we tried to lift him from his wheelchair into a taxi, the bandage began to unroll and catch in the spokes of the wheelchair. This seemed to be some unreasonableness on his part. My mother looked on sadly and tried to get him to co-operate.

That was the dream. I shared it with no one. Once when I woke, crying out, my brother turned on the light. He wanted to know what I'd been dreaming but I pretended I didn't remember. The dream made me feel guilty. I felt guilty *in* the dream, too, because my enraged father knew we didn't want to live with him. The dream represented us taking him home, or trying to, but it was nevertheless understood by all of us that he was to live alone. He was this derelict back from death, but what we were doing was taking him to some place where he would live by himself without help from anyone until he died again.

At one point I became so fearful of this dream that I tried not to go to sleep. I tried to think of good things about my father and to remember him before his illness. He used to call me "matey". "Hello, matey," he would say when he came home from work. He always wanted us to go someplace—to the store, to the park, to a ball game. He loved to walk. When I went walking with him he would say, "Hold your shoulders back, don't slump. Hold your head up and look at the world. Walk as if you mean it!" As he strode down the street his shoulders moved from side to side, as if he was hearing some kind of cakewalk. He moved with a bounce. He was always eager to see what was around the corner.

The next request for a letter coincided with a special occasion in the house: my brother Harold had met a girl he liked and had gone out with her several times. Now she was coming to our house for dinner.

We had prepared for this for days, cleaning everything in sight, giving the house a going-over, washing the dust of disuse from the glasses and good dishes. My mother came home early from work to get the dinner going. We opened the gateleg table in the living room and brought in the kitchen chairs. My mother spread the table with a laundered white cloth and put out her silver. It was the first family occasion since my father's illness.

I liked my brother's girlfriend a lot. She was a thin girl with very straight hair and she had a terrific smile. Her presence seemed to excite the air. It was amazing to have a living breathing girl in our house. She looked around and what she said was, "Oh, I've never seen so many books!" While she and my brother sat at the table my mother was in the kitchen putting the food into serving bowls and I was going from the kitchen to the living room, kidding around like a waiter, with a white cloth over my arm and a high style of service, placing the serving dish of green beans on the table with a flourish. In the kitchen my mother's eyes were sparkling. She looked at me and nodded and mimed the words, "She's adorable!"

My brother suffered himself to be waited on. He was wary of what we might say. He kept glancing at the girl—her name was Susan—to see if we met her approval. She worked in an insurance office and was taking courses in accounting at City College. Harold was under a terrible strain but he was excited and happy too. He had bought a bottle of Concord-grape wine to go with the roast chicken. He held up his glass and proposed a toast. My mother said, "To good health and happiness," and we all drank, even I. At that moment the phone rang and I went into the bedroom to get it.

"Jonathan? This is your Aunt Frances. How is everyone?"

"Fine, thank you."

"I want to ask one last favour of you. I need a letter from Jack. Your grandma's very ill. Do you think you can?"

"Who is it?" my mother called from the living room.

"OK, Aunt Frances," I said quickly. "I have to go now, we're eating dinner." And I hung up the phone.

"It was my friend Louie," I said, sitting back down. "He didn't know the math pages to review."

The dinner was very fine. Harold and Susan washed the dishes and by the time they were done my mother and I had folded up the gateleg table and put it back against the wall and I had swept the crumbs up with the carpet sweeper. We all sat and talked and listened to records for a while and then my brother took Susan home. The evening had gone very well.

Once when my mother wasn't home my brother had pointed out something: the letters from Jack weren't really necessary. "What is this ritual?" he said, holding his palms up. "Grandma is almost totally blind, she's half deaf and crippled. Does the situation really call for a literary composition? Does it need verisimilitude? Would the old lady know the difference if she was read the phone book?"

"Then why did Aunt Frances ask me?"

"That is the question, Jonathan. Why did she? After all, she could write the letter herself—what difference would it make? And if not Frances, why not Frances' sons, the Amherst students? They have learned by now to write."

"But they're not Jack's sons," I said.

"That's exactly the point," my brother said. "The idea is *service*. Dad used to bust his balls getting them things wholesale, getting them deals on things. Frances of Westchester really needed things at cost. And Aunt Molly. And Aunt Molly's husband, and Aunt Molly's ex-husband. Grandma, if she needed an errand done. He was always on the hook for something. They never thought his time was important. They never thought every favour he got was one he had to pay back. Appliances, records, watches, china, opera tickets, any goddamn thing. Call Jack."

"It was a matter of pride to him to be able to do things for them," I said. "To have connections."

"Yeah, I wonder why," my brother said. He looked out of the window.

Then suddenly it dawned on me that I was being implicated.

"You should use your head more," my brother said.

Yet I had agreed once again to write a letter from the desert and so I did. I mailed it off to Aunt Frances. A few days later, when I came home from school, I thought I saw her sitting in her car in front of our house. She drove a black Buick Roadmaster, a very large clean car with whitewall tyres. It was Aunt Frances all right. She blew the horn when she saw me. I went over and leaned in at the window.

"Hello, Jonathan," she said. "I haven't long. Can you get in the car?"

"Mom's not home," I said. "She's working."

"I know that. I came to talk to you."

"Would you like to come upstairs?"

"I can't. I have to get back to Larchmont. Can you get in for a moment, please?"

I got in the car. My Aunt Frances was a very pretty white-haired woman, very elegant, and she wore tasteful clothes. I had always liked her and from the time I was a child she had enjoyed pointing out to everyone that I looked more like her son than Jack's. She wore white gloves and held the steering wheel and looked straight ahead as she talked, as if the car was in traffic and not sitting at the curb.

"Jonathan," she said, "there is your letter on the seat. Needless to say I didn't read it to Grandma. I'm giving it back to you and I won't ever say a word to anyone. This just between us. I never expected cruelty from you. I never thought you were capable of doing something so deliberately cruel and perverse."

I said nothing.

"Your mother has very bitter feelings and now I see she has poisoned you with them. She has always resented the family. She is a very strong-willed, selfish person."

"No she isn't," I said.

"I wouldn't expect you to agree. She drove poor Jack crazy with her demands. She always had the highest aspirations and he could never fulfil them to her satisfaction. When he still had his store he kept your mother's brother, who drank, on salary. After the war when he began to make a little money he had to buy Ruth a mink jacket because she was so desperate to have one. He had debts to pay but she wanted a mink. He was a very special person, my brother, he should have accomplished something special, but he loved your mother and devoted his life to her. And all she ever thought about was keeping up with the Joneses."

I watched the traffic going up the Grand Concourse. A bunch of kids were waiting at the bus stop at the corner. They had put their books on the ground and were horsing around.

"I'm sorry I have to descend to this," Aunt Frances said. "I don't like talking about people this way. If I have nothing good to say about someone, I'd rather not say anything. How is Harold?"

"Fine."

"Did he help you write this marvellous letter?"

"No."

After a moment she said more softly, "How are you all getting along?"

"Fine."

"I would invite you up for Passover if I thought your mother would accept."

I didn't answer.

She turned on the engine. "I'll say good-bye now, Jonathan. Take your letter. I hope you give some time to thinking about what you've done."

That evening when my mother came home from work I saw that she wasn't as pretty as my Aunt Frances. I usually thought my mother was a good-looking woman, but I saw now that she was too heavy and that her hair was undistinguished.

"Why are you looking at me?" she said.

"I'm not."

"I learned something interesting today," my mother said. "We may be eligible for a VA pension because of the time your father spent in the Navy."

That took me by surprise. Nobody had ever told me my father was in the Navy.

"In World War I," she said, "he went to Webb's Naval Academy on the Harlem River. He was training to be an ensign. But the war ended and he never got his commission."

After dinner the three of us went through the closets looking for my father's papers, hoping to find some proof that could be filed with the Veterans Administration. We came up with two things, a Victory medal, which my brother said everyone got for being in the service during the Great War, and an astounding sepia photograph of my father and his shipmates on the deck of a ship. They were dressed in bell-bottoms and T-shirts and armed with mops and pails, brooms and brushes.

"I never knew this," I found myself saying. "I never knew this."

"You just don't remember," my brother said.

I was able to pick out my father. He stood at the end of the row, a thin, handsome boy with a full head of hair, a moustache, and an intelligent smiling countenance.

"He had a joke," my mother said. "They called their training ship the SS *Constipation* because it never moved."

Neither the picture nor the medal was proof of anything, but my brother thought a duplicate of my father's service record had to be in Washington somewhere and that it was just a matter of learning how to go about finding it.

"The pension wouldn't amount to much," my mother said. "Twenty or 30 dollars. But it would certainly help."

I took the picture of my father and his shipmates and propped it against the lamp at my bedside. I looked into his youthful face and tried to relate it to the Father I knew. I looked at the picture a long time. Only gradually did my eye connect it to the set of Great Sea Novels in the bottom shelf of the bookcase a few feet away. My father had given that set to me: it was uniformly bound in green with gilt lettering and it included works by Melville, Conrad, Victor Hugo and Captain Marryat. And lying across the top of the books, jammed in under the sagging shelf above, was his old ship's telescope in its wooden case with the brass snap.

I thought how stupid, and imperceptive, and self-centred I had been never to have understood while he was alive what my father's dream for his life had been.

On the other hand, I had written in my last letter from Arizona—the one that had so angered Aunt Frances—something that might allow me, the writer in the family, to soften my judgement of myself. I will conclude by giving the letter here in its entirety.

Dear Mama,

This will be my final letter to you since I have been told by the doctors that I am dying.

I have sold my store at a very fine profit and am sending Frances a check for five thousand dollars to be deposited in your account. My present to you, Mamaleh. Let Frances show you the passbook.

As for the nature of my ailment, the doctors haven't told me what it is, but I know that I am simply dying of the wrong life. I should never have come to the desert. It wasn't the place for me.

I have asked Ruth and the boys to have my body cremated and the ashes scattered in the ocean.

                                              Your loving son, Jack

alice adams

A Public Pool

Swimming

Reaching, pulling, gliding through the warm blue chlorinated water, I am strong and lithe: I am not oversized, not six feet tall, weighing one eighty-five. I am not myself, not Maxine.

I am fleet, possessed of powerful, deep energy. I could swim all day, swim anywhere. Sometimes I even wonder if I should try the San Francisco Bay, that treacherous cold tide-wracked water. People do swim there, they call themselves Polar Bears. Maybe I should, although by now I like it here in the Rossi Pool, swimming back and forth, doing laps in the Fast Lane, stretching and pulling my forceful, invisible body.

Actually the lane where I swim is not really Fast. I swim during Recreational Swimming, and during Rec hours what was Fast during Laps is roped off for anyone to use who does laps—Slow, Medium, or genuinely Fast, which I am not.

Last summer I started off in Slow, and then I could not do many lengths at a time, 16 or 18 at most, and only sidestroke. But I liked it, the swimming and the calm, rested way it seemed to make me feel. And I thought that maybe, eventually I might get thinner, swimming. Also, it takes up a certain amount of time, which for an out-of-work living-at-home person is a great advantage. I have been laid off twice in the past five years, both times by companies going out of business; I have a real knack, my mother says. And how many hours a day can a young woman read? That is a question my mother often asks. She is a down-town saleslady, old but blonde, and very thin. So—swimming.

After a month or so I realised that I was swimming faster than most of the people in Slow, and that some people who could barely swim at all were in my way. For another two or three weeks I watched Medium, wondering if I dare try to swim in there. One day I forced myself, jumping into Medium, the middle lane. I felt very anxious, but that was hardly an unfamiliar or unusual sort of emotion; sometimes shopping for groceries can have the same effect. And actually Medium turned out to be OK. There were a few hotshots who probably belonged in Fast but were too chicken to try it there, but quite a few people swam about the same as I did, and some swam slower.

Sometime during the Fall—still warm outside, big dry yellow sycamore leaves falling down to the sidewalks—the pool schedule changed so that all the lap swimming was geared to people with jobs: Laps at noon and after five. Discouraging: I knew that all those people would be eager, pushy aggressive swimmers, kicking big splashes into my face as they swam past, almost shoving me aside in their hurry to get back to their wonderful jobs.

However, I found out that during Rec there is always a lane roped off for laps, and the Rec hours looked much better: mid to late afternoon, and those can be sort of cold hours at home, a sad end of daytime, with nothing accomplished.

In any case, that is why I now swim my laps during Rec in the Fast lane. In the rest of the pool some little kids cavort around, and some grownups, some quite fat, some hardly able to swim at all. Sometimes a lot of school kids, mostly girls, mostly black, or Asian. A reflection of this neighbourhood.

To Meet Someone

Of course I did not begin swimming with any specific idea that I might meet someone, any more than meeting someone is in my mind when I go out to the Ninth Avenue Library. Still, there is always that possibility: the idea of someone is always there, in a way, wherever I go. Maybe everywhere everyone goes, even if most people don't think of it that way?

For one thing, the area of the Rossi Recreation Centre,

where the pool is, has certain romantic associations for me: a long time ago, in the 'Sixties, when I was only in junior high (and still thin!), that was where all the peace marches started; everyone gathered there on the Rossi playing field, behind the pool house, with their placards and flags and banners, in their costumes or just plain clothes. I went to all the marches; I loved them, and I hated LBJ, and I knew that his war was crazy, wicked, killing off kids and poor people, mostly blacks, was how it looked to me.

Anyway, one Saturday in May, I fell in love with a group of kids from another school, and we spent the rest of that day together, just messing around, walking almost all over town—eating pizza in North Beach and smoking a little dope in the park. Sort of making out, that night, at one of their houses, over on Lincoln Way. Three guys and a couple of girls, all really nice. I kept hoping that I would run into them somewhere again, but I never did. Or else they, too, underwent sudden changes, the way I did, and grew out-of-sight tall, and then fat. But I still think of them sometimes, walking in the direction of Rossi.

Swimming, though: even if you met someone it would be hard to tell anything about them, beyond the most obvious physical facts. For one thing almost no one says anything, except for a few super polite people who say Sorry when they bump into you, passing in a lane. Or, there is one really mean-looking black woman, tall, and a very fast swimmer, who one day told me, "You ought to get over closer to the side." She ought to have been in Fast, is what I would like to have said, but did not.

The men all swim very fast, and hard, except for a couple of really fat ones; most men somersault backward at the end of each length, so as not to waste any time. A few women do that, too, including the big mean black one. There is one especially objectionable guy, tall and blond (but not as tall as I am) with a little blond beard; I used to watch him zip past, ploughing the water with his violent crawl, in Fast, when I was still pushing along in Medium. Unfortunately, now he, too, comes to swim in Rec, and mostly at the same times that I do. He swims so fast, so roughly cutting through the water; he doesn't even know I am there, nor probably anyone else. He is just the kind of guy who used to act as though I was air, along the corridors at Washington High.

I have noticed that very few old people come to swim at Rossi. And if they do you can watch them trying to hide their old bodies, slipping down into the water. Maybe for that reason, body shyness, they don't come back; the very old never come more than once to swim, which is a great pity, I think. The exercise would be really good for them, and personally I like very old people, very much. For a while I had a job in a home for old people, a rehabilitation centre, so-called, and although in many ways it was a terrible job, really exhausting and sometimes very depressing, I got to like a lot of them very much. They have a lot to say that's interesting, and if they like you it's more flattering, I think, since they have more people to compare you with. I like *real* old people, who look their age.

People seem to come and go, though, at Rossi. You can see someone there regularly for weeks, or months, and then suddenly never again, and you don't know what has happened to that person. They could have switched over to the regular lap hours, or maybe found a job so that now they come very late, or early in the morning. Or they could have died, had a heart attack, or been run down by some car. There is no way you could ever know, and their sudden absences can seem very mysterious, a little spooky.

Garlic for Lunch

Since my mother has to stay very thin to keep her job (she has to look much younger than she is), and since God knows I should lose some weight, we usually don't eat much for dinner. Also, most of my mother's money goes for all the clothes she has to have for work, not to mention the rent and the horrible utility bills. We eat a lot of eggs.

However, sometimes I get a powerful craving for something really good, like a pizza, or some pasta, my favourite. I like just plain spaghetti, with scallions and garlic and butter and some Parmesan, mostly stuff we have already in the house. Which makes it all the harder not to yield to that violent urge for pasta, occasionally.

One night there was nothing much else around to eat, and so I gave in to my lust, so to speak. I made a big steaming bowl of oniony, garlicky, buttery spaghetti, which my mother, in a worse than usual mood, ate very little of. Which meant that the next day there was a lot left over, and at noontime, I was unable not to eat quite a lot of it for lunch. I brushed my teeth before I went off to swim, but of course that doesn't help a lot, with garlic. However, since I almost never talk to anyone at Rossi it didn't much matter, I thought.

I have worked out how to spend the least possible time undressed in the locker room: I put my bathing suit on at home, then sweatshirt and jeans, and I bring along underthings wrapped up in a towel. That way I just zip off my clothes to swim, and afterwards I can rush back into them, only naked for an instant; no one has to see me. While I am swimming I leave the towel with the understuff wrapped up in it on the long bench at one side of the pool, and sometimes I have fantasies of someone walking off with it; however, it is comforting to think that no one would know whose it was, probably.

I don't think very much while swimming, not about my bra and panties, nor about the fact that I ate all that garlic for lunch. I swim fast and freely, going up to the end with a crawl, back to Shallow with my backstroke, reaching wide, stretching everything

Tired, momentarily winded, I pause in Shallow, still crouched down in the water and ready to go, but resting.

Just then, startlingly, someone speaks to me, a man's conversational voice. "It's nice today," he says. "Not too many people, right?"

Standing up, I see that I am next to the blond-bearded man, the violent swimmer. Who has spoken.

Very surprised, I say, "Oh yes, it's really terrific, isn't it? Monday it was awful, so many people I could hardly move, really terrible. I hate it when it's crowded like that, hardly worth coming at all on those days, but how can you tell until you get there?" I could hear myself saying all that; I couldn't stop.

He looks up at me in—amazement? disgust? great fear, that I will say even more. It is hard to read the expression in his small blue bloodshot eyes, and he only mutters, "That's right," before plunging back into the water.

Was it my garlic breath or simply my height, my incredible *size* that drove him off like that? In a heavy way I wondered, as I continued to swim, all the rest of my laps, which seemed laborious. It could have been either, easily, or in fact anything about me could have turned him off, off and away, for good; I knew that he would never speak to me again. A pain which is close to and no doubt akin to lust lay heavily in my body's lower quadrant, hurtful and implacable.

Sex

The atmosphere in the pool is not exactly sexy, generally, although you might think that it would be, with everyone so stripped down, wearing next to nothing, and some of the women looking really great, so slim and trim, high-breasted, in their thin brief bathing suits.

Once, just as I was getting in I overheard what looked like the start of a romance between a young man, fairly good-looking, who was talking to a very pretty Mexican girl.

The girl said, "You're Brad?"

"No, Gregory."

"Well, Greg, I'll try to make it. Later."

But with brief smiles they then both plunged back into doing their laps, seeming not to have made any significant (sexual) contact.

I have concluded that swimming is not a very sexual activity. I think very infrequently of sex while actually swimming. Well, all sports are supposed to take your mind off sex, aren't they? They are supposed to make you miss it less.

The lifeguards, during swimming hours, usually just sit up on their high wooden lifeguard chairs, looking bored. A couple of youngish, not very attractive guys. Every now and then one of the guys will walk around the pool very slowly, probably just to break his own monotony, but trying to look like a person on patrol.

One afternoon I watched one of those guys stop at Shallow, and stare down for a long time at a little red-haired girl who was swimming there. She was a beautiful child, with narrow blue eyes and long wet red hair, a white little body, as lithe as a fish, as she laughed and slipped around, The lifeguard stared and stared, and I knew—I could tell that sex was on his mind. Could he be a potential child molester?

I myself think of sex more often, in spite of swimming, since the day Blond Beard spoke to me, the day I'd had all that garlic for lunch. I hate to admit this.

The Shrink

An interesting fact that I have gradually noticed as I come to Rossi, to swim my laps, is that actually there is more variety among the men's trunks than among the bathing suits the women wear. The men's range from cheap, too-tight Lastex to the khaki shorts with thin blue stripes that they advertise at Brooks, or Robert Kirk. Whereas, as I noted early on, all the women wear quite similar-looking dark suits. Do the men who are rich, or at least getting along OK in the world, not bother to hide it when they come to a cheap public school pool, while the women do? A puzzle. I cannot quite work it out. Blond Beard wears new navy Lastex trunks, which might mean anything at all.

Most people, including a lot of the men, but not Blond Beard, wear bathing caps, which makes it even harder to tell people apart, and would make it almost impossible, even, to recognise someone you knew. It is not surprising that from time to time I see someone I think I know, or have just met somewhere or other. At first, remembering the peace march kids, I imagined that I saw one or all of them, but that could have been just hope, a wishful thought. I thought I saw my old gym teacher, also from junior high-days. And one day I saw a man who looked like my father, which was a little crazy, since he split for Seattle when I was about five years old; I probably wouldn't know him if I did see him somewhere, much less in a pool with a bathing cap on.

But one day I saw an old woman with short white hair,

swimming very fast, whom I really thought was the shrink I went to once in high school, as a joke.

Or, going to the shrink started out to be a joke. The school had a list of ones that you could go to, if you had really "serious problems", and to me and my girlfriend then, Betty, who was black, it seemed such a ludicrous idea, paying another person just to listen, telling them about your sex life, all like that, that we dreamed up the idea of inventing some really serious problems, and going off to some fool doctor and really putting him on, and at the same time finding out what it was like, seeing shrinks.

Betty, who was in most ways a lot smarter than me, much faster to catch on to things, chickened out early on; but she kept saying that I should go; Betty would just help me make up some stuff to say. And we did; we spent some hilarious afternoons at Betty's place in the project, making up lists of "serious problems": heavy drugs, of course, and dealers. And stepfathers or even fathers doing bad sex things to you, and boys trying to get you to trick. All those things were all around Betty's life, and I think they scared her, really, but she laughed along with me, turning it into one big joke between us.

I made the appointment through the guidance office, with a Dr Sheinbaum, and I went to the address, on Steiner Street. And that is where the joke stopped being a joke.

A nice-looking white-haired lady (a surprise right there; I had expected some man) led me into a really nice-looking living room, all books and pictures and big soft comfortable leather furniture. And the lady, the doctor, asked me to sit down, to try to tell her about some of the things that upset me.

I sat down in a soft pale-coloured chair, and all the funny made-up stuff went totally out of my mind—and I burst into tears. It was horrible, great wracking sobs that I absolutely could not stop. Every now and then I would look up at the doctor, and see that gentle face, that intelligent look of caring, and for some reason that made me cry much harder, even.

Of course I did not tell Betty—or anyone—about crying like that. All I said about going to the shrink was that it was all right, no big deal. And I said about the good-looking furniture. Betty was interested in things like that.

But could the fast-swimming older woman be that shrink? Well, she could be; it seemed the kind of thing that she might do, not caring what anyone thought, or who might see her. But she would never remember or recognise me—or would she?

Looking for Work

The job search is something that I try not think about, along with sex, general deprivation. It is what I should be doing, naturally; and in theory that is what I do all day, look for work. However, these days I seldom get much further than the want ads in the paper, those columns and columns of people saying they want secretaries, or sales people. And no one, not in a million years, would think of hiring me for either of those slots. Secretaries are all about the same size, very trim and tidy-looking, very normal, and so are people in sales—just ask my mother.

Sometimes an ad for a waitress sounds possible, and that is something I've done; I had a part-time waitress job the summer I got out of Washington High. But in those days I was thinner, and just now my confidence is pretty low. In my imagination, prospective employers, restaurant owners take one look at me and they start to sneer: "We don't even have the space for a person your size," or some such snub.

Instead I swim, and swim, swim—for as long as I can, every day. I can feel my muscles stretching, pulling, getting longer, in the warm strong water.

Hello

An odd coincidence: on a Tuesday afternoon—short Rec hours, one-thirty to three—both Blond Beard *and* the big black woman who told me to swim closer to the side, so crossly—both those people on that same day say Hello to me, very pleasantly.

First, I had just jumped down into the pool, the shallow end of the lap section, when Blond Beard swam up and stood beside me for a minute. Looking up at me, he said Hello, and he smiled. However, his small pale eyes were vague; very likely he did not remember that we sort of talked before (hopefully, he did not remember the garlic).

I concentrated on not making too much of that encounter.

Later, when I had finished swimming and was drying off and dressing in the locker room, I was half aware that someone else was in there, too, on the other side of a row of lockers. Hurrying, not wanting to see anyone (or anyone to see me!), I was about to rush out of the room when at the exit door I almost bumped into the big black woman. In fact, it was a little funny, we are so nearly the exact same size. We both smiled; maybe she saw the humour in it, too? And then she said, "Say, your stroke's coming along real good."

"Oh. Uh, thanks."

"You're a real speeder these days."

I felt a deep pleasure in my chest. It was like praise from a teacher, someone in charge. We walked out of the building together, the black woman going up across the playground, where the peace marches gathered, maybe towards Geary Boulevard. And I walked down Arguello, out into the avenues. Home.

Warmth

The water in the pool is warm. In our cold apartment, where my mother screams over the higher and higher utility bills and keeps the heat down, I only have to think about that receiving warmness, touching all my skin, to force myself out into the cold and rain, to walk the long blocks to Rossi Pool, where quickly undressed I will slip down into it.

And swim.

In January, though, the weather got suddenly warmer. The temperature in the pool also seemed to have suddenly changed; it was suddenly cooler. Distrustful, as I guess I tend to be regarding my perceptions, I wondered if the water only seemed cooler. Or, had they turned it down because of the warmer weather, economising, as my mother does? In any case it was disappointing, and the pool was much less welcoming, no matter how falsely spring-like the outside air had turned.

"Do you think the water's colder?" It was Blond Beard who asked this of me one day; we were standing momentarily in the shallow end. But although I was the person he had chosen to ask, I was still sure that for him I was no one; he remembers nothing of me from one tiny, minor contact to another. I am a large non-person.

I told him, "Yes, it seems a little colder to me," (not wanting to say too much—again).

"They must have turned it down."

Swimming

Since the pool is 100 feet long, a half a mile is 26 lengths, which is what I try to do every day. "I swim three miles a week," would sound terrific, to anyone, or even, "I swim a little over two miles a week." Anyone would be impressed, except my mother.

On some days, though, I have to trick myself into swimming the whole 26. "I'm tired, didn't sleep too well, 16 lengths is perfectly okay, respectable," I tell myself. And then, having done the 16, I will say (to myself) that I might as well do a couple more, or four more. And if you get to 20 you might as well go on to 26, as I almost always do.

On other, better days I can almost forget what I am doing; that is, I forget to count. I am only aware of a long strong body (mine) pulling through the water, of marvellous muscles, a strong back, and long, long legs.

The Neighbourhood

Sometimes, walking around the neighbourhood, I see swimmers from the pool—or, people I think I have seen in swimming; in regular clothes it is hard to be sure.

Once, passing a restaurant out on Clement Street I was almost sure that the waitress with her back to the window was the big black woman, formerly cross but now friendly and supportive. Of course I could go in and check it out, even say Hello, but I didn't want to do that, really. But I was pleased with just the idea that she might be there, with a waitress job in such a nice loose-seeming coffee place. I even reasoned that if they hired that woman, big as she is, mightn't someone hire me, about the same size? (I think swimming is making me more optimistic, somehow.) Maybe I should look harder, not be so shy about applying for waitress jobs?

However, one day in late June, there is no mistaking Blond Beard, who comes up to me on Arguello, near Clement: I am just coming out of the croissant place where I treated myself to a cup of hot chocolate. I am celebrating, in a way: the day before I had pulled all my courage together and went out to a new "rehabilitation place" for old people, out in the Sunset, and they really seemed to like me. I am almost hired, I think. They would give me a place to live—I could leave home!

"Hey! I know you from swimming, don't I? In Rossi?" Blond Beard has come up close to me; he is grinning confidently up into my face. His clothes are very sharp, all clean and new, like from a window at Sears.

"You look so good, all that swimming's really trimmed you down," he tells me. And then, "This is a coincidence, running into you like this when I was needing a cup of coffee. Come on back in and keep me company. My treat."

He is breathing hard up into my face, standing there in the soft new sunlight. I am overwhelmed by the smell of Juicy Fruit—so much, much worse than garlic, I suddenly decide. And I hate sharp clothes.

Stepping back I say, "Thanks, but I have to go home now," and I move as smoothly as though through water.

I leave him standing there.

I swim away.

penelope lively

Black Dog

John Case came home one summer evening to find his wife huddled in the corner of the sofa with the sitting-room curtains drawn. She said there was a black dog in the garden, looking at her through the window. Her husband put his briefcase in the hall and went outside. There was no dog; a blackbird fled shrieking across the lawn and next door someone was using a mower. He did not see how any dog could get into the garden: the fences at either side were five feet high and there was a wall at the far end. He returned to the house and pointed this out to his wife, who shrugged and continued to sit hunched in the corner of the sofa. He found her there again the next evening and at the weekend she refused to go outside and sat for much of the time watching the window.

The daughters came, big girls with jobs in insurance companies, wardrobes full of bright clothes and £20,000 mortgages. They stood over Brenda Case and said she should get out more. She should go to evening classes, they said, join a Health Club, do a language course, learn upholstery, go jogging, take driving lessons. And Brenda Case sat at the kitchen table and nodded. She quite agreed, it would be a good thing to find a new interest—jogging, upholstery, French; yes, she said, she must pull herself together, and it was indeed up to her in the last resort, they were quite right. When they had gone she drew the sitting-room curtains again and sat on the sofa staring at a magazine they had brought. The magazine was full of recipes the daughters had said she must try; there were huge bright glossy photographs of puddings crested with alpine peaks of cream, of dark glistening casseroles and salads like an artists' palette. The magazine costed each recipe; a four-course dinner for six worked out at £3.89 a head. It also had articles advising her on life insurance, treatment for breast cancer and how to improve her love-making.

John Case became concerned about his wife. She had always been a good housekeeper; now, they began to run out of things. When one evening there was nothing but cold meat and cheese for supper he protested. She said she had not been able to shop because it had rained all day; on rainy days the dog was always outside, waiting for her.

The daughters came again and spoke severely to their mother. They talked to their father separately, in different tones, proposing an autumn holiday in Portugal or the Canaries, a new three-piece for the sitting-room, a musquash coat.

John Case discussed the whole thing with his wife, reasonably. He did this one evening after he had driven the Toyota into the garage, walked over to the front door and found it locked from within. Brenda, opening it, apologised; the dog had been round at the front today, she said, sitting in the middle of the path.

He began by saying lightly that dogs have not been known to stand up on their hind legs and open doors. And in any case, he continued, there is no dog. No dog at all. The dog is something you are imagining. I have asked all the neighbours, nobody has seen a big black dog. Nobody round here owns a big black dog. There is no evidence of a dog. So you must stop going on about this dog because it does not exist. "What is the matter?" he asked, gently. "Something must be the matter. Would you like to go away for a holiday? Shall we have the house re-decorated?"

Brenda Case listened to him. He was sitting on the sofa, with his back to the window. She sat listening carefully to him and from time to time her eyes strayed from his face to the lawn beyond, in the middle of which the dog sat, its tongue hanging out and its yellow eyes glinting. She said she would go away for a holiday if he wished, and she would be perfectly willing for the house to be re-decorated. Her husband talked about travel agents and decorating firms and once he got up and walked over to the window to inspect the condition of the paintwork; the dog, Brenda saw, continued to sit there, its eyes always on her.

They went to Marrakesh for 10 days. Men came and turned the kitchen from primrose to eau de nil and the hallway from magnolia to parchment. September became October and Brenda Case fetched from the attic a big gnarled walking stick that was a relic of a trip to the Tyrol many years ago; she took this with her every time she went out of the house which nowadays was not often. Inside the house, it was always somewhere near her—its end protruding from under the sofa, or hooked over the arm of her chair.

The daughters shook their tousled heads at their mother, towering over her in their baggy fashionable trousers and their big gay jackets. It's not fair on Dad, they said, can't you see that? You've only got one life, they said sternly, and Brenda Case replied that she realised that, she did indeed. Well then . . . said the daughters, one on each side of her, bigger than her, brighter, louder, always saying what they meant, going straight to the point and no nonsense, competent with income tax returns and contemptuous of muddle.

When she was alone, Brenda Case kept doors and windows closed at all times. Occasionally, when the dog was not there, she would open the upstairs windows to air the bedrooms and the bathroom; she would stand with the curtains blowing, taking in great gulps and draughts. Downstairs, of course, she could not risk this, because the dog was quite unpredictable; it would be absent all day, and then suddenly there it would be squatting by the fence, or leaning hard up against the patio doors, sprung from nowhere. She would draw the curtains, resigned, or move to another room and endure the knowledge of its presence on the other side of the wall, a few yards away. When it was there she would sit doing nothing, staring straight ahead of her; silent and patient. When it was gone she moved around the house, prepared meals, listened a little to the radio, and sometimes took the old photograph albums from the bottom drawer of the bureau in the sitting room. In these albums the daughters slowly mutated from swaddled bundles topped with monkey faces and spiky hair to chunky toddlers and then to spindly-limbed little girls in matching pinafores. They played on Cornish beaches or posed on the lawn, holding her hand (that same lawn on which the dog now sat on its hunkers). In the photographs, she looked down at them, smiling, and they gazed up at her or held out objects for her inspection—a flower, a sea-shell. Her husband was also in the photographs, a smaller man than now, it seemed, with a curiously vulnerable look, as though surprised in a moment of privacy. Looking at herself, Brenda saw a pretty young woman who seemed vaguely familiar, like some relative not encountered for many years.

John Case realised that nothing had been changed by Marrakesh and re-decoration. He tried putting the walking stick back up in the attic; his wife brought it down again. If he opened the patio doors she would simply close them as soon as he had left the room. Sometimes he saw her looking over his shoulder into the garden with an expression on her face that chilled him. He asked her, one day, what she thought the dog would do if it got into the house; she was silent for a moment and then said quietly she supposed it would eat her.

He said he could not understand, he simply did not understand, what could be wrong. It was not, he said, as though they had a thing to worry about. He gently pointed out that she wanted for nothing. It's not that we have to count the pennies any more, he said, not like in the old days.

"When we were young," said Brenda Case. "When the girls were babies."

"Right. It's not like that now, is it?" He indicated the 24″ colour TV set, the video, the stereo, the micro-wave oven, the English Rose fitted kitchen, the bathroom with separate shower. He reminded her of the BUPA membership, the index-linked pension, the shares and dividends. Brenda agreed that it was not, it most certainly was not.

The daughters came with their boyfriends, nicely-spoken confident young men in very clean shirts, who talked to Brenda of their work in firms selling computers and Japanese cameras while the girls took John into the garden and discussed their mother.

"The thing is, she's becoming agoraphobic."

"She thinks she sees this black dog," said John Case.

"We know," said the eldest daughter. "But that, frankly, is neither here nor there. It's a mechanism, simply. A ploy. Like children do. One has to get to the root of it, that's the thing."

"It's her age," said the youngest.

"Of course it's her age," snorted the eldest, "but it's also her. She was always inclined to be negative, but this is ridiculous."

"Negative?" said John Case. He tried to remember his wife—his wives—who—one of whom—he could see inside the house, beyond the glass of the patio window, looking out at him from between two young men he barely knew. The reflections of his daughters, his strapping prosperous daughters, were superimposed upon their mother, so that she looked at him through the cerise and orange and yellow of their clothes.

"Negative. A worrier. Look on the bright side, *I* say, but that's not Mum, is it?"

"I wouldn't have said . . ." he began.

"She's unmotivated," said the youngest, "that's the real trouble. No job, no nothing. It's a generation problem, too."

"I'm trying . . ." their father began.

"We know, Dad, we know. But the thing is, she needs help. This isn't something you can handle all on your own. She'll have to see someone."

"No way," said the youngest, "will we get Mum into therapy."

"Dad can take her to the surgery," said the eldest, "for starters."

The doctor—the new doctor, there was always a new doctor—was about the same age as her daughters, Brenda Case saw. Once upon a time doctors had been older men, fatherly and reliable. This one was good-looking, in the manner of men in knitting pattern photographs. He sat looking at her, quite kindly, and she told him how she was feeling. In so far as this was possible.

When she had finished he tapped a pencil on his desk. "Yes," he said. "Yes, I see." And then he went on, "There doesn't seem to be any very specific trouble, does there, Mrs Case?"

She agreed.

"How do you think you would define it yourself?"

She thought. At last she said that she supposed there was nothing wrong with her that wasn't wrong with—well, everyone.

"Quite," said the doctor busily, writing now on his pad. "That's the sensible way to look at things. So I'm giving you this . . . Three a day . . . Come back and see me in two weeks."

When she came out John Case asked to see the doctor for a moment. He explained that he was worried about his wife. The doctor nodded sympathetically. John told the doctor about the black dog, apologetically, and the doctor looked reflective for a moment and then said, "Your wife is 54."

John Case agreed. She was indeed 54.

"Exactly," said the doctor. "So I think we can take it that, with some care and understanding, these difficulties will . . . disappear. I've given her something." He smiled, confidently; John Case smiled back. That was that.

"It will go away," said John Case to his wife, firmly. He was not entirely sure what he meant, but it did not do, he felt sure, to be irresolute. She looked at him without expression.

Brenda Case swallowed each day the pills that the doctor had given her. She believed in medicines and doctors, had always found that aspirin cured a headache and used to frequent the surgery with the girls when they were small. She was prepared for a miracle. For the first few days it did seem to her just possible that the dog was growing a little smaller but after a week she realised that it was not. She continued to take the pills and when, at the end of a fortnight, she told the doctor that there was no change he said that these things took time, one had to be patient. She looked at him, this young man in his swivel chair on the other side of a cluttered desk, and knew that whatever was to be done would not be done by him, or by cheerful yellow pills like children's sweets.

The daughters came, to inspect and admonish. She said that yes, she had seen the doctor again, and yes, she was feeling rather more . . . herself. She showed them the new sewing machine with many extra attachments that she had not tried and when they left she watched them go down the front path to their cars, swinging their bags and shouting to each other, and saw the dog step aside for them, wagging his tail. When they had gone she opened the front door again and stood there for a few minutes, looking at it, and the dog, five yards away, looked back, not moving.

The next day she took the shopping trolley and set off for the shops. As she opened the front gate she saw the dog come out from the shadow of the fence but she did not turn back. She continued down the street, although she could feel it behind her, keeping its distance. She spoke in a friendly way to a couple of neighbours, did her shopping and returned to the house, and all the while the dog was there, 20 paces off. As she walked to the front door she could hear the click of its claws on the pavement and had to steel herself so hard not to turn round that when she got inside she was bathed in sweat and shaking all over. When her husband came home that evening he thought her in a funny mood, she asked for a glass of sherry and later she suggested they put a record on instead of watching TV—*West Side Story* or another of those shows they went to years ago.

He was surprised at the change in her. She began to go out daily, and although in the evenings she often appeared to be exhausted, as though she had been climbing mountains instead of walking suburban streets, she was curiously calm. Admittedly, she had not appeared agitated before, but her stillness had not been natural; now, he sensed a difference. When the daughters telephoned he reported their mother's condition and listened to their complacent comments: that stuff usually did the trick, they said, all the medics were using it nowadays, they'd always known Mum would be OK soon. But when he put the telephone down and returned to his wife in the sitting-room he found himself looking at her uncomfortably. There was an alertness about her that worried him; later, he thought he heard something outside and went to look. He could see nothing at either the front or the back and his wife continued to read a magazine. When he sat down again she looked across at him with a faint smile.

She had started by meeting its eyes, its yellow eyes. And thus she had learned that she could stop it, halt its patient shadowing of her, leave it sitting on the pavement or the garden path. She began to leave the front door ajar, to open the patio window. She could not say what would happen next, knew only that this was inevitable. She no longer sweated or shook; she did not glance behind her when she was outside, and within she hummed to herself as she moved from room to room.

John Case, returning home on an autumn evening, stepped out of the car and saw light streaming through the open front door. He thought he heard his wife speaking to someone in the house. When he came into the kitchen, though, she was alone. He said, "The front door was open," and she replied that she must have left it so by mistake. She was busy with a saucepan at the stove and in the corner of the room, her husband saw, was a large dog basket towards which her glance occasionally strayed.

He made no comment. He went back into the hall, hung up his coat and was startled by his own face, caught unawares in the mirror by the hatstand and seeming like someone else's— that of a man both older and more burdened than he knew himself to be. He stood staring at it for a few moments and then took a step back towards the kitchen. He could hear the gentle chunking sound of his wife's wooden spoon stirring something in the saucepan and then, he thought, the creak of wickerwork.

He turned sharply and went into the sitting room. He crossed to the window and looked out. He saw the lawn, blackish in the dusk, disappearing into darkness. He switched on the outside light and flooded it all with an artificial glow— the grass, the little flight of steps up to the patio and the flower-bed at the top of them, from which he had tidied away the spent summer annuals at the weekend. The bare earth was marked all over, he now saw, with what appeared to be animal footprints, and as he stood gazing it seemed to him that he heard the pad of paws on the carpet behind him.

He stood for a long while before at last he turned round.

david lodge

Hotel des Boobs

"**H**otel des Pins!" said Harry. "More like Hotel des Boobs."

"Come away from that window," said Brenda. "Stop behaving like a Peeping Tom."

"What d'you mean, a Peeping Tom?" said Harry, continuing to squint down at the pool area through the slats of their bedroom shutters. "A Peeping Tom is someone who invades someone else's privacy, isn't he?"

"This is a private hotel."

"Hotel des Tits. Hotel des Bristols. Hey, that's not bad!" He turned his head to flash a grin across the room. "Hotel Bristols, in the plural. Geddit?"

If Brenda got it, she wasn't impressed. Harry resumed his watch. "I'm not invading anyone's privacy," he said. "If they don't want people to look at their tits, why don't they cover them up?"

"Well go and look, then. Don't peep. Go down to the pool and have a good look." Brenda dragged a comb angrily through her hair. "Hold an inspection."

"You're going to have to go topless, you know, Brenda, before this holiday's over."

Brenda snorted derisively.

"Why not? You've nothing to be ashamed of." He turned his head again to leer encouragingly at her. "You've still got a fine pair."

"Thanks very much, I'm sure," said Brenda. "But I intend to keep them covered as per usual."

"When in Rome," said Harry.

"This isn't Rome, it's the Côte D'Azur."

"Côte des Tits," said Harry. "Côte des Knockers."

"If I'd known you were going to go on like this," said Brenda, "I'd never have come here."

For years Harry and Brenda had taken family holidays every summer in Guernsey, where Brenda's parents lived. But now that the children were grown up enough to make their own arrangements, they had decided to have a change. Brenda had always wanted to see the South of France, and they felt they'd earned the right to treat themselves for once. They were quite comfortably off, now that Brenda, a recent graduate of the Open University, had a full-time job as a teacher. It had caused an agreeable stir in the managerial canteen at Barnard Castings when Harry dropped the name of their holiday destination in among the Benidorms and Palmas, the Costas of this and that, whose merits were being debated by his colleagues.

"The French Riviera, Harry?"

"Yes, a little hotel near St Raphael. Brenda got the name out of a book."

"Going up in the world, aren't we?"

"Well, it *is* pricey. But we thought, well, why not be extravagant, while we're still young enough to enjoy it?"

"Enjoy eyeing all those topless birds, you mean?"

"Is that right?" said Harry, with an innocence that was not entirely feigned. Of course he knew in theory that in certain parts of the Mediterranean girls sunbathed topless on the beach, and he had seen pictures of the phenomenon in his secretary's daily newspaper, which he filched regularly for the sake of such illustrations. But the reality had been a shock. Not so much the promiscuous, anonymous breast-baring of the beach, as the more intimate and socially complex nudity around the hotel pool. What made the pool different, and more disturbing, was that the women who lay half-naked around its perimeter all day were the same as those you saw immaculately dressed for dinner in the evening, or nodded and smiled politely to in the lobby, or exchanged small talk about the weather with, in the bar. And since Brenda found the tree-shaded pool, a few miles inland, infinitely preferable to the heat and glare and crowdedness of the beach (not to mention the probable pollution of the sea), it became the principal theatre of Harry's initiation into the new code of mammary manners.

Harry—he didn't mind admitting it—had always had a thing about women's breasts. Some men went for legs, or bums, but Harry had always been what the boys at Barnard's called a tit-fancier. "You were weaned too early," Brenda used to say, a diagnosis that Harry accepted with a complacent grin. He always glanced, a simple reflex action, at the bust of any sexually interesting female that came within his purview, and had spent many idle moments speculating about the shapes that were concealed beneath their sweaters, blouses and brassieres. It was disconcerting, to say the least, to find this harmless pastime rendered totally redundant under the Provençal sun. He had scarcely begun to assess the figures of the women at the Hotel des Pins before they satisfied his curiosity to the last pore. Indeed, in most cases he saw them half-naked before he met them, as it were, socially. The snooty Englishwoman, for instance, mother of twin boys and wife to the tubby stockbroker never seen without yesterday's *Financial Times* in his hand and a smug smile on his face. Or the female partner of the German couple who worshipped the sun with religious zeal, turning and annointing themselves according to a strict timetable and with the aid of a quartz alarm clock. Or the deeply tanned brunette of a certain age whom Harry had privately christened Carmen Miranda, because she spoke an eager and rapid Spanish, or it might have been Portuguese, into the cordless telephone which the waiter Antoine brought to her at frequent intervals.

Mrs Snooty had hardly any breasts at all when she was lying down, just boyish pads of what looked like muscle, tipped with funny little turned-up nipples that quivered like the noses of two small rodents when she stood up and moved about. The German lady's breasts were perfect cones, smooth and firm as if turned on a lathe, and never seemed to change their shape whatever posture she adopted; whereas Carmen Miranda's were like two brown satin bags filled with a viscous fluid that ebbed and flowed across her rib-cage in continual motion as she turned and twisted restlessly on her mattress, awaiting the next phone call from her absent lover. And this morning there were a pair of teenage girls down by the pool whom Harry hadn't seen before, reclining side by side, one in green bikini pants and the other in yellow, regarding their recently acquired breasts, hemispheres smooth and flawless as jelly moulds, with the quiet satisfaction of housewives watching scones rise.

"There are two newcomers today," said Harry. "Or should I say, four."

"Are you coming down?" said Brenda, at the door. "Or are you going to spend the morning peering through the shutters?"

"I'm coming. Where's my book?" He looked around the room for his Jack Higgins paperback.

"You're not making much progress with it, are you?" said Brenda sarcastically. "I think you ought to move the bookmark every day, for appearance's sake."

A book was certainly basic equipment for discreet boob-watching down by the pool: something to peer over, or round, something to look up from, as if distracted by a sudden noise or movement, at the opportune moment, just as the bird a few yards away slipped her costume off her shoulders, or rolled onto her back. Another essential item was a pair of sunglasses, as dark as possible to conceal the precise direction of one's gaze. For there was, Harry realised, a protocol involved in topless-ness. For a man to stare at, or even let his eyes rest for a measurable span of time upon, a bared bosom, would be bad form, because it would violate the fundamental principle upon which the whole practice was based, namely, that there was nothing noteworthy about it, that it was the most natural, neutral thing in the world. (Antoine was particularly skilled in managing to serve his female clients cold drinks, or take their orders for lunch, stooped low over their prone figures, without seeming to notice their nakedness.) Yet this principle was belied by another, which confined toplessness to the pool and its margins. As soon as they moved on to the terrace, or into the hotel itself, the women covered their upper halves. Did bare tits gain and lose erotic value in relation to arbitrary territorial zones? Did the breast eagerly gazed upon, fondled and nuzzled by husband or lover in the privacy of the bedroom, become an object of indifference, a mere anatomical protuberance no more interesting than an elbow or kneecap, on the concrete rim of the swimming pool? Obviously not. The idea was absurd. Harry had little doubt that, like himself, all the men present, including Antoine, derived considerable pleasure and stimulation from the toplessness of most of the women, and it was unlikely that the women themselves were unaware of this fact. Perhaps they found it exciting, Harry speculated, to expose themselves knowing that the men must not betray any sign of arousal; and their own menfolk might share, in a vicarious, proprietorial way in this excitement. Especially if one's own wife was better endowed than some of the others. To intercept the admiring and envious glance of another man at your wife's tits, to think silently to yourself, "*Yes, all right matey, you can look, as long as it's not too obvious, but only I'm allowed to touch 'em, see?*" That might be very exciting.

Lying beside Brenda at the poolside, dizzy from the heat and the consideration of these puzzles and paradoxes, Harry was suddenly transfixed by an arrow of perverse desire: to see his wife naked, and lust after her, through the eyes of other men. He rolled over on to his stomach and put his mouth to Brenda's ear.

"If you'll take your top off," he whispered, "I'll buy you that dress we saw in St Raphael. The one for twelve hundred francs."

The author had reached this point in his story, when he was writing seated at an umbrella-shaded table on the terrace overlooking the hotel pool, using a fountain pen and ruled foolscap, as was his wont, and having accumulated many cancelled and rewritten pages, as was also his wont, when without warning a powerful wind arose. It made the pine trees in the hotel grounds shiver and hiss, raised wavelets on the surface of the pool, knocked over several umbrellas, and whirled the leaves of the author's manuscript into the air. Some of these floated back on to the terrace, or the margins of the pool, or into the pool itself, but many were funnelled with astonishing speed high into the air, above the trees, by the hot breath of the wind. The author staggered to his feet and gaped unbelievingly at the leaves of foolscap rising higher and higher, like escaped kites, twisting and turning in the sun, white against the azure sky. It was like the visitation of some god or demon, a pentecost in reverse, drawing words away instead of imparting them. The author felt raped. The female sunbathers around the pool, as if similarly conscious, covered their naked breasts as they stood and watched the whirling leaves of paper recede into the distance. Faces were turned towards the author, smiles of sympathy mixed with *Schadenfreude*. Bidden by the sharp voice of their mother, the English twins scurried round the pool's edge collecting up loose sheets, and brought them with doggy eagerness back to their owner. The German, who had been in the pool at the time of the wind, came up with two sodden pages, covered with weeping longhand, held between finger and thumb, and laid them carefully on the author's table to dry. Pierre, the waiter, presented another sheet on his tray. "*C'est le petit Mistral,*" he said with a *moue* of commiseration. "*Quel dommage!*" The author thanked them mechanically, his eyes still on the airborne pages, now mere specks in the distance, sinking slowly down into the pine woods. Around the hotel the air was quite still again. Slowly the guests returned to their loungers and mattresses. The women discreetly uncovered their bosoms, renewed the application of *Ambre Solaire*, and resumed the pursuit of the perfect tan.

"Simon! Jasper!" said the Englishwoman, "Why don't you go for a walk in the woods and see if you can find any more of the gentleman's papers?"

"Oh, no," said the author urgently. "Please don't bother. I'm sure they're miles away by now. And they're really not important."

"No bother," said the Englishwoman. "They'll enjoy it."

"Like a treasure hunt," said her husband. "Or rather, paperchase." He chuckled at his own joke. The boys trotted off obediently into the woods. The author retired to his room, to await the return of his wife, who had missed all the excitement, from St Raphael.

"I've brought the most darling little dress," she announced as she entered the room. "Don't ask me how much it cost."

"Twelve hundred francs?"

"Good God, not, not as much as that. Seven hundred and fifty, actually. What's the matter, you look funny."

"We've got to leave this hotel."

He told her what had happened.

"I shouldn't worry," said his wife. "Those little brats probably won't find any more sheets."

"Oh yes they will. They'll regard it as a challenge, like the Duke of Edinburgh Award. They'll comb the pine woods for miles around. And if they find anything, they're sure to read it."

"They wouldn't understand."

"Their parents would. Imagine Mrs Snooty finding her nipples compared to the nose tips of small rodents."

The author's wife spluttered with laughter. "You are a fool," she said.

"It wasn't my fault," he protested. "The wind sprang out of nowhere."

"An act of God?"

"Precisely."

"Well, I don't suppose He approved of that story. I can't say I cared much for it myself. How was it going to end?"

The author's wife knew the story pretty well as far as he had got with it, because he had read it out to her in bed the previous night.

"Brenda accepts the bribe to go topless."

"I don't think she would."

"Well, she does. And Harry is pleased as Punch. He feels that he and Brenda have finally liberated themselves, joined the sophisticated set. He imagines himself telling the boys back at Barnard Castings about it, making them ribaldly envious. He gets such a hard-on that he has to lie on his stomach all day."

"Tut, tut!" said his wife. "How crude."

"He can't wait to get to bed that night. But just as they're retiring, they separate for some reason I haven't worked out yet, and Harry goes up to their room first. She doesn't come at once, so Harry gets ready for bed, lies down, and falls asleep. He wakes up two hours later and finds Brenda is still missing. He is alarmed and puts on his dressing gown and slippers to go in search of her. Just at that moment, she comes in. *Where the hell have you been?* he says. She has a peculiar look on her face, goes to the fridge in their room and drinks a bottle of Perrier water before she tells him her story. She says that Antoine intercepted her downstairs to present her with a bouquet. It seems that each week all the male staff of the hotel take a vote on which female guest has the shapeliest breasts, and Brenda has come top of the poll. The bouquet was a mark of their admiration and respect. She is distressed because she left it behind in Antoine's room."

"Antoine's room?"

"Yes, he had coaxed her into seeing his room, a little chalet in the woods, and gave her a drink, and one thing led to another, and she ended up letting him make love to her."

"How improbable."

"Not necessarily. Taking off her bra in public released some dormant streak of wantonness in Brenda that Harry had never seen before. She is rather drunk and quite shameless. She taunts him with graphic testimony of Antoine's skill as a lover, and compares Harry's genital equipment unfavourably to the Frenchman's."

"Worse and worse," said the author's wife.

"At that point Harry hits her."

"Oh, nice. Very nice."

"Brenda half undresses and crawls into bed. A couple of hours later, she wakes up. Harry is standing by the window staring down at the empty pool, a ghostly blue in the light of the moon. Brenda gets out of bed, comes across and touches him gently on the arm. *Come to bed,* she says. *It wasn't true, what I told you.* He turns his face slowly towards her. *Not true? No,* she says, *I made it up. I went and sat in the car for two hours with a bottle of wine, and I made it up. Why?* he says. *I don't know why,* she says. *To teach you a lesson, I suppose. But I shouldn't have. I don't blame you for hitting me. Come to bed.* But Harry just shakes his head and turns back to stare out of the window. *I never knew,* he says, in a dead sort of voice, *that you cared about the size of my prick. But I don't,* she says. *I made it all up.* Harry shakes his head disbelievingly, gazing down at the blue, breastless margins of the pool. That's how the story was going to end, with those words, 'the blue, breastless margins of the pool'."

As he spoke these words, the author was himself standing at the window, looking down at the hotel pool from which all the guests had departed to change for dinner. Only the solitary figure of Pierre moved among the umbrellas and tables, collecting bathing towels and tea-trays. "Hmmm," said the author's wife.

"Harry's fixation on women's breasts, you see," said the author, "has been displaced by an anxiety about his own body from which he will never be free."

"Yes, I see that. I'm not stupid, you know." The author's wife came to the window and looked down. "Poor Pierre," she said. "He wouldn't dream of making a pass at me, or any of the other women. He's obviously gay."

"Fortunately," said the author, "I didn't get that far with my story before the wind scattered it all over the countryside. But you'd better get out the Michelin and find another hotel. I can't stand the thought of staying on here, on tenterhooks all the time in case one of the guests comes back from a walk in the woods with a compromising piece of fiction in their paws. What an extraordinary thing to happen."

"You know," said the author's wife. "It's really a better story."

"Yes," said the author. "I think I shall write it. I'll call it 'Tit for Tat'."

"No, call it 'Hotel des Boobs'," said the author's wife. "Theirs and yours."

"What about yours?"

"Just leave them out of it, please."

Much later that night, when they were in bed and just dropping off to sleep, the author's wife said:

"You don't really wish I would go topless, do you?"

"No, of course not," said the author. But he didn't sound entirely convinced, or convincing.

joyce carol oates

Adulteress

She was in love with two men, one of them her husband. The men were approximately the same age, approximately the same height and weight. The lover had greying brown hair with a slight curl, the husband had greying blond hair with a just perceptible wave. One was coiled tight as a spring, the other hummed to himself, absorbed in his thoughts. She had fallen in love with her lover out of loneliness for the early years of her marriage. She could not recall why she had fallen in love with her husband.

She and her husband had no children but lived in an old spacious house on a street of similar houses. There she arranged her life in a sequence of time slots that dazzled like sheets of plate glass: for adultery involves acrobatic feats, tricks of navigation regarding time, space. The precise relationship of the clock face to the distance that must be travelled. Had she not had her own automobile she could never have become an adulteress.

Her lover was separated from his family and lived alone on the twentieth floor of a building that shone in the sun like a Christmas tree ornament. From one wall of windows the river was visible on clear days, from another an expressway cloverleaf. He seemed at times not to know where he was, he kept speaking of home. He was crazy with love for her, he said. He said often. When she came to him his eyes were clear as washed glass with his need for her. Afterwards he said, "I hate to be deceiving your husband like this." He said reproachfully, "I hate any kind of deception."

Early in her marriage she and her husband had talked vaguely of having children, but for some reason the time for the first baby was never right. Then they went to Europe, travelled by car through the Alps, and when they returned home the talk of children was not resumed. Much of her conversation with her lover had to do with his children. How desperately he loved them, did not want to hurt them. How desperately he wanted to behave in an intelligent and responsible way. His own father, he said bitterly, had been a weak, self-pitying man, prone to histrionic outbursts. Hardly a man at all. "I'd want to kill myself," her lover said passionately, "if I discovered I was turning into him." It was her task and privilege to assure him he was not.

Sleeping with two men left her breathless, giddy. On the edge of euphoria. She wept easily, laughed easily. It was like being in the mountains at 12,000 feet. The pulse races and careens, the blood thins. She lay in bed with one man, cradling him in her arms, and saw the twists and coils of expressway she would have to navigate to get to the other man, with whom she would also lie in bed, thinking of the return trip. She had memorised most of the exits on the expressway and might have boasted that she could drive the route blindfolded.

The first time she travelled high in the mountains she had not known what was wrong with her—the quickened heartbeat, the rapid shallow breath, the feather sensation of panic, dread—until someone explained. It's the altitude. It's a touch of altitude sickness. Never fatal, she was told, unless you had cardiac problems.

The love affair continued for months, a year. A year and a half. Her lover pressed her to get a divorce though he and his wife talked occasionally of attempting a reconciliation for the sake of the children. To pacify him she fell in with his plans though if she herself initiated the topic he became upset. Sometimes she invited her lover to parties at her house, or even to small dinners—he was a friend, to a degree, of her husband, the two men liked each other quite well—but most of the time their love affair was a matter of telephone calls, discreetly placed, and meetings in his apartment or on neutral ground (the palatial new Hyatt Regency, for instance, just off the expressway).

Years after the affair was over she would recall the almost unbearable excitement, the apprehension, with which she telephoned her lover: from a pay phone, for instance; in a department store; once from her doctor's office. At such times her hands shook and her throat constricted with the terrible need to cry. I wish I could be with you right now, she would say, and he would say, I wish I could be with you. Sometimes she did cry, and he would console her, soothe her. They would be together after all the next day, most likely. And she knew he loved her, didn't she.

After these telephone calls she felt both exhausted and ecstatic. She might have said that her heart sang, her spirits soared. Her power had been confirmed. Her beauty. It was so treacherous, sleeping with two men. It would not be fatal.

During much of this time her lover's wife behaved strangely. She took the children away on mysterious trips, she telephoned from distant cities, hinting at danger. She needed money. She needed advice about dental work, schools, household repairs. Sometimes she threatened to do injury, as she put it, to herself and the children.

Her lover telephoned her to speak of these matters, his voice was raw, frantic, sick with guilt. He would dial her number and let the phone ring just once, then hang up; which meant that she should telephone him when she was free to do so. Often she had to wait until her husband was asleep, then she would slip out of the bedroom and dial her lover's number, barefoot and shivering in the kitchen, not having troubled to put on a bathrobe.

Was his wife serious, was it nothing but emotional blackmail? They discussed the subject endlessly. He said again that he wanted to behave decently, intelligently. He wanted to do the right thing, if only he knew what the right thing was.

(Once her lover confessed that his wife's violent emotion had always intimidated him. Her passion. Her sexual need. She had seemed to want more, always more, than he could give her, he said, his voice rising with anger. They were in a cool bright airy room on the twenty-third floor of the Hyatt Regency, the filmy white curtains drawn, the air humming from a window unit. "You can't imagine what some women are like," he said. He was stroking her sides, her thighs. Her breasts. She lay with her eyes closed as if asleep. A small heartbeat pulsed in her forehead. "Some women . . .!" he said, his voice trailing off into silence. She did not move, she held herself intact.)

It was not altogether clear when the love affair ended, but she thought it must have been when she placed an emergency call to her lover at his office, from an Exxon station on the expressway. She had had a minor accident: a driver passing her carelessly on the right had cut sharply in front of her, she hadn't been able to brake swiftly enough to avoid a collision, she was badly shaken and could not seem to get her breath though no one was injured and the accident was assuredly not her fault. She was being punished, she thought. Her mind had wandered and she was being punished even if the accident hadn't been her fault.

Her car was towed to the Exxon station and she telephoned her lover at once. She telephoned her lover before she telephoned her husband. What if she had been injured, she said. What if she had been hospitalised. What would they do, she said. What would they do.

Her lover was distracted, upset. He commiserated with her. But she wasn't hurt, was she?—and her car wasn't badly damaged?

"But what would we do," she said, beginning to cry, "if one of us was hospitalised? If one of us died?"

She could hear her voice rising in hysteria but she could not control it. Even the fact that people in the service station could overhear her seemed to make no difference. Her eyes welled with tears, her face burned. She was saying, "What would we do, what would we do," again and again, helplessly, "what if one of us died?" Her breath came in harsh stinging slivers like slivers of glass though she was not injured, she hadn't even struck her forehead on the windshield or been thrown against the steering wheel.

Then she was saying, "I don't want to live like this, I want to die."

Her lover spoke reasonably, calmly. He pointed out that she had had a shock and she must telephone her husband at once and tell him what happened. She should take a taxi home. She should see a doctor. Surely she wasn't injured but she had suffered a shock and should see a doctor as soon as possible, did she understand? It was no good to get hysterical.

She understood.

She and her husband happened to meet her lover for drinks at a downtown hotel. The occasion was casual, incidental, her lover's birthday perhaps. They would order a bottle of champagne, they would sit and chat for an hour. It seemed to be so rare, her husband said, that the three of them saw one another.

When she was alone with her husband she thought of her lover and when she was alone with her lover she thought of her husband, but now that she was seated at a small table with both men her mind wandered and lost itself amidst the gentle silver tinkling of a waterfall close by. The cocktail lounge was situated at the base of an atrium that rose for a dozen floors; it was lavishly decorated with mosaics in jade, emerald, and gold, and potted orange trees, and tall narrow strips of mirrored glass.

She had a glass of champagne, and then another. Her husband and her lover were talking about a mutual acquaintance who was rumoured to be close to bankruptcy. Her lover would not look at her; he sat tense and unnaturally straight in his chair, looking at her husband. Both men were eating Brazil nuts out of a little glass bowl.

She excused herself and went to the ladies' room, some distance away. The carpet was so thick, so new, her heels sank in, and the air hummed and smelled of a slightly acidic spray perfume. She saw her mirrored reflection, that grim gloating sallow face, the too-dark lipstick she supposed fashionable, the limp fading hair that had been cut the day before. Beautiful, one of them had said of her, stroking her belly, her breasts, framing her face in his hands, or had it been both men? and when? She wasn't drunk and she wasn't hysterical but she ran cold water to splash onto her wrists. She soaked paper towels, pressed them against her forehead and that throbbing artery in her throat. Her lover was now telling her husband that he loved her and wanted to marry her. His voice was faltering, brave. He had not wanted to hurt anyone and he had not wanted to deceive anyone but somehow it had happened. He hated deception. He wanted to behave decently and responsibly. But he was in love. And it was necessary to . . .

She was drying her face, slapping at her cheeks. Her eyes shone with a steely triumph. She smeared dark lipstick on her mouth and blotted it savagely and rather liked the effect, there *was* something savage about her, a woman with a long history of deceit, an adulteress. A pretty fluffy jewel-laden woman of late middle age entered the powder room, stooped a little to regard her in the mirror, giggled, cried out in a sweet drunken Virginia drawl, "Now *there's* a happy girl." The remark was not at all rude, it seemed quite the right thing, the necessary thing. Yet a moment later the older woman tripped and fell heavily, uttering a wild little scream.

She turned at once from the mirror and tried to help the woman to her feet. Drunk! A drunkard! In fact she had been uneasily aware of the woman in the cocktail lounge, seated at a table near her own with an elderly gentleman and a loud-voiced younger man, their son perhaps. While her husband and her lover talked she had observed that filmy floating bleached hair, impeccably styled, the pale powdered skin, the restless eyes, the wink of diamonds on thin trembling fingers. The woman wore a lacy ruffled white pantsuit that would have looked ludicrous on most women her age. And high-heeled sling-back open-toed white kidskin Italian sandals. And beneath her elaborate make-up mask she was a beautiful woman, still, or would surely have been were she not now suddenly stricken by a spasm of vomiting.

Her husband and her lover seemed to be waiting for her, had she been gone that long? Ten minutes. Fifteen. But they were smiling, too. They had devoured all the Brazil nuts, the waitress was bringing a fresh bowl. Should they order a second bottle of champagne? What did she think? Both men stood in deference to her, or, rather, made motions at standing, her lover in awkward haste, her husband more mechanically, pulling her flimsy wire-backed chair away from the table so that she could sit. What had they been talking about, she asked, what had she missed, and they said they'd been talking about, well what *had* they been talking about?—one thing or another. But why had she been gone so long, her husband asked, and she said with a pretty shrug of one shoulder, "There was a sick woman in the ladies' room, I couldn't just leave her."

fiona cooper

Mirror, Mirror

At the sound of the nightingale, seven good fairies drifted through the open window. A gentle breeze lifted the air and a bird of paradise preened by a sparkling waterfall in the dusk. Silently, the seven good fairies gathered round the sleeping child. And the first spoke:

"I will give him eyes as blue as tender violets drenched in dew."

Said the second:

"I will give him a graceful body to cut a dash in a velvet doublet, silken hose and boots of Spanish-leather-o! He will dance like an angel—oh, the samba, the mamba! He will run like the wind!"

The third said:

"From me he will have a voice as true as doves cooing on a summer evening. He will . . ."

She broke off with a gasp of fear as a dark shape cycloned over the crib, spitting lightning crackles of venomous laughter.

"He will? Go on . . . he WILL? He will NOTHING!" jeered the bad fairy, lurching over to the child. "This one is MINE! Mine to nurse, and mine to curse! Samba! Mamba! Viol da Gamba! Tender heart and true! Pretty boy, you're going to the . . . twentieth century!"

The good fairies fluttered, pale and helpless in the ghastly shadow. A chill wind fingered the baby's cheeks. He whimpered in his sleep.

"Nasty dreams, my precious?" sneered the bad fairy, "I'll give you nightmares before I'm through!"

"There's summat wrong wi' that child," his gran sentenced

him as he stumbled over something he hadn't noticed on the swirling patterned carpet. "He needs glasses. That'll put him right."

But Kevin saw nothing wrong with the living-room at Christmas; he loved the dazzling blur of gaudy purple, scarlet, green, gold; the dancing silver shimmer of tinsel against the dark mass of the tree.

"Falling over his own feet."

Gran sat back, folded her hands and waited.

"Leave the boy," said his mum, looping gilt-papered chocolate snowmen over the blue-green needles.

"Are you daft or what?" his dad snapped, slamming the newspaper onto his lap.

"I'll make a cup of tea," said his mum. "Come on, useless, give me a hand."

Father Christmas was a huge robe with cottonwool edges; his dad sherry-seasonal, loud and hearty. Children milling round his skirts, as he ho-ho-ho-ed the gleaming gifts from the tree. His fingers dug into Kevin's ribs and he banged him onto his knee.

"Kiss for Santa, little man?"

Kevin kissed his dad.

"And what do you want off the tree, old man, eh?"

"I want the fairy!" he shouted, "give me the fairy!"

She was an angel, a froth of white twinkling way above his head; she was the winter moon and the rainbow dazzle on the snow—she was beauty, beauty, with her fluffed-out skirts and glittering wand, her feathery white-gold hair.

"The *fairy*?" said his dad in his dad's voice slurred with no ho-ho, oh no, "the *fairy*?"

"Give him the fairy," said his mum, "he's only seven."

"No lad of mine will have a fairy, not even on Christmas Day. Kevin, you don't want the fairy!"

But he did, wanted it like he'd never wanted anything before, and his dad set him down hard on the carpet. He cried and cried till his face was wet and red, his fists were hot and sticky.

"This is *your* present," said his dad, and pulled his son's fingers round Action Man with his suede hair, his rough camouflage battle-dress, his dull black boots, his brown plastic gun.

Kevin looked into the square-jawed face, the black dot eyes. Miles away, at the top of the tree, the fairy angel glowed like a candleflame through his brimming tears. That afternoon, his parents and aunties and uncles and Gran dozing over the Queen's speech and stuffed with turkey, he scratched a pit in the hard winter earth and buried Action Man alive, stamping the earth flat with his plastic boots.

It was neither winter nor spring when the world snapped into sombre focus behind tortoise-shell frames, curved wires stabbing into his ears. His dad said:

"That's better."

The children jeered at playtime:

"Specky-four-eyes, can't catch me!"

And he punched them out to arms length until the jeering stopped.

"A proper little lad," said his dad to his bruises and scowl. "A right little tough, just like his dad."

But he lit up for school plays, he stole the show year after year—Buttons, Aladdin, Prince Florizel, Jack; his voice broke gently into song. His teacher wrote home urging that his gifts should be explored.

"He does seem to have a talent for music, Dad. We can afford it."

"Afford it's neither here nor there. He'll not make his living at it."

"So it's no?" said Kevin.

"Yes, it's no. And no going behind my back to your mam. And another thing—there'll be no more plays. My lad clarted up with grease-paint, and getting ideas. Dear God, Kevin, it's not healthy. Why can't you make a go of something proper, like sport? You're champion at football."

"I can do football as well, Dad."

"A job worth doing's worth doing well. Do something I can

be proud of you for. Singing! Dancing! Acting! Folk'll think you're a cissy."

"What do you mean, Dad?"

"Never mind what I mean. Get to bed."

The bad fairy leered through swirls of pipe-smoke. On the stairs, Kevin heard his dad shouting:

"He's had too much schooling, mam. Time he was out and earning."

His mum said something, but too softly for him to hear. Out and earning? Just like that? At school they talked about qualifications and careers, at church it was *vocations*. What could he do for a job? He'd only ever day-dreamed about "being on the stage".

His dad put in a word for him, and he got a position in the same haulage firm. His dad drove lorries; he was tea-boy, messenger-boy, office-boy.

"You stick with us, young Kevin. You'll go far. Maybe on the lorries like your dad. See the world," the manager told him, bristling with good-living.

The best thing about work was money. He togged up in all the right gear like the other lads were wearing, greased his hair to an Elvis quiff, drew on match-thin roll-ups, lounged in coffee-bars, eyed up the talent. He thought of it as acting. He did it very well.

"Our Kev can pull the birds," said his dad proudly, and let him stay out later and later.

He walked his girlfriend home, they kissed in the porch. For this he always took his glasses off.

"You're dead romantic, you," she said, "and you're dead sexy out of those glasses."

Then he was seventeen.

"You can get a motorbike now," said his dad. "I had my first bike at your age. From my own savings."

Kevin got himself contact lenses, stuffed his glasses in the bottom of a drawer, went through three months of blinking hell. He stuck with it, so that when he passed plate-glass windows, he liked what he saw. There were no blurred bits at the edges any more; he could see everything clearly, even in the rain.

He was the Whortley Players' gem, noble in the highbrow costume dramas, saucy for Gilbert and Sullivan—but the pantomimes were best. The only time he was allowed to sit at a mirror, making free with Nu-lash mascara, Kandi-floss lipstick, sponging himself pan-pink, filling in his eyelids with soft gold—transforming to a thing of beauty, neither man nor woman, in net flounces, satin bodice, falsies, a beehive blonde wig.

And how they clapped as he shimmied onto stage with his tinsel wand.

"Cinders, I come, I hear your call,
I shall get you to the ball!
With my wand of magic power
You'll be there within the hour!
No rags for you—a silver gown!
Your coach of gold the best in town!"

And then a puff of violet smoke, a crack of stage lightning, and the glittering coach paraded round, with Cinders waving, blowing kisses, and Kevin looking modest and curtseying.

"Our Kev's got a lovely voice!" his mum said fondly. Even his dad laughed. It was Christmas after all. In the pub afterwards, men crowded to buy him drinks, make risqué comments, flirt with him.

"You daft beggar!" said his dad. "You can't wear that stuff in the streets!"

He felt suddenly cold, pale under the rouge, smiling all the time.

On those rare days when his dad was away long-distance, and his mum out, he would drop the front-door catch and sneak into their bedroom. To his mother's wardrobe. She had three lovely party dresses, hanging in polythene.

The first time, he looked.

The second time, he touched.

The third time, he couldn't stop himself; he slid the lamé fabric from the hanger and held it against his body. After that first step, it was routine; it took him about half an hour to do himself up and sit at the mirror.

"And what's your name?" he would ask the pretty creature looking back at him. She only smiled and tossed her hair.

Once he walked as far as the landing, wanted to sweep down the stairs like a movie-star, sit in the living room, legs elegantly crossed, sipping sherry, smoking Silver Thins. His heart almost stopped as he thought he heard the front door. But it was only the thin March wind rattling the letter-box.

And his mother's shoes didn't fit or suit him. He flexed his feet, and wished for high-heeled elegance, as he laced up suede boots for Saturday nights with the lads, black lace-ups for work.

There was a fancy-dress party, and he decided to go as the nameless lovely no one else had ever seen. No question of going from home: he offered to work late and lock up, and changed there. He kept make-up in his locker, had found a pair of patent stilettoes with a diamanté spray in Oxfam. His dress he'd made himself, in secret. It was pearl-grey moiré, dissolving to a frou of silver lace at the hem. He had twenty-denier silver tights. He was stunning.

He teetered through the lamp-lit streets, wincing at wolf-whistles, sure that everyone could see and know. Through the spray of drizzle, he saw his dad walking towards him, too late to cross the road. Only when they had passed each other did he start breathing again. He didn't know his own son!

Perfect, it was perfect! He slowed to a smooth pace, and knocked at the door. Only in the hall was he recognised.

"Kevin!" cried his hostess. "You are a one!"

"Kay, if you don't mind," he said haughtily, and Kay had her christening with a gulp of lethal punch.

"The little girls' room is upstairs, Kay," said the hostess, screeching with laughter.

He knew how to manage stairs—"One foot in front of the other, and give a little wiggle," said Kay archly.

The men flocked to light his cigarettes, get him drinks, smiling at him, laughing with him.

"I shall have to change," he slurred, hours later. "My dad wouldn't like it . . ."

He heard one of his work-mates in the hall say belligerently:

"He does it too well, the bloody poofter, I shouldn't be surprised."

"He's no poofter," said the hostess angrily. "This is fancy dress. I've been out with him. He's all fella I can tell *you*!"

He creamed his face back to normal, combed his hair flat, and Kevin looked back out of the mirror. It was him all right. All wrong. He swaggered down the stairs and said:

"Give us a roll-up, I can't stand those ladies cigarettes."

Liar, liar, pants on fire, jeered Kay, locked under his skin.

He tried to put her away with the clothes in his locker, but out of sight was never out of mind. Her eyes accused him every time he pissed. He made a pact with her: one enchanted evening every month, he would be Kay, in some bar in some other town. Now he drove a van for the firm, he could be away for a night every so often, and sling his bag in the cab, find an anonymous B&B, and be the only freak in town. Men would buy him drinks and dinner, and be surprised at his grip stopping them trying it on. He always felt better the next day, Kay took him out of himself.

He knew he was walking a tightrope; he knew he couldn't stop.

"A word with you, miss."

Dear God, it was the law.

"You're not from round here, are you? I've not seen you before. This is a respectable neighbourhood."

Oh, Jesus, Mr Plod thought he was on the game, pulling out his little black pad, and licking his pencil.

"Perhaps you'd let me know where you're staying?"

That he could not: Mrs Morgan's Guest House . . . yes, I have a young man, officer, very quiet . . . no, I don't let to *single women, no,* you can't be too careful . . .

"Well, you'd better come down to the station."

He knew it was *wrong,* but was it a crime? Did people get arrested for it? Kay would have fainted.

We should have got a taxi, she scolded him.

"Right," said the sergeant, past the knowing looks at the desk, behind a locked door in a windowless room.

"Name?"

Which would take them to his parents door. He went numb.

"Age?"

"Nineteen," he murmured.

"Cup of tea? You girls are silly, nice-looking girl like you could get herself a decent bloke, not wander round the streets. It's not right, you know."

He held the mug in his hands, frozen with fear.

A WPC came in.

"Perhaps you'd rather talk to me," she said, disapprovingly. The feminine touch.

"It's not what you think," he said.

"It never is," she said, opening her notebook. "You'd better tell me all about it."

Kevin told her.

"Sarge," she called up the corridor. "You'd better come in here."

The judge sat in his long black robes, the bad fairy a vulture on his shoulder.

"It is the recommendation of this court that you seek psychiatric help. This is your first offence, and you have been found guilty as charged. We feel that you need help rather than punishment."

He stared at Kevin over his gold-rimmed glasses.

"I wouldn't be seen dead in that wig," thought Kay.

"If you appear before the courts again, you will be dealt with—and with the utmost severity prescribed by law. You are a young man, at the beginning of your life, and let us hope that this distasteful incident has taught you a lesson."

His mother sat white-faced in the court. Kevin fainted. It was that, he thanked Kay, that convinced them he had seen the error of his ways.

The next few weeks he spent in a place "for people like him", as his dad bitterly called it. He acted Kevin, full-time likely lad, making the right responses to female nudes: he'd always liked women—didn't they know? He liked everything about them.

"Just hang on, dear," soothed Kay. "This is the most important performance you've ever given."

"I've brought Father O'Rourke to see you, Kevin," said his mother, every syllable a reproach. "He's come straight from a Christening—listen to him, Kevin."

The red-cheeked man in black, an ivory lace sash across his shoulders. His ringed hands clutched Kevin's—touching the leper. The priest sat and arranged his long skirts over crossed legs.

Kevin fixed on the gold-capped tooth, and nodded with fatuous humility.

"My son," said the celibate boom, "I hum you harry tumbles. Everyone gum thrum diddle-de-dum . . ."

Stay cool, hang loose, admit nothing, said Kay—*and look at the weight of that lace!*

Father O'Rourke's blessing boomeranged round the room.

"Mum, the Gumbalumba blezzumba yumba and guide you, Kevin, there's always a place frum yumbum in the Humdeum-dum um Gumb."

See you in church, love, said Kay. She wouldn't shut up. And he really didn't want her to. She was keeping him alive, after all.

"So," the psychiatrist twinkled at him. "We can put this down to a boyish prank, eh, a young man away from home— you're a bit of an actor, aren't you, Kevin? Get yourself a nice steady girl. Nothing wrong in that department."

"Yeah, no," said Kevin, dragging on a cigarette.

He read the upside-down notes on the desk.

"At this stage I would not recommend ECT, although this may become appropriate at a later date, depending on Kevin's full adjustment to normal life. He is fortunate that his family are willing to accept him at home, and put this behind them."

The nurse gave him his personal belongings from the ward safe and unlocked the door. He walked down the corridor and out into the street.

Home life?

Home?

Get thee behind me, Satan?

His town was the sort where headline news would be:

"MRS SMITH HAS RECORD DAHLIA CROP."

or: "HAVE YOU PUT YOUR CLOCKS BACK?"

So a scoop like KEVIN THE CROSS-DRESSER IN COURT would be legend for the rest of his life in this town. Everyone knew everyone else's business and made it their own. And the town where It had happened—and, he felt, anywhere in the Midlands, lines of yobboes ending their Saturday night out with a bit of queer-bashing, paki-bashing, bashing anything that crossed their path and didn't take their fancy.

He took a one-way ticket to Kings Cross.

To London, where all the wicked people live, fretted his mother.

There was a nice girl in packing at his firm, who took to him and his gentle ways. After three months he took her to bed. After six months she was talking about a ring.

"I'd love to walk down the aisle with you, Kev," she told him. She thought he was a bit shy; she knew he was different from all the other boys, so kind and considerate. They sat in his bed-sit, and he could see himself in the mirror with her beside him, promising *Forever*. But Kay, bundled to suffocation in the wardrobe drawer, nagged at him.

"If she wants you, she'll meet me sooner or later . . . And why don't *I* get a ring? I've got lovely hands."

So he told his girlfriend about her.

But she wouldn't believe him, she cried:

"If you want to pack me in, you could just tell me straight!"

"I don't want to pack you in," he said, holding her, "but I am what I am."

Still she wouldn't believe him.

He opened the drawer like Pandora's box. Kay spilled onto the floor.

She looked at the clothes and then at him. She shook her head.

"All right," he said. "I'll have to show you."

She watched like a rabbit trapped in headlights, as her boyfriend—my Kevin—zipped his dress, rolled on stockings, teased his hair, made his face up, and finally stood in front of her.

Then she cried, rose to hysteria and tore from the room. He ran after her, ran up the street, begging her to stop.

"Bloody lesbians!"

He stopped at the corner, and walked unsteadily home. Well, he demanded of Kay, well, where do I go from here?

"For a start," she said out loud. "You stop driving that bloody van, and start taking care of your nails. Get your flaming act together!"

"It's worse than come-bloody-dancing," complained the queen in the powder-room, sweating under the lights as he pencilled in his eye-brows.

"Shit! Can I borrow your mascara?"

"I can't get this wig to sit right . . ."

"Love the dress, dear—did you make it yourself?"

"Yes," said Kay. "All my own work."

"Are those contacts tinted?"

"No," said Kay. "I'm a blue-eyed girl."

"Some people are born lucky—you've got lovely thick hair too—I send mine away to get it washed—hoo!"

Kay wriggled through yards of net and chiffon and escaped to the dance floor, lights dipping and swirling everywhere. She could have worn that tiara—you couldn't overdress here. Tonight she had the spot she'd been working for: The Sensational Lady Kay. She had the gardenia skewered in her hair, and sat at a table, eyes bathed in the extravaganza of sequins and gilt lace. To think she'd thought she was the only one!

She swept onto the stage.

"I'm going to give you a number you all know and love," she breathed into the mike. The tape of Lover Man started—she was on—she was magnificent . . .

"Your own voice, dear? Let's hear it," they'd said doubtfully at the audition.

And then:

"All *right*! Where have *you* been hiding it?"

The jewelled, gloved hands fountained applause.

In the wings, the bad fairy cursed. The nightmares were receding.

pamela painter

The Real Story

It starts simply enough when the son, back from a volunteer job abroad with Vietnamese refugees, discovers that he has become a minor character in one of his father's novels. In Chapter 10 the "son" returns from the "Peace Corps", sleeps a lot, and makes exits and entrances talking of El Salvador—not Vietnamese refugees.

"So this is how real people and things are transformed into fiction," the young man says to his father after reading the father's manuscript. They are in the father's downstairs study.

"Real? One never knows another human being that well," his father says, leaning back in his chair, closing the subject.

Nevertheless, the son determines to read more of his father's work, and his mother's too.

His parents' library and files are illuminating. He discovers he has lived with them in fiction, in various permutations, for a long time. Perhaps he, too, is a writer. The cleaning woman seems cheered to have him home again and helps him clear out the storage space over the garage. There he sets up shop. The first story he writes is about a son who returns from the Vietnam War to discover that his parents, both writers, have used material from his letters, from his life—the mother in stories and the father in a novel.

"But we wouldn't do that," his parents say, when he shows them his manuscript for comment. "How could you write such a thing?"

The parents follow the son to his study over the garage, where they all sit on orange crates. The son begins addressing s.a.e.'s. "You wrote about a kid who thinks the laundry is washed in the laundry chute," he accuses his mother.

"But it was so funny," she says, trying not to smile.

"And there's a son in your latest novel who gets three graduate degrees before deciding he wants to be a garlic farmer."

"You're not a garlic farmer," his father says.

"Maybe you should be a poet," his mother says.

The mother's next story is about a brilliant young poet who writes mystically about nature and its life cycles, yet refuses to "examine" his two years in Vietnam. Critics wait expectantly for a decade. Finally, as the poet is dying of something related to Agent Orange, it is revealed that he has been writing about Vietnam ever since he returned, but only on the walls of buildings, the seats of subway trains, the tiles of public bathrooms. Instantly, scholars find themselves with a new terrain. Bespectacled, bearded men and lank-haired young women armed with Nikons begin the task of gathering his epic graffiti poem. Each "line" is numbered. He used a red magic marker. His scrawled lines are spotted in Albuquerque, Peoria, Memphis; he has been everywhere, Bangor, Maine. "I ended with number 352," are the poet's last words. The hunt intensifies. Female scholars claim discrimination and demand escorts into the men's johns. This indignity ends the story.

"Just because I haven't written about Vietnam yet doesn't mean I'm not going to," the son says to his mother in her study, where her black Underwood typewriter rests on an old sewing machine.

"Of course you will write about Vietnam," his mother says. "But you had such a normal childhood. My poet is an orphan."

"A Normal Childhood," the son's next story, tells of a boy of nine who reads his mother's journal, which indirectly recounts a series of affairs she has while he is growing up, all with men closely associated with his father: his dissertation adviser, his squash partner, his dentist, his star graduate student. But the writing in her journal is so oblique that it isn't until the boy has his first sexual experience that he knows his mother's "friends" were actually her lovers. He has come of age.

The story is accepted immediately by his father's old editor.

His parents uncork a bottle of Piper-Heidsieck to celebrate this first publication. Even the cleaning woman is given a glass. But later that night the son overhears the mother angrily assert that since she didn't have any affairs, their son must be writing about his father. She asks her husband if, in addition to having affairs, he also wrote them down for the scrutiny of future biographers.

"You know I think journal writing depletes creative energy," the husband says as he undresses.

"Affairs don't!" she says.

Her husband ignores her. Shaking his head he says, "That kid. Didn't he write a great sexual-awakening scene."

So: the wife writes a story about a woman who understands her husband's sexual inadequacies only after she finally meets his mother, who chatters about the unusual methods of discipline she employed to stop her son from wetting his pants. The mother-in-law enjoys telling how she dressed him up as a little girl and sent him out on the front porch for all the neighbours to see (those she alerted by phone), and how he later had hormone treatments for undeveloped genitals and late-staying baby fat.

When the wife's story is published the husband storms into his wife's study, pounds on her Underwood. "I resent your using painful details from my childhood."

"But after all the affairs you've had, no one could possibly think the man with the sexual problems is you," his wife says, already at work on another story. She writes them in two to four hours, which makes both her son and her husband nervous when they compare the day's output over dinner. But she, she reminds them—she works on her stories for weeks after. "And your mother, thank God, lives in New Mexico and never reads a thing."

In the husband's next story, his first in several years, a man is married to a woman who suspects him of having affairs. He is innocent, of course, which the reader knows, but the increasingly distraught and suspicious wife proceeds to become a master domestic spy. She draws up elaborate charts and graphs for his meetings, his out-of-town trips. She charts gas receipts, restaurant checks, long-distance calls. These "clues" are colour-coded by both paper and ink, and soon the wife begins to think of the charts as works of art. A select committee at the Institute of Contemporary Art actually admits a chart titled *Infidelity* #4 to a juried exhibit. Finally, in a cataclysmic scene, the wife is confronted by a museum guard as she is adding another name, "Gloria," to the collage.

"Why don't you stick with novels," the wife says, barging into her husband's dishevelled study, an open *New Yorker* in her hand. He whispers something into the phone and quickly hangs up the phone, but she ignores this. She points to the thin shiny column of prose. "How dare you. Until I learned to tolerate your affairs, drawing up those charts kept me away from my work for two whole years."

"It was a detail I couldn't resist. There are those, I have discovered," the husband admits sheepishly. "Besides, friends know you're not crazy."

"Your affairs are real."

"But only your psychiatrist saw your charts."

Her psychiatrist is a closet writer with three novels in his bottom drawer. He plans to use a pseudonym, not because he might be breaking his Hippocratic oath by revealing his patients' secrets (which he is), but because he doesn't want to disturb his patients' progress by introducing a personal side of himself into their lives. In fact, he has an irresistible temptation to write about a wife's—he changes it—a husband's elaborate system of charting the suspected course of his wife's affairs as if they were stock market fluctuations. It rings familiar. Commodities? No. He makes the husband an oil tycoon obsessed with fat phallic oil wells (now who designed them?). Their locations appear as blue pushpins on his eight-colour topographic map of Texas. Red pushpins represent his wife's gas receipts, her platinum American Express card bill, her extended visits to the ranches of rich Texan relatives. (Alliteration pleases the psychiatrist.) Then the psychiatrist calls a patient who is a writer (the free-association of this escapes him) and asks for the name of her agent.

"Jesus, my shrink called me for an agent. He says he's beginning to write fiction," the mother complains to a friend. She cancels future appointments, risking writer's block, but her anger has energy. Consequently her next story is about an analyst whose most interesting patient is a writer of stories that appear in *Esquire*, the *Atlantic*, *Playboy*. Soon this writer realises that the analyst is not treating him but rather his characters—the flat ones on some glossy page. In their sessions, the analyst asks the writer to explain: why a father reveals a daughter's real mother to be an aunt the daughter can't stand; why a woman creates a second set of journals when she suspects her husband is reading the first; why a criminal, given a new identity through the government's witness protection programme, leaves clues as to who and where he is, even though it means certain death. "Where do these stories come from?" the analyst asks. Enraged, the writer retaliates by writing a story about a patient who poses as a transvestite in order to seduce his analyst and bring about his downfall. At their next session, just after "The Couch" has appeared, the writer and the analyst agree to part ways. The mother mails the story off to her agent. Writing is therapy!

The son's next stories are about: a mother who reveals a son's real father to be an uncle the son has always hated; a husband who keeps a second set of journals when he suspects his wife is reading the first; a woman spy who, given a new identity under the government's witness protection programme, leaves clues as to who and where she is, even though it means certain death.

"Those are my stories," his mother accuses.

In defence, the son says he read that a young Algerian woman recently wrote to Doris Lessing and asked if she could write Paul's novel, whose first line is given to him by Anna Wolfe in *The Golden Notebook*, and Lessing said yes.

"But you didn't ask me," the mother persists, though she is secretly mollified by his comparison of her with Lessing. She is even more pleased when the stories appear in a magazine that has been turning down her husband's latest work.

Flushed with success, the son buys an IBM Displaywriter and gives his old typewriter away. Now the most prolific member of his family, he writes a story about an artist, a son of well-known artists, who finally confronts what it meant to grow up in their shadow, of needing to find his own light.

"Good image," his father says. "But I wonder if your artist's career would have taken off so smartly if he hadn't used the family name."

Furious, the son locks himself in his study and pours out a story in which a dying composer accuses his son of trading on his father's name in order to get his own, less accomplished concertos performed.

"What will people think?" His father rants and raves (clichés are true, the son discovers, but you still can't use them). "I mean, what kind of father would say a thing like that?"

"You tell me," the son says.

"But you are the one who wrote it," the father says. "Stories demand motivation, consistent behaviour. Real people aren't held accountable for what they say, but characters are. Besides, I'll be besieged by reporters' morbid phone calls, neighbours' discreet condolences for an illness you neglected to name."

"But the father has to be dying," the son says. "Why else would a father say a thing like that—accusing the son of using his name." Suddenly he looks at his father with curiosity—and false enlightenment.

"I am not dying," his father says. "The answer is no."

But it makes the father think. In the next five weeks the father finds a new well of creative energy and begins to write brutally honest memoirs of his childhood, his teenage years, his marriage and his lovers. He loves his son, his wife, but he loves immortality more. He will pre-empt the biographers, the memoirs of a wife and a son, by telling more than any son or wife could ever imagine. All his life he wrote fiction in order to tell the truth, but now he will write the truth in order to avoid becoming a fiction. His latest affair is allowed to wither and he instructs the cleaning woman to screen all his calls. The son must do his own editing; his wife has stories of her own to write. He retreats to his study. Furthermore, the cleaning woman is expressly forbidden to disturb a thing in his study. "Come to think of it," the husband tells her, "you really needn't clean it again at all."

The cleaning woman, of course, takes offence. She also has been taking notes for years, ever since she heard some writer ask on *All Things Considered*, "Why aren't there any novels by cleaning women?" She's ready to quit. They have ceased to surprise her, this quasi-famous family (her vocabulary has improved while cleaning their toilets, changing their sheets, baking their casseroles). She has enough material: habits, plots, lines of dialogue; the charts and graphs of adultery; the son's letters from Thailand; the husband's wimpy affairs; the line "My shrink called me for an agent." She tells her employers she wants to work only part-time because she has other things to accomplish. Somehow, and truth is stranger than fiction, she finds a job with a therapist who fancies himself a writer and has all the books on technique—books the family used to ridicule—next to Freud. She makes sure before taking the job that he never locks his files. There is an efficiency about all this the missus often accused her of lacking. But she feels efficient as she assembles her cast of characters. Heavily into symbols, she begins her saga by recalling a story Robert Graves told of the Scilly Isles, a place that had no industry and where the people had to make do by taking in each other's laundry. An island setting appeals to her. Three famous writers all live under one red-tiled roof, in a white stucco house overlooking a cerulean sea. Mother, father, son—and of course the cleaning woman. It will be a *roman à clef*. She types on an old typewriter the family gave her, gave her the way folks always give things to the help.

william trevor

Kathleen's Field

" I'm after a field of land, sir."

Hagerty's tone was modest to the bank agent, careful and cautious. He was aware that Mr Ensor would know what was coming next. He was aware that he constituted a risk, a word Mr Ensor had used a couple of times when endeavouring to discuss the overdraft Hagerty already had with the bank.

"I was wondering, sir . . ." His voice trailed away when Mr Ensor's head began to shake. He'd like to say yes, the bank agent assured him. He would say yes this very instant, only what use would it be when Head Office wouldn't agree? "They're bad times, Mr Hagerty."

It was a Monday morning in 1948. Leaning on the counter, his right hand still grasping the stick he'd used to drive three bullocks the seven miles from his farm, Hagerty agreed that the times were as bad as ever he'd known them. He'd brought the bullocks in to see if he could get a price for them, but he hadn't been successful. All the way on his journey he'd been thinking about the field old Lally had spent his lifetime carting the rocks out of. The widow the old man left behind him had sold the nineteen acres on the other side of the hill but the last of her fields was awkwardly placed for anyone except Hagerty. They both knew it would be convenient for him to have it; they both knew there'd be almost as much profit in that single pasture as there was in all the land he possessed already. Gently sloping, naturally drained, it was free of weeds and thistles, and the grass it grew would do your heart good to look at. Old Lally had known its value from the moment he'd inherited it. He had kept it ditched, with its gates and stone walls always cared for. And for miles around no one had ever cleared away rocks like old Lally had.

"I'd help you if I could, Mr Hagerty," the bank agent assured him. "Only there's still a fair bit owing."

"I know there is, sir."

Every December Hagerty walked into the bank with a plucked turkey as a seasonal statement of gratitude: the overdraft had undramatically continued for seventeen years. It was less than it had been, but Hagerty was no longer young and he might yet be written off as a bad debt. He hadn't had much hope when he'd raised the subject of the field he coveted.

"I'm sorry, Mr Hagerty," the bank agent said, stretching his hand across the width of the counter. "I know that field well. I know you could make something of it, but there you are."

"Ah well, you gave it your consideration, sir."

He said it because it was his way to make matters easier for a man who had lent him money in the past: Hagerty was a humble man. He had a tired look about him, his spare figure stooped from his shoulders, a black hat always on his head. He hadn't removed it in the bank, nor did he in Shaughnessy's Provisions and Bar, where he sat in a corner by himself, with a bottle of stout to console him. He had left the bullocks in Cronin's yard in order to free himself for his business in the bank, and since Cronin made a small charge for this fair day service he'd thought he might as well take full advantage of it by delaying a little longer.

He reflected as he drank that he hardly needed the bank agent's reminder about the times being bad. Seven of his ten children had emigrated, four to Canada and America, the other three to England. Kathleen, the youngest, now sixteen, was left, with Biddy, who wasn't herself, and Con, who would inherit the farm. But without the Lally's field it wouldn't be easy for Con to keep on going. Sooner or later he would want to marry the Kilfedder girl, and there'd always have to be a home for Biddy on the farm, and for a while at least an elderly mother and father would have to be accommodated also. Sometimes one or other of the exiled children sent back a cheque and

Hagerty never objected to accepting it. But none of them could afford the price of the field, and he wasn't going to ask them. Nor would Con accept these little presents when his time came to take over the farm entirely, for how could the oldest brother be beholden like that in the prime of his life? It wasn't the same for Hagerty himself: he'd been barefoot on the farm as a child, which was when his humility had been learnt.

"Are you keeping yourself well, Mr Hagerty?" Mrs Shaughnessy enquired, crossing the small bar to where he sat. She'd been busy with customers on the grocery side since soon after he'd come in; she'd drawn the cork out of his bottle, apologising for her busyness when she gave it to him to pour himself.

"I am," he said. "And are you, Mrs Shaughnessy?"

"I have the winter rheumatism again. But thank God it's not severe."

Mrs Shaughnessy was a tall, big-shouldered woman whom he remembered as a girl before she'd married into the shop. She wore a bit of make-up, and her clothes were more colourful than his wife's, although they were hidden now by her green shop overall. She had been flighty as a girl, so he remembered hearing, but in no way could you describe her as that in her late middle age: "well-to-do" was the description that everything about Mrs Shaughnessy insisted upon.

"I was wanting to ask you, Mr Hagerty. I'm on the look-out for a country girl to assist me in the house. If they're any good they're like gold dust these days. Would you know of a country girl out your way?"

Hagerty began to shake his head and was at once reminded of the bank agent shaking his. It was then, while he was still actually engaged in that motion, that he recalled a fact which previously had been of no interest to him: Mrs Shaughnessy's husband lent people money. Mr Shaughnessy was a considerable businessman. As well as the Provisions and Bar, he owned a barber's shop and was an agent for the Property & Life Insurance Company; he had funds to spare. Hagerty had heard of people mortgaging an area of their land with Mr Shaughnessy, or maybe the farmhouse itself, and as a consequence being able to buy machinery or stock. He'd never yet heard of any unfair or sharp practice on the part of Mr Shaughnessy after the deal had been agreed upon and had gone into operation.

"Haven't you a daughter yourself, Mr Hagerty? Pardon me now, if I'm guilty of a presumption, but I always say if you don't ask you won't know. Haven't you a daughter not long left the nuns?"

Kathleen's round, open features came into his mind, momentarily softening his own. His youngest daughter was inclined to plumpness and to freckles, but her wide, uncomplicated smile often radiated moments of prettiness in her face. She had always been his favourite, although Biddy, of course, had a special place also.

"No, she's not long left the convent."

Her face slipped away, darkening to nothing in his imagination. He thought again of the Lallys' field, the curving shape of it like a teacloth thrown over a bush to dry. A stream ran among the few little ash trees at the bottom, the morning sun lingered on the heart of it.

"I'd never have another girl unless I knew the family, Mr Hagerty. Or unless she'd be vouched for by someone the like of yourself."

"Are you thinking of Kathleen, Mrs Shaughnessy?"

"Well, I am. I'll be truthful with you, I am."

At that moment someone rapped with a coin on the counter of the grocery and Mrs Shaughnessy hurried away. If Kathleen came to work in the house above the Provisions and Bar, he might be able to bring up the possibility of a mortgage. And the grass was so rich in the field it wouldn't be too many years before a mortgage could be paid off. Con would be left secure, Biddy would be provided for.

Hagerty savoured a slow mouthful of stout. He didn't want Kathleen to go to England. *I can get her fixed up*, her sister, Mary Florence, had written in a letter not long ago. "I'd rather Kilburn than Chicago," he'd heard Kathleen herself saying to Con, and at the time he'd been relieved because at least Kilburn was nearer. Only Biddy would always be with them, for you couldn't count on Con not being tempted by Kilburn or Chicago the way things were at the present time. "Sure, what choice have we in any of it?" their mother had said, but enough of them had gone, he'd thought. His father had struggled for the farm and he'd struggled for it himself.

"God, the cheek of some people!" Mrs Shaughnessy exclaimed, re-entering the bar. "Tinned pears and ham, and her book unpaid since January! Would you credit that, Mr Hagerty?"

He wagged his head in an appropriate manner, denoting amazement. He'd been thinking over what she'd put to him, he said. There was no girl out his way who might be suitable, only his own Kathleen. "You were right enough to mention Kathleen, Mrs Shaughnessy." The nuns had never been displeased with her, he said as well.

"Of course, she would be raw, Mr Hagerty. I'd have to train every inch of her. Well, I have experience in that all right. You train them, Mr Hagerty, and the next thing is they go off to get married. There's no sign of that, is there?"

"Ah, no, no."

"You'd maybe spend a year training them and then they'd be off. Sure, where's the sense in it? I often wonder why I bother."

"Kathleen wouldn't go running off, no fear of that, Mrs Shaughnessy."

"It's best to know the family. It's best to know a father like yourself."

As Mrs Shaughnessy spoke, her husband appeared behind the bar. He was a small man, with grey hair brushed straight back from his forehead, and a map of broken veins dictating a warm redness in his complexion. He wore a collar and tie, which Mr Hagerty did not, and the waistcoat and trousers of a dark blue suit. He carried a number of papers in his right hand and a packet of Sweet Afton cigarettes in his left. He spread the papers out on the bar and having lit a cigarette proceeded to scrutinise them. While he listened to Mrs Shaughnessy's further exposition of her theme, Hagerty was unable to take his eyes off him.

"You get in a country girl and you wouldn't know was she clean or maybe would she take things. We had a queer one once, she used to eat a raw onion. You'd go into the kitchen and she'd be at it. "What are you chewing, Kitty?" you might say to her politely. And she'd open her mouth and you'd see the onion in it."

"Kathleen wouldn't eat onions."

"Ah, I'm not saying she would. Des, will you bring Mr Hagerty another bottle of stout. He has a girl for us."

Looking up from his papers but keeping a finger in place on them, her husband asked her what she was talking about.

"Kathleen Hagerty would come in and assist me, Des."

Mr Shaughnessy asked who Kathleen Hagerty was, and when it was revealed that her father was sitting in the bar in need of another drink he bundled his papers into a pocket and drew the corks from two bottles of stout. His wife winked at Hagerty. He liked to have a maid about the house, she said. He pretended he didn't, but he liked the style of it.

All the way back to the farm, driving home the bullocks, Hagerty reflected on that stroke of luck. In poor spirits he'd turned into Shaughnessy's, it being the nearest public house to the bank. If he hadn't done so, and if Mrs Shaughnessy hadn't mentioned her domestic needs, and if her husband hadn't come in when he had, there wouldn't have been one bit of good news to carry back. "I'm after a field of land," he'd said to Mr Shaughnessy, making no bones about it. They'd both listened to him, Mrs Shaughnessy only going away once, to pour herself half a glass of sherry. They'd understood immediately the thing about the field being valuable to him, because of its position. "Doesn't it sound a grand bit of land, Des?" Mrs Shaughnessy had remarked with enthusiasm. "With a good hot sun on it?" He'd revealed the price old Lally's widow was asking; he'd laid every fact he knew down before them.

In the end, on top of four bottles of stout, he was poured a glass of Paddy, and then Mrs Shaughnessy made him a spreadable cheese sandwich. He would send Kathleen in, he promised, and after that it would be up to Mrs Shaughnessy. "But, sure, I think we'll do business," she confidently predicted.

Biddy would see him coming, he said to himself as he urged the bullocks on. She'd see the bullocks and she'd run back into the house to say they hadn't been sold. They'd be long faces then, but he'd take it easy when he entered the kitchen and reached out for his tea. A bad old fair it had been, he'd report, which was nothing only the truth, and he'd go through the offers that had been made to him. He'd go through the conversation with Mr Ensor and then explain how he'd gone into Shaughnessy's to rest himself before the journey home.

On the road ahead he saw Biddy waving at him and then doing what he'd known she'd do: hurrying back to precede him with the news. As he murmured the words of thanksgiving, his youngest daughter again filled his mind. The day Kathleen had been born it had rained from dawn till dusk. People said that was lucky for the family of an infant, and it might be they were right.

Kathleen was led from room to room and felt alarmed. She had never experienced a carpet beneath her feet before. There were boards or linoleum in the farmhouse, and only linoleum in the Reverend Mother's room at the convent. She found the papered walls startling: flowers cascaded in the corners, and ran in a narrow band around the room, close to the ceiling. "I see you admiring the frieze," Mrs Shaughnessy said. "I had the house redone a year ago." She paused and then laughed, amused by the wonder in Kathleen's face. "Those little borders," she said. "I think they call them friezes these days."

When Mrs Shaughnessy laughed her chin became long and smooth, and the skin tightened on her forehead. Her very white false teeth—which Kathleen was later to learn she referred to as her "delf"—shifted slightly behind her reddened lips. The laugh was a sedate whisper that quickly exhausted itself.

"You're a good riser, are you, Kathleen?"

"I'm used to getting up, ma'am."

Always say ma'am, the Reverend Mother had adjured, for Kathleen had been summoned when it was known that Mrs Shaughnessy was interested in training her as a maid. The Reverend Mother liked to have a word with any girl who'd been to the convent when the question of local employment arose, or if emigration was mooted. The Reverend Mother liked to satisfy herself that a girl's future promised to be what she herself would have chosen for the girl; and she liked to point out certain hazards, feeling it her duty to do so. The Friday fast was not observed in Protestant households, where there would also be an absence of sacred reminders. Conditions met with after emigration left even more to be desired.

"Now, this would be your own room, Kathleen," Mrs Shaughnessy said, leading her into a small bedroom at the top of the house. There was a white china wash-basin with a jug standing in it, and a bed with a mattress on it, and a cupboard. The stand the basin and the jug were on was painted white, and so was the cupboard. A net curtain covered the bottom half of a window and at the top there was a brown blind like the ones in the Reverend Mother's room. There wasn't a carpet on the floor and there wasn't linoleum either; but a rug stretched on the boards by the bed, and Kathleen couldn't help imagining her bare feet stepping on its softness first thing every morning.

"There'll be the two uniforms the last girl had," Mrs Shaughnessy said. "They'd easily fit although I'd say you were bigger on the chest. You wouldn't be familiar with a uniform, Kathleen?"

"I didn't have one at the convent, ma'am."

"You'll soon get used to the dresses."

That was the first intimation that Mrs Shaughnessy considered her suitable for the post. The dresses were hanging in the cupboard, she said. There were sheets and blankets in the hot press.

"I'd rather call you Kitty," Mrs Shaughnessy said. "If you wouldn't object. The last girl was Kitty, and so was another one we had."

Kathleen said that was all right. She hadn't been called Kitty at the convent, and wasn't at home because it was the pet name of her eldest sister.

"Well, that's great," Mrs Shaughnessy said, the tone of her voice implying that the arrangement had already been made.

"I was never better pleased with you," her father said when Kathleen returned home. "You're a great little girl."

When she'd packed some of her clothes into a suitcase that Mary Florence had left behind after a visit one time, he said it was hardly like going away at all because she was only going seven miles. She'd return every Sunday afternoon; it wasn't like Kilburn or Chicago. She sat beside him on the cart and he explained that the Shaughnessys had been generous to a degree. The wages he had agreed with them would be held back and set against the debt: it was that that made the whole thing possible, reducing his monthly repayments to a figure he was confident he could manage, even with the bank overdraft. "It isn't everyone would agree to the convenience of that, Kathleen."

She said she understood. There was a new sprightliness about her father; the fatigue in his face had given way to an excited pleasure. His gratitude to the Shaughnessys, and her mother's gratitude, had made the farmhouse a different place during the last couple of weeks. Biddy and Con had been affected by it, and so had Kathleen even though she had no idea what life would be like in the house above the Shaughnessys' Provisions and Bar. Mrs Shaughnessy had not outlined her duties beyond saying that every night when she went up to bed she should carry with her the alarm clock from the kitchen dresser, and carry it down again every morning. The most important thing of all appeared to be that she should rise promptly from her bed.

"You'll listen well to what Mrs Shaughnessy says," her father begged her. "You'll attend properly to all the work, Kathleen?"

"I will of course."

"It'll be great seeing you on Sundays, girl."

"It'll be great coming home."

A bicycle, left behind also by Mary Florence, lay in the back of the cart. Kathleen had wanted to tie the suitcase on to the carrier and cycle in herself with it, but her father wouldn't let her. It was dangerous, he said, a suitcase attached like that, it could easily unbalance you.

"Kathleen's field is what we'll call it," her father said on their journey together, and added after a moment: "They're decent people, Kathleen. You're going to a decent house."

"Oh, I know, I know."

But after only half a day there Kathleen wished she was back in the farmhouse. She knew at once how much she was going to miss the comfort of the kitchen she had known all her life, and the room along the passage she shared with Biddy, where Mary Florence had slept also, and the dogs nosing up to her in the yard. She knew how much she would miss Con, and her father and her mother, and how she'd miss looking after Biddy.

"Now, I'll show you how to set a table," Mrs Shaughnessy said. "Listen to me carefully, Kitty."

Cork mats were put down on the tablecloth so that the heat of the dishes wouldn't penetrate to the polished surface beneath. Small plates were placed on the left of each cork mat, to put the skins of potatoes on. A knife and a fork were arranged on each side of the mats and a spoon and a fork across the top. The pepper and salt was placed so that Mr Shaughnessy could easily reach them. Serving spoons were placed by the bigger mats in the middle. The breakfast table was set the night before, with the cups upside down on the saucers so that they wouldn't catch the dust when the ashes were taken from the fire-place.

"Can you cut kindling, Kitty? I'll show you how to do it with the little hatchet."

She showed her, as well, how to sweep the carpet on the stairs with a stiff hand-brush, and how to use the dust-pan. She explained that every mantelpiece in the house had to be dusted every morning, and all the places where grime would gather. She showed her where saucepans and dishes were kept, and instructed her in how to light the range, the first task of the day. The backyard required brushing once a week, on Saturday between four o'clock and five. And every morning after breakfast water had to be pumped from the tank in the yard, fifteen minutes' work with the hand lever.

"That's the WC you'd use, Kitty," Mrs Shaughnessy

indicated, leading her to a privy in another part of the backyard. "The maids always use this one."

The dresses of the uniforms didn't fit. She looked at herself in the blue one and then in the black. The mirror on the dressing-table was tarnished but she could tell that neither uniform enhanced her in any way whatsoever. She looked as fat as a fool, she thought, with the hems all crooked, and the sleeves too tight on her forearms. "Oh now, that's really very good," Mrs Shaughnessy said when Kathleen emerged from her bedroom in the black one. She demonstrated how the bodice of the apron was kept in place and how the afternoon cap should be worn.

"Is your father fit?" Mr Shaughnessy enquired when he came upstairs for his six o'clock tea.

"He is, sir." Suddenly Kathleen had to choke back tears because without any warning the reference to her father had made her want to cry.

"He was shook the day I saw him," Mr Shaughnessy said, "on account he couldn't sell the bullocks."

"He's all right now, sir."

The Shaughnessys' son re-appeared then too, a narrow-faced youth who hadn't addressed her when he'd arrived in the dining-room in the middle of the day and who didn't address her now. There were just the three of them, two younger children having grown up and gone away. During the day Mrs Shaughnessy had often referred to her other son and her daughter, the son in business in Limerick, the daughter married to a county surveyor. The narrow-faced son would inherit the business, she'd said, the barber's shop and the Provisions and Bar, maybe even the insurances. With a bout of wretchedness, Kathleen was reminded of Con inheriting the farm. Before that he'd marry Angie Kilfedder, who wouldn't hesitate to accept him now that the farm was improved.

Kathleen finished laying the table and went back to the kitchen, where Mrs Shaughnessy was frying rashers and eggs and slices of soda bread. When they were ready she scooped them on to three plates and Kathleen carried the tray, with a tea-pot on it as well, into the dining-room. Her instructions were to return to the kitchen when she'd done so and to fry her own rasher and eggs, and soda bread if she wanted it. "I don't know we will make much of that one," she heard Mrs Shaughnessy saying as she closed the dining-room door.

That night she lay awake in the strange bed, not wanting to sleep because sleep would too swiftly bring the morning, and another day like the day there'd been. She couldn't stay here: she'd say that on Sunday. If they knew what it was like they wouldn't want her to. She sobbed, thinking again of the warm kitchen she had left behind, the sheepdogs lying by the fire and Biddy turning the wheel of the bellows, the only household task she could do. She thought of her mother and father sitting at the table like they always did, her mother knitting, her father pondering, with his hat still on his head. If they could see her in the dresses they'd understand. If they could see her standing there pumping up the water they'd surely be sorry for the way she felt. "I haven't the time to tell you twice, Kitty," Mrs Shaughnessy said over and over again, her long, painted face not smiling in the least way whatsoever. If anything was broken, she'd said, the cost of it would have to be stopped out of her wages, and she'd spoken as though the wages actually changed hands. In Kathleen's dreams Mrs Shaughnessy kept laughing, her chin going long and smooth and her large white teeth moving in her mouth. The dresses belonged to one of the King of England's daughters, she explained which was why they didn't fit. And then Mary Florence came into the kitchen and said she was just back from Kilburn with a pair of shoes that belonged to someone else. The price of them could be stopped out of the wages, she suggested, and Mrs Shaughnessy agreed.

When Kathleen opened her eyes, roused by the alarm clock at half-past six, she didn't know where she was. Then one after another the details of the previous day impinged on her waking consciousness: the cork mats, the shed where the kindling was cut, the narrow face of the Shaughnessys' son, the greasy doorknobs in the kitchen, the impatience in Mrs Shaughnessy's voice. The reality was worse than the confusion of her dreams, and there was nothing magical about the softness of the rug beneath her bare feet: she didn't even notice it. She lifted her nightdress over her head and for a moment caught a glimpse of her nakedness in the tarnished looking-glass—plumply rounded thighs and knees, the dimple in her stomach. She drew on stockings and underclothes, feeling even more lost than she had when she'd tried not to go to sleep. She knelt by her bed, and when she'd offered her usual prayers she asked that she might be taken away from the Shaughnessys' house. She asked that her father would understand when she told him.

"The master's waiting on his breakfast, Kitty."

"I lit the range the minute I was down, ma'am."

"If you don't get it going by twenty to seven it won't be hot in time. I told you that yesterday. Didn't you pull the dampers out?"

"The paper wouldn't catch, ma'am."

"If the paper wouldn't catch you'll have used a damp bit. Or maybe paper out of a magazine. You can't light a fire with paper out of a magazine, Kitty."

"If I'd had a drop of paraffin, ma'am."

"My God, are you mad, child?"

"At home we'd throw on a half cup of paraffin if the fire was slow, ma'am."

"Never bring paraffin near the range. If the master heard you he'd jump out of his skin."

"I only thought it would hurry it, ma'am."

"Set the alarm for six if you're going to be slow with the fire, if the breakfast's not on the table by a quarter to eight he'll raise the roof. Have you the plates in the bottom oven?"

When Kathleen opened the door of the bottom oven a black kitten darted out, scratching the back of her hand in its agitation.

"Great God almighty!" exclaimed Mrs Shaughnessy. "Are you trying to roast the poor cat?"

"I didn't know it was in there, ma'am."

"You lit the fire with the poor creature inside there! What were you thinking of to do that, Kitty?"

"I didn't know, ma'am."

"Always look in the two ovens before you light the range, child. Didn't you hear me telling you?"

After breakfast, when Kathleen went into the dining-room to clear the table, Mrs Shaughnessy was telling her son about the kitten in the oven. "Haven't they brains like turnips?" she said even though Kathleen was in the room. The son released a half-hearted smile, but when Kathleen asked him if he'd finished with the jam he didn't reply. "Try and speak a bit more clearly, Kitty," Mrs Shaughnessy said later. "It's not everyone can understand a country accent."

The day was similar to the day before except that at eleven o'clock Mrs Shaughnessy said:

"Go upstairs and take off your cap. Put on your coat and go down the street to Crawley's. A half pound of round steak, and suet. Take the book off the dresser. He'll know who you are when he sees it."

So far, that was the pleasantest chore she had been asked to do. She had to wait in the shop because there were two other people before her, both of whom held the butcher in conversation. "I know your father," Mr Crawley said when he'd asked her name, and he held her in conversation also, wanting to know if her father was in good health and asking about her brothers and sisters. He'd heard about the buying of Lally's field. She was the last uniformed maid in town, he said, now that Nellie Broderick at O'Mara's had had to give up because of her legs.

"Are you mad?" Mrs Shaughnessy shouted at her on her return. "I should be down in the shop and not waiting to put that meat on. Didn't I tell you yesterday not to be loitering in the mornings?"

"I'm sorry, ma'am, only Mr Crawley—"

"Go down to the shop and tell the master I'm delayed over cooking the dinner and you can assist him for ten minutes."

But when Kathleen appeared in the grocery Mr Shaughnessy asked her if she'd got lost. The son was weighing sugar into grey paper-bags and tying string round each of them. A murmur of voices came from the bar.

"Mrs Shaughnessy is delayed over cooking the dinner,"

Kathleen said. "She was thinking I could assist you for ten minutes."

"Well, that's a good one!" Mr Shaughnessy threw back his head, exploding with laughter. A little shower of spittle damped Kathleen's face. The son gave his half-hearted smile. "Can you make a spill, Kitty? D'you know what I mean by a spill?" Mr Shaughnessy demonstrated with a piece of brown paper on the counter. Kathleen shook her head. "Would you know what to charge for a quarter pound of tea, Kitty? Can you weigh out sugar, Kitty? Go back to the missus, will you, and tell her to have sense."

In the kitchen Kathleen put it differently, simply saying that Mr Shaughnessy hadn't required her services. "Bring a scuttle of coal up to the dining-room," Mrs Shaughnessy commanded. "And get out the mustard. Can you make mustard?"

Kathleen had never tasted mustard in her life; she had heard of it but did not precisely know what it was. She began to say she wasn't sure about making some, but even before she spoke Mrs Shaughnessy sighed and told her to wash down the front steps instead.

"I don't want to go back there," Kathleen said on Sunday. "I can't understand what she says to me. It's lonesome the entire time."

Her mother was sympathetic, but even so she shook her head. "There's people I used to know," she said. "People placed like ourselves whose farms failed on them. They're walking on the roads now, no better than tinkers. I have ten children, Kathleen, and seven are gone from me. There's five of them I'll maybe never see again. It's that you have to think of, pet."

"I cried the first night. I was that lonesome when I got into bed."

"But isn't it a clean room you're in, pet? And aren't you given food to eat that's better than you'd got here? And don't the dresses she supplies save us an expense again? Wouldn't you think of that, pet?"

A bargain had been struck, her mother also reminded her,

and a bargain was a bargain. Biddy said it sounded great, going out into the town for messages. She'd give anything to see a house like that, Biddy said, with the coal fires and the stairs.

"I'd say they were well pleased with you," Kathleen's father said when he came in from the yard later on. "You'd have been back here inside a day if they weren't."

She'd done her best, she thought as she rode away from the farmhouse on Mary Florence's bicycle; if she'd done everything badly she would have obtained her release. She wept because she wouldn't see Biddy and Con and her father and mother for another seven days. She dreaded the return to the desolate bedroom which her mother had reminded her was clean, and the kitchen where there was no one to keep her company in the evenings. She felt as if she could not bear it, more counting of the days until Sunday and when Sunday came the few hours passing so swiftly. But she knew, by now, that she would remain in the Shaughnessys' house for as long as was necessary.

"I must have you back by half six, Kitty," Mrs Shaughnessy said when she saw her. "It's closer to seven now."

Kathleen said she was sorry. She'd had to stop to pump the back tyre of her bicycle, she said, although in fact this was not true: what she'd stopped for was to wipe away the signs of her crying and to blow her nose. In the short time she had been part of Mrs Shaughnessy's household she had developed the habit of making excuses, and obscuring her inadequacies beneath lies that were easier than the truth.

"Fry the bread like I showed you, Kitty. Get it brown on both sides. The master likes it crisp."

There was something Mr Shaughnessy liked also, which Kathleen discovered when seven of her free Sunday afternoons had gone by. She was dusting the dining-room mantelpiece one morning when he came and stood very close to her. She thought she was in his way, and moved out of it, but a week or so later he stood closer to her again, his breath warm on her cheek. When it happened the third time she felt herself blushing.

It was in this manner that Mr Shaughnessy rather than his

wife came to occupy, for Kathleen, the central role in the household. The narrow-faced son remained as he had been since the day of her arrival, a dour presence, contributing little in the way of conversation and never revealing the fruits of his brooding silence. Mrs Shaughnessy, having instructed, had apparently played out the part she'd set herself. She came into the kitchen at midday to cook meat and potatoes and one of the milk puddings her husband was addicted to, but otherwise the kitchen was Kathleen's province now, and it was she who was responsible for the frying of the food for breakfast and for the six o'clock tea. Mrs Shaughnessy preferred to be in the shop. She enjoyed the social side of that, she told Kathleen; and she enjoyed the occasional half glass of sherry in the bar. "That's me all over, Kitty. I never took to housework." She was more amiable in her manner, and confessed that she always found training a country girl an exhausting and irksome task and might therefore have been a little impatient. "Kitty's settled in grand," she informed Kathleen's father when he looked into the bar one fair day to make a mortgage payment. He'd been delighted to hear that, he told Kathleen the following Sunday.

Mr Shaughnessy never said anything when he came to stand close to her, although on other occasions he addressed her pleasantly enough, even complimenting her on her frying. He had an easy way with him, quite different from his son's. He was more like his other two children, the married daughter and the son who was in Limerick, both of whom Kathleen had met when they had returned to the house for an uncle's funeral. He occasionally repeated a joke he'd been told, and Mrs Shaughnessy would laugh, her chin becoming lengthy and the skin tightening on her forehead. On the occasion of the uncle's funeral his other son and his daughter laughed at the jokes also, but the son who'd remained at home only smiled. "Wait till I tell you this one, Kitty," he'd sometimes say, alone with her in the dining-room. He would tell her something Bob Crowe who ran the barber's shop for him had heard from a customer, making the most of the anecdote in a way that suggested he was anxious to entertain her. His manner and his tone of voice denied that it had ever been necessary for him to stand close to her, or else that his practice of doing so had been erased from his memory.

But the scarlet complexion of Mr Shaughnessy's face and the sharply brushed-back grey hair, the odour of cigarette smoke that emanated from his clothes, could not be so easily forgotten by Kathleen. She no longer wept from loneliness in her bedroom, yet was aware that the behaviour of Mr Shaughnessy lent the feeling of isolation an extra, vivid dimension, for in the farmhouse kitchen on Sundays the behaviour could not be mentioned.

Every evening Kathleen sat by the range, thinking about it. The black kitten which had darted out of the oven on her second morning had grown into a cat and sat blinking beside her chair. The alarm clock ticked loudly on the dresser. Was it something she should confess? Was it a sin to be as silent as she was when he came to stand beside her? Was it a sin to be unable to find the courage to tell him to leave her alone? Once in the village where the convent was, another girl in her class had pointed out a boy who was loitering with some other boys by the 1798 statue. That boy was always trying to kiss you, the girl said; he would follow you along a road if you were going home on your own, or he'd be hiding on the way. But although Kathleen often went home alone the boy never came near her. He wasn't a bad-looking boy, she'd thought, she wouldn't have minded much. She'd wondered if she'd mind the boys her sisters complained about, who tried to kiss you when they were dancing with you. Pests, her sisters called them, but Kathleen thought it was nice that they wanted to.

Mr Shaughnessy was different. When he stood close to her his breathing would become loud and unsteady. He always moved away quite quickly, when she wasn't expecting him to. He walked off, never looking back, soundlessly almost.

Then one day, when Mrs Shaughnessy was buying a new skirt and the son was in the shop, he came into the kitchen, where she was scrubbing the draining-boards. He came straight to where she was, as if between them there was some understanding that he should do so. He stood in a slightly different position from usual, behind her rather than at her side, and she felt for the first time his hands passing over her clothes.

"Mr Shaughnessy!" she whispered. "Mr Shaughnessy, now."

He took no notice. Some part of his face was touching her hair. The rhythm of his breathing changed.

"Mr Shaughnessy, I don't like it."

He seemed not to hear, she sensed that his eyes were closed. As suddenly, and as quickly as always, he went away.

"Well, Bob Crowe told me a queer one this evening," he said that same evening, while she was placing their plates of fried food in front of them in the dining room. "It seems there's a woman asleep in Clery's window in Dublin."

His wife expressed disbelief. Bob Crowe would tell you anything, she said.

"In a hypnotic trance, it seems. Advertising Odearest Mattresses."

"Ah, go on now! He's pulling your leg, Des."

"Not a bit of him. She'll stop there a week, it seems. The Guards have to move the crowds on."

Kathleen closed the dining-room door behind her. He had turned to look at her when he'd said there was a woman asleep in Clery's window, in an effort to include her in what he was retailing. His eyes had betrayed nothing of their surreptitious relationship, but Kathleen hadn't been able to meet them.

"We ploughed the field," her father said the following Sunday. "I've never tucked up earth as good."

She almost told him then. She longed so much she could hardly prevent herself. She longed to let her tears come and to hear his voice consoling her. When she was a child she'd loved that.

"You're a great girl," he said.

Mr Shaughnessy took to attending an earlier mass than his wife and son, and when they were out at theirs he would come into the kitchen. When she hid in her bedroom he followed her there. She'd have locked herself in the outside WC if there'd been a latch on the door.

"Well, Kitty and myself were quiet enough here," he'd say

in the dining-room later on, when the three of them were eating their midday dinner. She couldn't understand how he could bring himself to speak like that, or how he could so hungrily eat his food, as though nothing had occurred. She couldn't understand how he could act normally with his son or with his other children when they came on a visit. It was extraordinary to hear Mrs Shaughnessy humming her songs about the house and calling him by his Christian name.

"The Kenny girl's getting married," Mrs Shaughnessy said on another mealtime occasion. "Tyson from the hardware."

"I didn't know she was doing a line with him."

"Oh, that's been going on a long time."

"Is it the middle girl? The one with the peroxide?"

"Enid she's called."

"I wonder Bob Crowe didn't hear that. There's not much Bob misses."

"I never thought much of Tyson. But, sure, maybe they are well matched."

"Did you hear that, Kitty? Enid Kenny's getting married. Don't go taking ideas from her." He laughed, and Mrs Shaughnessy laughed, and the son smiled. There wasn't much chance of that, Kathleen thought. "Are you going dancing tonight?" Mr Crawley often asked her on a Friday, and she would reply that she might, but she never did because it wasn't easy to go alone. In the shops and at mass no one displayed any interest in her whatsoever, no one eyed her the way Mary Florence had been eyed, and she supposed it was because her looks weren't up to much. But they were good enough for Mr Shaughnessy, with his quivering breath and his face in her hair. Bitterly, she dwelt on that; bitterly, she heard herself turning on him in the dining-room, accusing him to his wife and son.

"Did you forget to sweep the yard this week?" Mrs Shaughnessy asked her. "Only it's looking poor."

She explained that the wind had blown in papers and debris from a knocked-over dustbin. She'd sweep it again, she said. "I hate a dirty backyard, Kitty."

Was this why the other girls had left, she wondered, the girls whom Mrs Shaughnessy had trained and who'd then gone off? Those girls, whoever they were, would see her, or would know about her. They'd imagine her in one uniform or the other, obedient to him because she enjoyed his attentions. That was how they'd think of her.

"Leave me alone, sir," she said when she saw him approaching her the next time, but he took no notice. She could see him guessing she wouldn't scream.

"Please sir," she said. "Please, sir. I don't like it."

But after a time she ceased to make any protestation and remained as silent as she had been at first. Twelve years or maybe fourteen, she said to herself, lying awake in her bedroom: as long as that, or longer. In the two different uniforms she would continue to be the outward sign of Mrs Shaughnessy's well-to-do status, and her ordinary looks would continue to attract the attentions of a grey-haired man. Because of the field, the nature of the farm her father had once been barefoot on would change. "Kathleen's field," her father would often repeat, and her mother would say again that a bargain was a bargain.

patrick süskind

Depth Wish

At her first exhibition, a young lady from Stuttgart who drew beautifully, received a comment from a critic, who actually meant no harm and even wanted to encourage her. He said: "What you do is interesting and gifted, but as yet you show too little depth."

The young lady did not understand what the critic meant, and had soon forgotten his remark. However, two days later a review of the show appeared in the paper, written by the same critic, in which he stated: "The young artist possesses a lot of talent, and at first glance her work is very pleasing; unfortunately, however, she lacks a little depth."

The young lady now began to think about this. She looked at her drawings, and rummaged in her old portfolios. She looked at all her drawings, including those which she was working on at present. Then she screwed the tops on to her ink-bottles, washed out her pens, and went for a walk.

That same evening she was invited out. The people there seemed to have learnt the reviews by heart, and spoke repeatedly of the great pleasure that her pictures aroused at first glance, and of the talent that this affirmed. But from the murmur in the background, and from those who stood with their backs to her, the young lady could just make out, if she listened carefully: "No depth—she has no depth. That's it. She's not bad, but sadly she has no depth."

During the whole of the following week the young lady drew nothing. She sat silent in her flat, brooding, with only one simple question in her head, which like an octopus, embraced and devoured all remaining thoughts: "Why do I have no depth?"

In the second week the lady tried to draw again, but she could not get beyond clumsy scratchings. Sometimes she couldn't even make a mark. Finally, she was shaking so much that she couldn't dip her pen into the ink-pot anymore. Then she started to sob, and cried: "Yes, it's true, I have no depth!"

In the third week she started to look at art books, to study the works of other draughtsmen, and to wander through galleries and museums. She read books on art theory. She went into a bookshop and demanded that the salesman bring her the deepest book that he had in stock; she was given a work by a certain Mr Wittgenstein. She couldn't get into it.

At an exhibition at the City Museum (500 years of European Drawing), she attached herself to a class of schoolchildren who were being shown around by their art teacher. Suddenly, by one of Leonardo da Vinci's etchings, she stepped forward and asked, "Excuse me, but could you tell me if this work possesses depth?" The art teacher smiled at her, and replied, "My dear young lady, if you want to catch me out, you'll have to do better than that!"—and the class burst out laughing. She, however, went home and burst into tears.

The young lady now became more and more peculiar. She scarcely left her workroom, and yet she could not work. She took tablets to keep her from sleeping, but did not know why she ought to stay awake. When she felt tired she slept in her chair, as she was too scared of the depth of sleep to get into bed. She also started to drink, and she kept a light burning all night long. She no longer drew. When an art dealer from Berlin rang her and asked for some drawings, she screamed down the phone: "Leave me alone! I have no depth!" Occasionally she played with plasticine, but never made anything specific with it; she just buried her fingertips in it, or made little plasticine dumplings. She neglected herself. She no longer took care over her appearance, and she let the flat go to pieces.

Her friends became worried. They said, "We must try to help her, she's sliding into depression. Either she's reached a type of personal crisis, or she's got artistic problems; or maybe she's in financial difficulty. If it's the first, then there's nothing we can do; if it's the second, then she must pull through it herself; if it's the third, then we could organise a collection for her, but she might find that embarrassing." So, they decided to restrict themselves to inviting her out to dinner, or to parties. She always declined, excusing herself by saying that she had to work. But she never did work. Instead, she sat in her room staring straight ahead, kneading plasticine.

Once, she did in fact feel so desperate that she accepted an invitation. After an evening out, a young man who found her attractive wanted to take her home and sleep with her. She told him that he was most welcome to, as she also found him attractive; however, he must prepare himself totally for the fact that she was not deep. On hearing this, the young man took his leave.

The young lady who had once drawn so beautifully, now deteriorated noticeably. She no longer went out, and she ceased all intercourse. She became fat through lack of exercise, and the alcohol and tablets made her age prematurely. Her flat began to decay, and she herself started to smell acrid.

She had inherited 30,000 marks. She lived on this for three years. Once during this time, she journeyed to Naples—no one knew under what circumstances. Whoever tried to speak to her only received an unintelligible babble for an answer.

When she had used up all the money, the lady cut up and pierced holes in all her drawings, climbed to the top of the television broadcasting tower, which was 139 metres high, or deep, and jumped off. However, because a strong wind was blowing on that particular day, she did not dash against the gravelled square beneath the tower, but instead was carried away over an entire oat field to the edge of a forest, where she went down into the fir trees. In spite of this, she died instantly.

The tabloids seized upon this fall gratefully. The suicide, the unusual trajectory, the fact that it concerned a once promising artist who was pretty into the bargain—all these factors made the story newsworthy. The condition of her flat appeared to be so catastrophic, that one could take picturesque photos of it; thousands of empty bottles; signs of ruin everywhere; slashed pictures; lumps of plasticine on the walls; even excrement in the corners of the room! One could risk a second headline, and another report on page 3.

In a review paper, the aforementioned critic wrote a small paragraph in which he expressed his perplexity at the fact that the young lady had to have such a hideous end. "Once again," he wrote, "it is for us who are left behind after a shocking event, to bear witness—here a young and talented person did not find the strength to assert herself on the stage of life. It does not suffice to have public support and personal initiative, where one is primarily concerned with an affinity with the human realm, and an accompanying understanding of the artistic sphere. Certainly, it seems that the seed of this tragic end was planted long ago. Was it not discernible in her early, still apparently naïve work—the terrifying discord, visible in her wilful and significant use of mixed technique; that mono-maniacal aggression turned in upon itself; that introspective revolt, spirally boring within her, which is both highly emotional and obviously useless—that very rebellion of man against his own being? That fatal, I almost want to say: reckless depth-wish?"

Translated by Peter Howarth

ruth rendell

A Pair of Yellow Lilies

A famous designer, young still, who first became well-known when she made a princess's wedding dress, was coming to speak to the women's group of which Bridget Thomas was secretary. She would be the second speaker in the autumn programme which was devoted to success and how women had achieved it. Repeated requests on Bridget's part for a biography from Annie Carter so that she could provide her members with interesting background information had met with no response. Bridget had even begun to wonder if she would remember to come and give her talk in three weeks' time. Meanwhile, obliged to do her own research, she had gone into the public library to look Annie Carter up in *Who's Who*.

Bridget had a precarious job in a small and not very prosperous bookshop. In her mid-thirties, with a rather pretty face that often looked worried and worn, she thought that she might learn something from this current series of talks. Secrets of success might be imparted, blueprints for achievement, even short cuts to prosperity. She never had enough money, never knew security, could not have dreamed of aspiring to an Annie Carter ready-to-wear even when such a garment had been twice marked down in a sale. Clothes, anyway, were hardly a priority, coming a long way down the list of essentials which was headed by rent, fares, food, in that order.

In the library she was not noticeable. She was not, in any case and anywhere, the kind of woman on whom second glances were bestowed. On this Wednesday evening, when the shop closed at its normal time and the library later than usual, she could be seen by those few who cared to look, wearing a long black skirt with a dusty appearance, a tee shirt of a slightly different shade of black—it had been washed fifty times at least—and a waistcoat in dark striped cotton. Her shoes were black velvet Chinese slippers with instep straps and there was a hole she did not know about in her turquoise blue tights, low down on the left calf. Bridget's hair was wispy, long and fair, worn in loops. She was carrying an enormous black leather bag, capacious and heavy, and full of unnecessary things. Herself the first to admit this, she often said she meant to make changes in the matter of this bag but she never got around to it.

This evening the bag contained: a number of crumpled tissues, some pink, some white, a spray bottle of "Wild Musk" cologne, three ballpoint pens, a pair of nail scissors, a pair of nail clippers, a London tube pass, a British Telecom Phonecard, an address book, a mascara wand in a shade called "After-midnight blue", a cheque book, a notebook, a postcard from a friend on holiday in Brittany, a calculator, a paperback of Vasari's *Lives of the Artists*, which Bridget had always meant to read but was not getting on very fast with, a container of nasal spray, a bunch of keys, a book of matches, a silver ring with a green stone, probably onyx, a pheasant's feather picked up while staying for the weekend in someone's cottage in Somerset, three quarters of a bar of milk chocolate, a pair of sunglasses and her wallet which contained the single credit card she possessed, her bank cheque card, her library card, her never-needed driving licence and seventy pounds, give or take a little, in five- and ten-pound notes. There was also about four pounds in change.

On the previous evening Bridget had been to see her aunt. This was the reason for her carrying so much money. Bridget's Aunt Monica was an old woman who had never married and whom her brother, Bridget's father, referred to with brazen insensitivity as "a maiden lady". Bridget thought this outrageous and remonstrated with her father but was unable to bring him to see anything offensive in this expression. Though Monica had never had a husband, she had been successful in other areas of life, and might indeed almost have qualified to join Bridget's list of female achievers fit to speeak to her women's group. Inherited money wisely invested brought her in a substantial income, and this added to the pension derived from having been quite high up the ladder in the Civil Service made her nearly rich.

Bridget did not like taking Monica Thomas's money. Or she told herself she didn't, actually meaning that she liked the money very much but felt humiliated as a young healthy woman who ought to have been able to keep herself adequately, taking money from an old one who had done so and still did. Monica, not invariably during these visits but often enough, would ask her how she was managing.

"Making ends meet, are you?" was the form this enquiry usually took.

Bridget felt a little tide of excitement rising in her at these words because she knew they signified a coming munificence. She simultaneously felt ashamed at being excited by such a thing. This was the way, she believed, other women might feel at the prospect of love-making or discovering themselves pregnant or getting promotion.

She felt excited because her old aunt, her maiden aunt tucked away in a gloomy flat in Fulham, was about to give her fifty pounds.

Characteristically, Monica prepared the ground. "You may as well have it now instead of waiting till I'm gone."

And Bridget would smile and look away, or if she felt brave tell her aunt not to talk about dying. Once she had gone so far as to say, "I don't come here for the sake of what you give me, you know," but as she put this into words she knew she did. And Monica, replying tartly, "And I don't see my little gifts as paying you for your visits," must have known that she did and they did, and that the two of them were involved in a commercial transaction, calculated enough, but imbued with guilt and shame.

Bridget always felt that at her age, thirty-six, and her aunt's, seventy-two, it should be she who gave alms and her aunt who received them. That was the usual way of things. Here the order was reversed, and with a hand that she had to restrain forcibly from trembling with greed and need and excitement, she had reached out on the previous evening for the notes that were presented as a sequel to another of Monica's favourite remarks, that she would like to see Bridget better-dressed. With only a vague grasp of changes in the cost of living, Monica nevertheless knew that for any major changes in her niece's wardrobe to take place, a larger than usual sum would be required. Another twenty-five had been added to the customary fifty.

Five pounds or so had been spent during the course of the day. Bridget had plenty to do with the rest, which did not include buying the simple dark coat and skirt and pink twinset Monica had suggested. There was the gas bill, for instance, and the chance at last of settling the credit card account, on which interest was being paid at 21 per cent. Not that Bridget had no wistful thoughts of beautiful things she would like to possess and most likely never would. A chair in a shop window in Bond Street, for instance, a chair which stood alone in slender, almost arrogant, elegance, with its high-stepping legs and sweetly curved back, she imagined gracing her room as a bringer of daily-renewed happiness and pride. Only today a woman had come into the shop to order the new Salman Rushdie and she had been wearing a dress that was unmistakeably Annie Carter. Bridget had gazed at that dress as at some unattainable glory, at its bizarreries of zips round the sleeves and triangles excised from armpits, uneven hemline and slashed back, for if the truth were told it was the fantastic she admired in such matters and would not have been seen dead in a pink twinset.

She had gazed and longed, just as now, fetching *Who's Who* back to her seat at the table, she had stared, in passing at the back of a glorious jacket. Afterwards she could not have said if it was a man or woman wearing it, a person in jeans was all she could have guessed at. The person in jeans was pressed fairly close up against the science fiction shelves so that the back of the jacket, its most beautiful and striking area, was displayed to the best advantage. The jacket was made of blue denim with a design appliquéd on it. Bridget knew the work was appliqué because she had learned something of this technique herself at a handicrafts class, all part of the horizon-widening, life-enhancing programme with which she combated loneliness. Patches of satin and silk and brocade had been used in the work, and beads and sequins and gold thread as well. The design was of a flock of brilliant butterflies, purple and turquoise and vermilion and royal blue and fuchsia pink, tumbling and fluttering from the open mouths of a pair of yellow lilies. Bridget had gazed at this fantastic picture in silks and jewels and then looked quickly away, resolving to look no more, she desired so much to possess it herself.

Annie Carter's *Who's Who* entry mentioned a book she had written on fashion in the early eighties. Bridget thought it would be sensible to acquaint herself with it. It would provide her with something to talk about when she and the committee entertained the designer to supper after her talk. Leaving *Who's Who* open on the table and her bag wedged between the table legs and the leg of her chair, Bridget went off to consult the library's computer as to whether this book was in stock.

Afterwards she recalled, though dimly, some of the people she had seen as she crossed the floor of the library to where the computer was. An old man in gravy-brown clothes reading a newspaper, two old women in fawn raincoats and pudding basin hats, a child that ran about in defiance of its mother's threats and pleas. The mother was a woman about Bridget's own age, grossly fat, with fuzzy dark hair and swollen legs. There had been other people less memorable.

The computer told her the book was in stock but out on loan. Bridget went back to her table and sat down. She read the sparse *Who's Who* entry once more, noting that Annie Carter's interests were bob-sleighing and collecting netsuke, which seemed to make her rather a daunting person, and then she reached down for her bag and the notebook it contained.

The bag was gone.

The feeling Bridget experienced is one everyone has when they lose something important or think they have lost it, the shock of loss. It was a physical sensation as of something falling through her—turning over in her chest first and then tumbling down inside her body and out through the soles of her feet. She immediately told herself she couldn't have lost the bag, she couldn't have done, it couldn't have been stolen—who would have stolen it among that company?—she must have taken it with her to the computer. Bridget went back to the computer, she ran back, and the bag wasn't there. She told the two assistant librarians and then the librarian herself and they all looked round the library for the bag. It seemed to Bridget that by this time everyone else who had been in the library had swiftly disappeared, everyone that is but the old man reading the newspaper.

The librarian was extremely kind. They were about to close and she said she would go to the police with Bridget, it was on her way. Bridget continued to feel the shock of loss, sickening overturnings in her body and sensations of panic and disbelief. Her head seemed too lightly poised on her neck, almost as if it floated.

"It can't have happened," she kept saying to the librarian. "I just don't believe it could have happened in those few seconds I was away."

"I'm afraid it did," said the librarian who was too kind to say anything about Bridget's unwisdom in leaving the bag unattended even for a few seconds. "It's nothing to do with me, but was there much money in it?"

"Quite a lot. Yes, quite a lot." Bridget added humbly, "Well, a lot for me."

The police could offer very little hope of recovering the money. The bag, they said, and some of its contents might turn up. Meanwhile Bridget had no means of getting into her room, no means even of phoning the credit card company to notify them of the theft. The librarian, whose name was Elizabeth Derwent, saw to all that. She took Bridget to her own home and led her to the telephone and then took her to a locksmith. It was the beginning of what was to be an enduring friendship. Bridget might have lost so many of the most precious of her worldly goods, but as she said afterwards to her Aunt Monica, at least she got Elizabeth's friendship out of it.

"It's an ill wind that blows nobody any good," said Monica, pressing fifty pounds in ten-pound notes into Bridget's hand.

But all this was in the future. That first evening Bridget had to come to terms with the loss of seventy pounds, her driving licence, her credit card, her cheque book, *Lives of the Artists* (she would never read it now), her address book and the silver ring with the stone which was probably onyx. She mourned alone there in her room. She fretted miserably, shock and disbelief having been succeeded by the inescapable certainty that someone had deliberately stolen her bag. Several cups of strong hot tea comforted her a little. Bridget had more in common with her aunt than she would have liked to think possible, being very much a latter day maiden lady in every respect but maidenhood.

At the end of the week a parcel came. It contained her wallet (empty but for the library card), the silver ring, her address book, her notebook, the nail scissors and the nail clippers, the mascara wand in the shade called "After-midnight blue" and most of the things she had lost but for the money and the credit card and the cheque book, the driving licence, the paperback Vasari, and the bag itself. A letter accompanied the things. It said: "Dear Miss Thomas, This name and address were in the notebook. I hope they are yours and that this will reach you. I found your things inside a plastic bag on top of a litter bin in Kensington Church Street. It was the wallet which made me think they were not things someone had meant to throw away. I am afraid this is absolutely all there was, though I have the feeling there was money in the wallet and perhaps other valuable things. Yours sincerely, Patrick Baker.

His address and a phone number headed the sheet of paper. Bridget, who was not usually impulsive, was so immediately brimming with amazed happiness and restored faith in human nature, that she lifted the phone at once and dialled the number. He answered. It was a pleasant voice, educated, rather slow and deliberate in its enunciation of words, a young man's voice. She poured out her gratitude. How kind he was! What trouble he had been to! Not only to retrieve her things but to take them home, to parcel them up, pay the postage, stand in a queue no doubt at the Post Office! What could she do for him? How could she show the gratitude she felt?

Come and have a drink with him, he said. Well, of course she would, of course. She promised to have a drink with him and a place was arranged and a time, though she was already getting cold feet. She consulted Elizabeth.

"Having a drink in a pub in Kensington High Street couldn't do any harm," said Elizabeth, smiling.

"It's not really something I do." It wasn't something she had done for years, at any rate. In fact it was two years since Bridget had even been out with a man, since her sad affair with the married accountant which had dragged on year after year, had finally come to an end. Drinking in pubs had not been a feature of the relationship. Sometimes they had made swift furtive love in the small office where clients' VAT files were kept. "I suppose," she said, "it might make a pleasant change."

The aspect of Patrick Baker which would have made him particularly attractive to most women, if it did not repel Bridget, at least put her off. He was too good-looking for her. He was, in fact, radiantly beautiful, like an angel or a young Swedish tennis player. This, of course, did not specially matter that first time. But his looks registered with her as she walked across the little garden at the back of the pub and he rose from the table at which he was sitting. His looks frightened her and made her shy. It would not have been true, though, to say that she could not keep her eyes off him. Looking at him was altogether too much for her, it was almost an embarrassment, and she tried to keep her eyes turned away.

Nor would she have known what to say to him. Fortunately, he was eager to recount in detail his discovery of her property in the litter bin in Kensington Church Street. Bridget was good at listening and she listened. He told her also how he had once lost a briefcase in a tube train and a friend of his had had his wallet stolen on a train going from New York to Philadelphia. Emboldened by these homely and not at all sophisticated anecdotes, Bridget told him about the time her Aunt Monica had burglars and lost an emerald necklace which fortunately was insured. This prompted him to ask more about her aunt and Bridget found herself being quite amusing, recounting Monica's financial adventures. She didn't see why she shouldn't tell him the origins of the stolen money and he seemed interested when she said it came from Monica who was in the habit of bestowing like sums on her.

"You see, she says I'm to have it one day—she means when she's dead, poor dear—so why not now?"

"Why not indeed?"

"It was just my luck to have my wallet stolen the day after she'd given me all that money."

He asked her to have dinner with him. Bridget said all right but it mustn't be anywhere expensive or grand. She asked Elizabeth what she should wear. They were in a clothes mood, for it was the evening of the Annie Carter talk to the women's group which Elizabeth had been persuaded to join.

"He doesn't dress at all formally himself," Bridget said. "Rather the reverse." He and she had been out for another drink in the meantime. "He was wearing this kind of safari suit with a purple shirt. But, oh Elizabeth, he is amazing to look at. Rather too much so, if you know what I mean."

Elizabeth didn't. She said that surely one couldn't be too good-looking? Bridget said she knew she was being silly but it embarrassed her a bit—well, being seen with him, if Elizabeth knew what she meant. It made her feel awkward.

"I'll lend you my black lace if you like," Elizabeth said. "It would suit you and it's suitable for absolutely everything."

Bridget wouldn't borrow the black lace. She refused to sail in under anyone else's colours. She wouldn't borrow Aunt Monica's emerald necklace either, the one she had bought to replace the necklace the burglars took. Her black skirt and the velvet top from the secondhand shop in Hammersmith would be quite good enough. If she couldn't have an Annie Carter she would rather not compromise. Monica, who naturally had never been told anything about the married accountant or his distant predecessor, the married primary school teacher, spoke as if Patrick Baker were the first man Bridget had ever been alone with, and spoke too as if marriage were a far from remote possibility. Bridget listened to all this while thinking how awful it would be if she were to fall in love with Patrick Baker and become addicted to his beauty and suffer when separated from him.

Even as she thought in this way, so prudently and with irony, she could see his face before her, in hawk-like lineaments and its softnesses, the wonderful mouth and the large wide-set eyes, the hair that was fair and thick and the skin that was smooth and brown. She saw too his muscular figure, slender and graceful yet strong, his long hands and his tapering fingers, and she felt something long-suppressed, a prickle of desire that plucked very lightly at the inside of her and made her gasp a little.

The restaurant where they had their dinner was not grand or expensive, and this was just as well since at the end of the meal Patrick found that he had left his cheque book at home and Bridget was obliged to pay for their dinner out of the money Monica had given her to buy an evening dress. He was very grateful. He kissed her on the pavement outside the restaurant, or if not quite outside it, under the archway that was the entrance to the mews. They went back to his place in a taxi.

Patrick had quite a nice flat at the top of the house in Bayswater, not exactly overlooking the park but nearly. It was interesting what was happening to Bridget. Most of the time she was able to stand outside herself and view these deliberate acts of hers with detachment. She would have the pleasure of him, he was so beautiful, she would have it and that would be that. Such men were not for her, not at any rate for more than once or twice. But if she could once in a lifetime have one of them for once or twice, why not? Why not?

The life too, the lifestyle, was not for her. On the whole she was better off at home with a pot of strong hot tea and her embroidery or the latest paperback on changing attitudes to women in western society. Nor had she any intention of sharing Aunt Monica's money when the time came. She had recently had to be stern with herself about a tendency, venal and degrading, to dream of that distant prospect when she would live in a World's End studio with a gallery, fit setting for the arrogant Bond Street chair, and dress in a bold eccentric manner, in flowing skirts and antique pelisses and fine old lace.

Going home with Patrick, she was rather drunk. Not drunk enough not to know what she was doing but drunk enough not to care. She was drunk enough to shed her inhibitions while being sufficiently sober to know she had inhibitions, to know that they would be waiting to return to her later and to return quite unchanged. She went into Patrick's arms with delight, with the reckless abandon and determination to enjoy herself of someone embarking on a world cruise that must necessarily take place but once. Being in bed with him was not in the least like being in the VAT records office with the married accountant. She had known it would not be and that was why she was there. During the night the central heating went off and failed, through some inadequacy of a fragile pilot light, to restart itself. It grew cold but Bridget, in the arms of Patrick Baker, did not feel it.

She was the first to wake up. Bridget was the kind of person who is always the first to wake up. She lay in bed a little way apart from Patrick Baker and thought about what a lovely time she had had the night before and how that was enough and she would not see him again. Seeing him again might be dangerous and she could not afford, with her unmemorable appearance, her precarious job and low wage, to put herself in peril. Presently she got up and said to Patrick who had stirred a little and made an attempt in a kindly way to cuddle her, that she would make him a cup of tea.

Patrick put his nose out of the bedclothes and said it was freezing, the central heating had gone wrong. It was always going wrong. "Don't get cold," he said sleepily. "Find something to put on in the cupboard."

Even if they had been in the tropics Bridget would not have dreamt of walking about a man's flat with no clothes on. She dressed. While the kettle was boiling she looked with interest around Patrick's living room. There had been no opportunity to take any of it in on the previous evening. He was an untidy man, she noted, and his taste was not distinguished. You could see he bought his pictures ready-framed at Athena Art. He hadn't many books and most of what he had was science fiction, so it was rather a surprise to come upon Vasari's *Lives of the Artists* in paperback between a volume of fighting fantasy and a John Wyndham classic.

Perhaps she did after all feel cold. She was aware of a sudden unpleasant chill. It was comforting to feel the warmth of the kettle against her hands. She made the tea and took him a cup, setting it down on the bedside table, for he was fast asleep again. Shivering now, she opened the cupboard door and looked inside.

He seemed to possess a great many coats and jackets. She pushed the hangers along the rail, sliding tweed to brush against serge and linen against wild silk. His wardrobe was vast and complicated. He must have a great deal to spend on himself. The jacket with the butterflies slid into sudden brilliant view as if pushed there by some stage manager of fate. Everything conspired to make the sight of it dramatic, even the sun which came out and shed an unexpected ray into the open cupboard. Bridget gazed at the denim jacket as she had gazed with similar lust and wonder once before. She stared at the cascade of butterflies in purple and vermilion and turquoise, royal blue and fuchsia pink that tumbled and fluttered from the open mouths of a pair of yellow lilies.

She hardly hesitated before taking it off its hanger and putting it on. It was glorious. She remembered that this was the word she had thought of the first time she had seen it. How she had longed to possess it and how she had not dared look for long lest the yearning became painful and ridiculous! With her head a little on one side she stood over Patrick, wondering whether to kiss him goodbye. Perhaps not, perhaps it would be better not. After all, he would hardly notice.

She let herself out of the flat. They would not meet again. A more than fair exchange had been silently negotiated by her. Feeling happy, feeling very light of heart, she ran down the stairs and out into the morning, insulated from the cold by her coat of many colours, her butterflies, her rightful possession.

primo levi

The Great Mutation

For several days now Isabella had been restless; she ate little, had a slight fever, and complained about an itch on her back. Her family was busy running the store and did not have much time to devote to her. "She's probably developing," her mother said; she kept her on a diet and gave her massages with a salve, but the itch increased. The girl was no longer able to sleep; as she applied the salve, her mother noticed that the skin was rough: it was beginning to be covered with hairs, thick, stiff, short, and whitish. At that she got frightened, consulted with the father, and they sent for the doctor.

The doctor examined her. He was young and charming, and Isabella noticed with astonishment that at the beginning of the examination he appeared preoccupied and perplexed, then increasingly attentive and interested, and in the end he seemed as happy as though he had won the lottery. He announced that it wasn't anything serious, but that he had to review certain books of his and would come back the next day.

The next day, he returned with a magnifying glass and showed to her father and mother that those hairs were ramified and flat: in fact, they weren't hairs but rather feathers that were growing. He was even more cheerful than the day before.

"Buck up, Isabella," he said. "There's nothing to be afraid of. In four months you'll be able to fly."

Then, turning to the parents, he added a rather confused explanation. Was it possible that they did not know anything? Didn't they read the newspapers? Didn't they watch television? "It's a case of Major Mutation, the first in Italy, and it's actually in our parts, in this forgotten valley!" The wings would form little by little, without damage to the organism, and then there would probably be other cases in the neighbourhood, perhaps the girl's schoolmates, because this thing was contagious.

"But if it's contagious, it's an illness!" the father said.

"It is contagious, apparently it's a virus, but it's not an illness. Why should all viral infections be harmful? Flying is a beautiful thing; I would like it myself, if only to visit the patients in the outlying hamlets. This is the first case in Italy, as I already told you, and I'll report it to the provincial physician's office, but the phenomenon has already been described; several centres of infection have already been observed in Canada, Sweden, and Japan. But just think, what a piece of luck for you and for me!"

That it actually was a piece of luck Isabella wasn't all that convinced. The feathers were growing rapidly: they bothered her when she lay in bed, and you could see them through her blouse. Along about March the new bone structure was already quite visible, and by the end of May the separation of the wings from her back was almost complete.

Then came photographers, journalists, Italian and foreign medical committees: Isabella enjoyed herself and felt important, but she answered all questions seriously and with dignity, and in any case the questions were stupid and always the same. She did not dare discuss it with her parents, since she did not want to frighten them, but she was alarmed: very well, she would have wings, but where would she learn to fly? At the driving school in the provincial capital? Or the Poggio Merli airport? She would have liked to have the public-health doctor teach her: or what if he too sprouted wings, hadn't he said that they were contagious? So they would have gone together to see patients in the hamlets; and perhaps they would even have passed beyond the mountains and flown together over the sea, side by side, beating their wings in the same cadence.

In June, at the end of the school year, Isabella's wings were well formed and very beautiful to look at. They matched the colour of her hair (Isabella was blonde): on top towards the shoulders they were sprinkled with golden-brown dots, but the tips were snow-white, shiny and robust. A commission came from the National Research Council, a substantial grant came from UNICEF, and there also came a physiotherapist from Sweden: she stayed at the only inn in the village, didn't understand Italian very well, nothing suited her, and she got Isabella to do a series of very boring exercises.

Boring and useless: Isabella felt her new muscles quiver and stretch, she watched the sure flight of the swallows in the summer sky, she no longer had any doubts, and she had the definite sensation that she would be able to learn to fly by herself, that indeed she already knew how to fly: by now at night she dreamt of nothing else. The Swede was strict, she had made it clear to her that she must wait some more, that she mustn't expose herself to dangers, but Isabella was only waiting for the opportunity to present itself to her. When she was able to be by herself on a sloping meadow, or sometimes even in her closed room, she had tried to beat her wings; she had heard their harsh rustle in the air, and in her small adolescent shoulders she had felt a strength that almost frightened her. The gravity of her body had become hateful to her; when she fanned her wings, she felt it reduce her body weight, almost annul it: almost. The call of the earth was still too strong, a halter, a chain.

The opportunity arrived about the middle of August. The Swede on vacation had returned to her country, and Isabella's parents were at the store, busy with the summer visitors. Isabella took the Costalunga mule path, went past the ridge, and reached the steep meadows on the opposite slope: nobody was there. She crossed herself, as when you dive into the water, opened her wings, and began to run down the hill. At each step the impact with the ground became lighter and the earth vanished under her feet; she felt a great peace, and the air whistled in her ears. She stretched her legs out behind her: she regretted not having put on jeans, her skirt fluttered in the wind and got in her way.

Her arms and hands also got in her way, she tried to cross

them over her chest, then she held them stiffly along her sides. Who ever said that flying was difficult? There was nothing easier in the world, she wanted to laugh and sing. If she increased the slant of the wings, her flight slowed down and pointed upward, but only briefly; then her speed fell off too much, and Isabella felt in danger. She tried beating her wings, and she felt supported, gaining height with each beat, easily, without effort.

Also, changing direction was as easy as a game, you learned how immediately, all you had to do was give a light twist to the right wing and you immediately turned to the right. You didn't even have to think about it, the wings themselves thought of it, just as the feet think of making you turn right or left when you walk. Suddenly she sensed a swelling, a tension in her lower abdomen; she felt damp, she touched it, and her hand came away smeared with blood. But she knew what it was, she knew that one day or another it would happen, and she wasn't frightened.

She stayed in the air for a good hour and learned that from the Gravio's boulders rose a current of warm air that helped her gain altitude without effort. She followed the provincial highway and hovered right above the village, at a height of perhaps two hundred metres: she saw a passerby stop, then point at the sky for another passerby; the second looked up, then he ran to the store, and out of it came her mother and her father with two or three customers. Soon the streets were swarmed with people. She would have liked to land in the piazza, but in fact there were too many people and she was afraid of landing badly and being laughed at.

She let the wind carry her beyond the stream, over the meadows behind the mill. She descended, continued to descend until she could distinguish the clover's pink flowers. Also, when it came to landing it seemed the wings knew better than she did: it seemed to them natural to be set vertically and churn violently as though to fly backwards; she lowered her legs and found herself standing on the grass, just the slightest bit out of breath. She folded her wings and set out for home.

In the autumn four of Isabella's schoolmates sprouted wings, three boys and a girl; on Sunday mornings it was amusing to see them chase each other in midair around the church's bell tower. In December the mailman's son got wings, and he immediately replaced his father, to everyone's great advantage. The doctor grew wings the next year, but he no longer took an interest in Isabella, and in great haste he married a young woman without wings who came from the city.

Isabella's father sprouted wings when he was already over fifty. He did not draw great profit from them: with fear and vertigo he took a few dozen lessons from his daughter, and he twisted an ankle in landing. The wings wouldn't let him sleep, they filled his bed with feathers and down, and he found it difficult to put on his shirt, jacket, and coat. They also were a hindrance when he was behind the counter in the store, and so he had them amputated.

Translated by Raymond Rosenthal

christine harrison

La Scala Inflammata

Through the glass of the kitchen window Celia noticed that the twisted old apple tree had some blossoms on it. She thought of Stonehenge and the Aubrey holes where the ashes of the dead were buried. There were ashes buried under the apple tree. She had forgotten what they were.

She wrung out the washing she was doing at the sink. It was a good day for drying the clothes, a sharp little wind. But the clothesline was tied at one end to a branch of the apple tree, so she hung the things about the room to dry. It was getting hard to breathe in the little room. She gasped for air as if she were a creature from another element, a sea-creature with gills struggling for breath. The apple tree pressed its branches against the window. There was a crack right across one of the panes.

Little pools of water began to form on the floor under the dripping clothes.

With quiet movements she put on her jacket and put her purse in her pocket.

Outside, the garden path was edged with little jagged-toothed lilies of the valley, "babies teeth" someone had called them. She kept her eyes low and did not look at the branches of the tree which, from the corner of her eye, she saw dancing hideously in the breeze. She locked the tall garden gate after her. No one could see over the high wall and the high garden gate.

The shop at the end of the street was kept by a youngish woman with great freckled arms. Her husband was a shadowy creature who lived in the back room, the door always ajar. He never seemed to go out. Occasionally he made a dishevelled appearance in the shop, when his wife would stop serving her customers and stop talking while she waited for him to go, meanwhile looking at him with pure dislike as at some slimy animal that might have entered her shop leaving a stinking trail.

The old man from round the corner was buying a tin of cocoa. He was very old but stood back from the counter without leaning for support, though his knees bent a little. His large hands were like tools at the end of skinny arms which were nothing but skin and bone, but had hard muscles, like some ancient piece of machinery, found in a field, which still worked. "That'll warm your cockles, old feller,"—the woman shrieked with preposterous laughter, freckles stretching around her mouth. The old man had not heard. He was carefully turning his money over in his hand. Celia's head ached. She could hardly say what she wanted. A packet of seeds. Seeds of basil. It was basil, wasn't it, that Isabella had planted in the pot containing her lover's mouldering head? A packet of basil seeds. The woman gave her a furious and uncomprehending stare. What in God's name? Cress seeds, then. Cress seeds will do.

Back in the garden, Celia opened the packet of seeds. Her hand shook as she poured out the tiny black seeds on to her hand. They ran spilling between her closed fingers. Without looking up she scattered them under and around the apple tree, sowing them very shallowly so as not to disturb the ashes which must have been buried very hastily—for a piece of ash flew up in the cold spring air.

Her head still ached and she was very tired. But she lit her fire, swept the floor and made her bed. Night came down, but she did not sleep. She thought about the dark garden, the lilies with their tiny sharp teeth hidden under leaves. The shop and its inhabitants did not have any real existence during these night hours. The reality of their night existence was altogether too great to be borne; the woman lying on her back, her freckled eyelids closed, her husband curled like a mollusc in bed beside her.

Celia never drew the curtains at night. The high wall around the house made it unnecessary. Usually she liked to see the light dawn in the sky and to lie in bed watching the sky change colour. This morning the greenish light made the tree stand out black. She got out of bed and drew the curtains quickly to shut out the sight. She might saw down that tree today. There was a little saw she used for small logs for the fire. It was hung up in the shed . . .

This was not a practical idea. She could saw all she liked and never get through the black writhing trunk. Perhaps the old man would do it for her. He was old and frail but she remembered his large hands like tools, and the muscles in his skinny arms.

She washed under running cold tap water. As she dressed, her breath came in little gasps. She took a bottle of milk from the doorstep and drank it all, gasping for breath between each mouthful.

Out in the street she started to make her way to the old man's house. Becoming aware of a feeling of extreme fear, her entrails turned to water. For above the narrow streets hung a Presence. The Presence was palpable like a dark cloud. It would not go away, it blocked the skyline and the black chimney pots were etched against it. It brooded over the car park and walked up and down the narrow streets like the God of Genesis. But it would not talk to her as it had to Adam.

With clenched fists she banged desperately on the old man's door. After a long time he came suspiciously to the door and opened it a crack. He had been asleep; he was still half dressed. His dirty grey vest had broken buttons. She could not ask him to saw down her tree, she could not tell him about the Presence which hovered over the houses. This red-eyed old man, frail and cold, woken up out of his sleep from his poor ragged bed. "I'm going away," she said. "Will you look after my key until I get back?" She gave him the key and some money. She did not wait for his answer but turned away and fled down the street.

She ran up and down the maze of little narrow streets and then suddenly her way was blocked. She had run into a cul-de-sac. In the road was a young man tinkering with his car. "Will you take me up to the hospital?" asked Celia, panting for breath. It needed a great effort to speak calmly; her head was feeling very bad and inward shudders shook her body. "My mother has had a bad accident and I must get there . . . She's been run over." The young man said nothing; his hair had fallen over his eyes, he flicked it back and rubbed his oily hands on a rag. "She's lost a lot of blood," said Celia. The young man looked unyielding. Celia opened the door of the passenger seat and got in. The man slowly put away his tools and reluctantly got in too. "Which hospital?" he asked in a surly way. "Princess Beatrice," she said. "That's not an accident hospital, it's the nut house," he said. "My mother is insane," said Celia. She thought that would break the ice and make him laugh, but it did not. He looked suspicious. She just shut up and let him drive. It was quite a long way. When they got there she did not thank him but got out and left him to drive off very fast.

A steep flight of steps led up to the hospital's main doors. The steps shifted under her feet like moving water. She wondered what the old man was doing opening the door for her, his white hospital coat barely covering his dirty buttoned vest.

A nurse helped Celia into the high hospital bed, and took away her wedding ring. A doctor gave her an injection.

Now time itself shifted. She saw with an inward eye a landscape of the mind. Here the world was depicted as on an old parchment drawing and was surrounded by the Outer Darkness. Antique fish and sea monsters covered in precise scales marked where oceans were. Countries and mountain ranges, oceans and lakes were named in beautiful flowing lettering. The heavenly sphere was inscribed with the word "Order", the regions below with "Chaos". Order was presided over by the Presence she had encountered in the streets. A flaming ladder led up to the Presence and was inscribed, "La Scala Inflammata".

With one foot on the bottom rung of this fiery ladder she looked down into Chaos. Dreadful sight.

"O' I'll leape up to my God, who pulls me down?"

The doctor sat on her bed, stroking his ginger beard. He took

Celia's hand kindly and held it for a moment. "Stay with us and we'll get you better," he said.

Celia shook her head. "I must go to Wiltshire," she said. "My mother is very ill and she is expecting me."

"You won't be going anywhere for a bit," said the doctor. "We'll give you something to make you sleep." But Celia was afraid to sleep in case, off her guard, she was clawed down into hell's ravenous mouth. She put the tablets under her pillow. As the doctor went out he turned and asked where her baby was. "The old man is looking after it," she said. The doctor looked surprised but said nothing.

Celia walked quietly out of the hospital, leaving her wedding ring in payment.

She set off to walk back to the town; it was a long way. After she had been walking for an hour she thought she might as well spend the little money she had left on a drink. The cool little inn was dark inside after the bright sunlight of the dusty road. The only drink for sale was draught cider, it had a greenish look. The room was full of workmen. They seemed to Celia like characters in a dream. There was some wild parsley in a cracked flowery jug blocking out the light from a tiny window. Celia asked for a glass of water and was given warmish water in a smeared glass. As she drank she watched the sun's rays filtering through the lacy flowers on to the fair hairs on the backs of the men's brown arms and on the backs of their necks, damp with sweat.

As she left she noticed one of the men just about to climb into his lorry. She called out, "I have to get to Salisbury Plain. Are you going that way?" "Where are you making for exactly?" he asked. Celia went across to the lorry. "Well, Stonehenge will do," she said. Perhaps that sounded fishy, she thought, and added, "I have to draw a plan of it." The man looked interested. "Alright," he said, "hop in." After they had been travelling for a while he said, "You don't seem to have anything to draw with." "No," she said. "I left my sketchbook at the hospital. I was visiting my mother there. I expect my friends will have drawing things, I'm going to meet them at Stonehenge. We are an archaeological society." When they were near to the stone circle the man said, "Are you on the up and up then?" Celia looked at him coldly. "What does that mean?" she asked. "Oh, never mind," he said and pulled up. "This is as near as the road goes."

She could see Stonehenge from the road. Her heart gave a great thud.

The afternoon sun ran like bright water over the fields of moving barley. White clouds sailed under the vaulted sky. Great shadows moved quickly over the spread-eagled country followed, wave after wave, by shining moving areas of pure light. But what she had been drawn there for was buried underground. Celia felt her flesh shudder and fall from the bone.

The place was skipping with young schoolchildren. They were all looking for blood on the altar stone. "As I told you," yelled their young teacher against the wind, brushing his hair back from his face, "it is unlikely that this was a place of human sacrifice. It was created over a very long period in the same way as our cathedrals. In about 1660 by a man called John Aubrey . . ." But they were not listening as they scoured the stones for blood. The teacher smiled and shrugged at Celia. "I think I might just as well let them enjoy themselves." He flopped down on the grass beside her. "You were telling them about the Aubrey holes," said Celia. "Yes, they are the pits where they buried the ashes of their dead. Come on, I'll show you." As she went with him the huge stones rocked vertiginously around her. Giddily she reached out and took his arm. "I don't want to see them yet," she said. "You look a bit done in," he said. "What's up?" "I'm hungry," said Celia, and remembered the last meal she had had was the milk she had drunk the morning before. "Come with us," said the schoolteacher. "We're going to have a picnic on Silbury Hill. If you can manage the climb."

They walked single file through the waving barley, some of the children's heads scarcely showing above it, to the Avebury circle. There they picked up a coach to take them to the foot of Silbury.

The teacher held out his hand and helped her up. The children scrambled up on all fours like busy ants.

On top of Silbury all the children took out their sandwiches and apples. "Sir, Vernon hasn't got any, Sir." "Everybody give Vernon a sandwich," said Sir imperiously. Vernon's pile of sandwiches was nearly as tall as Silbury Hill itself. Vernon grinned, showing incredibly dirty teeth streaked with green. "What about Miss?" shrieked the children. "She hasn't got none either." "Miss can have some of mine," said the teacher.

"Down there you looked a bit off colour. Is there anything the matter?" He was not looking at her but raking about in his rucksack after apples and biscuits.

"Yes, there is something the matter. I'll tell you," she said. There, on top of Silbury Hill, she told him about the garden and the apple tree and the charred bundle buried under it. The teacher was silent. He was watching the children as they drank out of bottles, rolled down the slopes, made paper aeroplanes out of chocolate wrappers and threw them off the edge of the hill for the wind to blow straight back.

"When I get this lot back to school, I'll come down with you and we'll sort it out," he said. "What do you mean," said Celia, "sort it out?"

"We'll go and face it. You can't run across the length and breadth of England, can you?" Celia did not answer.

That evening she left the curtains drawn back and lay in the young man's arms, looking out at the branches of the apple tree. The branches moved and swayed in the wind, sometimes tapping lightly on the windowpanes like a fingernail tapping. "In the morning," whispered the young man, "I'll fell that tree and I'll find out what's buried there."

She slept that night. When she woke the young man was making some breakfast. He brought her some coffee and toast. When they had eaten he said, "Have you got a spade?" Celia shuddered. She dropped her head down between her knees to stop herself from fainting. "You stay here," he said.

She watched through the kitchen window. Great angels sat vulture-like in the tree, the breeze riffled their wings. Two more sat side-saddle on the garden wall. They watched and waited as the young man, a Crusader with a cross on his breast, dug under the apple tree.

Celia traced her finger down the crack in the window pane, pressing her finger on it and drawing blood. She closed her eyes.

When she looked out again the garden was a shipwreck, the fallen tree sprawled like a broken mast across the length of it.

She watched as the young man stooped to pick the lilies. He held them to his face to smell and then, seeing that she was watching him from the window, he raised his hand in a kind of salute, or a farewell.

lorrie moore

Starving Again

Dennis's ex-wife had fallen in love with a man she said was like out of a book. Dennis forgot to ask what book. He was depressed and barely dating. "I should have said to her, 'Yeah, and what book?' " Dennis was always kicking himself on the phone, not an easy thing, the tricky ouch of it. His friend Mave tended to doodle a lot when talking to him, slinky items with features, or a solitary game of tic-tac-toe. Sometimes she even interrupted him to ask what time it was. Her clock was in the other room.

"But you know," Dennis was saying, "I've got my own means of revenge: if she wants to go out with other men, I'm going to sit here and just let her."

"That's an incredibly powerful form of revenge," said Mave. She was not good on the phone. She needed the face, the pattern of eyes, nose, trembling mouth. When she was on the phone she often had to improvise Dennis's face from a window; the pugnose of the lock, the paned eyes, the lip-jut of the sill. Or else she drew another slinky item with features. People talking were meant to look at a face, the hide and seek of the heart dashing across. With a phone, you said words, but you never watched them go in. You saw them off at the airport, but never knew whether there was anyone there to greet them when they got off the plane.

They met for dinner at some sort of macrobiotic place because Dennis had recently become obsessed. Before his wife left him his idea of eating healthy had been to go to McDonald's and order the Filet-o-Fish, but now he had whole

books about miso. And about tempeh. Mostly, however, he
had books about love. He believed in studying his own heart
this way. Men were like that, Mave had noticed. They liked to
look in the mirror. For women mirrors were a chore: women
looked, frowned, got out equipment and went to work. But for
men mirrors were sex: men locked gazes with their own
reflections, undressed themselves with their eyes, and stared
for a shockingly long time. Mave believed that not being able to
see your life clearly, to scrutinise it intelligently, meant that
probably you were at the dead centre of it, and that couldn't
possibly be a bad thing.

This month Dennis was reading books written supposedly
for women, titles like *Get Real, Smarting Cookie, Get Real,* and
Why I Hate Myself. "Those books are trouble," said Mave.
"Too many well-adjusted people will endanger the arts in this
country. To say nothing of the professions." She studied
Dennis's flipped-over tie, the soft, torn eye of its clipped label.
"You choose to be healthy and you leave too many good people
behind."

But Dennis said he identified, that the books were amazing,
and he reached into the bookbag he now carried with him
everywhere and read passages aloud. "Here," he said to Mave,
who had brought her own whiskey to the place and was pouring
it into a water glass from which she had drunk all the water and
left only the ice. She had had to argue with the waitress to get
ice. "Oh, no, here," Dennis said. He had found another
passage from *Why I Hate Myself,* and started to read it, loud
and with expression, when suddenly he broke into a dis-
consolate weep, deep and from the belly. "Oh, God, I'm
sorry."

Mave shoved her whiskey glass across the table toward him.
"Don't worry about it," she murmured. He took a sip then put
his book away. He dug through his bookbag and found
Kleenex to dab at his nose.

"I didn't get like this on my own," he said. "There are
people responsible." Inside his bag Mave could see a news
magazine with the exasperated headline "Ethiopia: Why are
they starving *THIS* time?"

"Boredom is heartless," said Dennis, the tears slowing. He indicated the magazine. "When the face goes into a yawn, the blood to the chest gets constricted."

"Are you finished with my drink?"

"No." He took another gulp and winced. "I mean, yes," and he handed it back to Mave, wiped his mouth with a napkin. Mave looked at Dennis's face and was glad no one had broken up with her recently. When someone broke up with you, you became very unattractive, and it confirmed all the doubts that person had ever had about you to begin with. "Wait, just one more sip." Someone broke up with you and you yelled. You blistered, withered, and flushed. You apologised to inanimate objects and drank when you swore you wouldn't. You went around humming the theme to *Valley of the Dolls*, doing all the instruments even, lingering on the line about *gotta get off, gonna get; have to get* . . . It wasn't good to go out on that kind of limb for love. You went out on a limb for food, but not for love. Love was not food. Love, thought Mave, was more like the restrooms at the Ziegfield: sinks in the stalls big deal. Mave worked hard to forget very quickly afterwards what the men she went out with even looked like. This was called *sticking close to the trunk*.

"All yours," said Dennis. He was smiling. The whiskey brought the blood to his face in a nice way.

Mave looked down at her menu. "There's no spaghetti and meatballs here. I wanted to order the child's portion of the spaghetti and meatballs."

"Oh, that reminds me," said Dennis shaking a finger for emphasis. With his books away and the whiskey in him, he seemed more confident. "Did I tell you the guy my wife's seeing is Italian? Milanese, not Brooklyn. What do you suppose that means, her falling in love with an Italian?"

"It means she's going to feel scruffy all the time. It means that he will stare at all the fuzzies on her shirt while she is telling him something painful about a childhood birthday party nobody came to. Let's face it: she's going to start to miss the fact, Dennis, that your hair zooms out all over the goddamn place."

"I'm getting it cut tomorrow."

Mave put on her reading glasses. "This is not a restaurant. Restaurants serve different things from this."

"You know, one thing about these books for women, I have to tell you. The whole emphasis on locating and accepting your homosexual side is really very powerful. It frees and expands some other sort of love in you."

Mave looked up at him and smiled. She was drawn to the insane because of their blazing minds. "So you've located and accepted?"

"Well, I've realised this. I like boys. *And* I like girls." He leaned toward her confidentially. "I just don't like *berls*." Dennis reached again for Mave's whiskey. "Of course, I am completely in the wrong town. May I?" He leaned his head back and the ice cubes knocked against his teeth. Water beaded up on his chin. "So, Mave, who are *you* romancing these days?" Dennis was beginning to look drunk. His lips were smooth and thick and hung open like a change purse.

"These days?" There were little ways like this of stalling for time.

"These right here."

"Right here. These. I've been seeing Mitch again a little." Dennis dropped his forehead into his palm, which had somehow flown up from the table so that the two met mid-air in an unsightly smack. "Mitch! Mave, he's such a womaniser!"

"So I needed to be womanised. I was losing my sheen."

"You know what you do? You get all your boyfriends on sale. It's called Bargain Debasement. Immolation by desire."

"Look, you need to be womanised, you go to a womaniser. I don't take these things seriously anymore. I make it a point now to forget what everybody looks like. I'm being Rudolph Bing. I've lost my mind and am traipsing around the South Seas with an inappropriate lover, and I believe in it. I think everybody in a love affair is being Rudolph Bing anyway, and they're vain to believe otherwise—Oh, my God, that man in the sweater is feeling his girlfriend's lymph nodes." Mave put away her reading glass and fumbled around in her bag for the whiskey flask. That was the thing with hunger: it opened up something dangerous in you, something endless, like a universe, or a cliff. "I'm sorry Rudolph Bing is on my mind. He's really been on my mind. I feel like we're all almost like him."

"Almost like Bing in love," said Dennis. "What a day this has been. What a rare mood I'm in." Mave was in a long sip. "I've been listening to that *Live at Carnegie Hall* tape too much."

"Music! Let's talk about music! Or death! Why do we always have to talk about love?"

"Because our parents were sickos and we're starved for it."

"You know what I've decided? I don't want to be cremated. I used to, but now I think it sounds just a little too much like a blender speed. Now I've decided I want to be embalmed, and then I want a plastic surgeon to come put in silicone implants everywhere. Then I want to be laid out in the woods like Snow White with a gravestone that reads *Gotta Dance*." The whiskey was going down sweet. That was what happened after a while, with no meal to assist, it had to do the food work on its own. "There. We talked about death."

"That's talking about death?"

"What is *kale*? I don't understand why they haven't taken our order yet. I mean, it's crowded now, but it wasn't ten minutes ago. Maybe it was the ice thing."

"You know what else my wife says about this Italian? She says he goes around singing this same song to himself. You know what it is?"

"*Santa Lucia.*"

"No. It's 'Their house is a museum, when people come to see-um, they really are a scree-um, the Addams family.' "

"Your wife tells you this?"

"We're friends."

"Don't tell me you're friends. You hate her."

"We're friends. I don't hate her."

"You think she's a user and a tart. She's with some guy with great shoes whose coif doesn't collapse into hairpin turns across his part."

"You used to be a nice person."

"I never was a nice person. I'm still a nice person."

"I don't like this year," said Dennis, his eyes welling again.

"I know," said Mave. " '88. It's too Sergio Mendes or something."

"You know, it's OK not to be a nice person."

"I need your permission? Thank you." This was what Dennis had been doing lately: granting everyone permission to feel the way they were going to feel regardless. It was the books. Dennis's relationship to his own feelings had become tender, curatorial. Dismantling. Entomological. Mave couldn't be like that. She treated her emotional life like she treated her car: she let it go, let it tough it out. To friends she said things like, "I know you're thinking this looks like a '79, but it's really an '87." She finally didn't care to understand all that much about her emotional life; she just went ahead and did it. The point, she thought, was to attend the meagre theatre of it, quietly, and not stand up in the middle and shout, "Oh, my God, you can see the crew backstage!" There was a point at which the study of something became a frightening and naive thing.

"But Dennis, really, why do you think so much about love, of someone loving you or not loving you? That is all you read about, all you talk about."

"Put the starving people of the world together in a room and what you get is a lot of conversation about roast beef. They should be talking about the Napoleonic Code?" At the mention of roast beef Mave's face lit up, greenish, fluorescent. She looked past Dennis and saw the waitress coming toward their table at last; she was moving slowly, meanly, scowling. There was a large paper doily stuck to her shoe. "I mean . . ." Dennis was saying, looking pointedly at Mave, but Mave was watching the waitress approach. *Oh, life, oh sweet, forgiven for the ice*— He grabbed Mave's wrist. There was always an emergency. And then there was love. And then there was another emergency. That was the sandwiching of it. Emergency. Love. Emergency. "I mean, it's not as if you've been dozing off," Dennis was saying, his voice reaching her now, high and watery. "I mean, correct me if I'm wrong," he said, "but I don't think I've been having this conversation alone." He tightened his grip. "I mean, have I?"

rose tremain

Tradewind over Nashville

It was July and hot. At five in the morning, vapour rose from the tarmac parking lots.

"Know somethin', Willa?" said an Early Breakfast customer at the counter of Mr Pie's restaurant. "You look so pretty in that waitress cap, it's like yore dyin' a' beauty!"

"I declare!" said Willa. "I never heard such a thing in the world!"

The waitress cap was lace. Polyester and cotton lace. Then there was the gingham dress that Willa had to wear. With that on, you didn't see the last days of her thirtieth year passing. No, sir. What you saw were her pushed-up tits and the waist she kept trim and the sweet plumpness of her arms. And as she passed the early customer—one of her six a.m. regulars—his plate of egg, sausage and biscuit, he took all of her in—into his crazed head and into his belly.

She lived in a trailer in a trailer park off the airport freeway. Her lover, Vee, had painted the trailer inside and out bright staring white, to keep out the Tennessee sun. Willa had a Polaroid picture of Vee with his paint roller and bucket, wearing shorts and a singlet and his cowboy boots. She nailed it up over her bunk, just low enough to reach and touch with her stubby hand. Shoot! she sometimes thought, what kills me dead 'bout Vee is his titchy short legs! And she'd lie there smiling to herself and dealing poker hands in her mind so as to stay awake till he came home. And then, when he did, she'd whisper: "Vee? That you, Vee, wakin' me up in here?"

"Who else?" he'd ask. "Who else you got arrivin'?"

"Well then?"

"Well what?"

"Why ain't ya doin' it to me?"

So, on the next lot, at two in the morning, frail Mr Zwebner would wake to hear them shouting and pounding the hell out of their white walls. Zwebner had dreams of Viennese chocolate. Patisseries eaten with a little fork. And what he felt when Willa and Vee woke him was an old, unassuageable greed. "That Willa," he'd sigh, "she's got it coming to her. She's got something, one day soon, gonna come along."

At Mr Pie's, she poured coffee, set up a side order of doughnuts next to the plate of sausage. Seeing her arm reflected in the shiny counter, she said: "Lord! Ain't that a terrible sight, the elbow of a person. Look at that, will ya?"

The customer looked up. His mouth was full of egg. He stared at Willa's arm.

"If Vee ever did see that, how wizened an' so forth it is, well, I swear he'd leave me right off. He'd jes take his gee-tar and his boots an' all his songs an' fly away."

The man wiped his jowls with a chequered napkin. "He sold any a' his songs yet, that Vee?"

"No. Not a one."

"Then he ain't gonna leave ya yet."

"What's that gotta do with him leavin' me or not?"

"Got everythin' to do with it, Willa."

"I don't see how."

"Only one thing'll make him quit, honey. And it ain't no piece a' your elbow. It's fame."

Willa stared at the fat customer with her wide-apart eyes. Trouble with a place like Mr Pie's, she said to herself, is everyone sticks their noses in your own private thoughts.

Out at Green Hills, in the actual hills that looked away from Mr Pie's and all the other roadside diners and all the gas stations and glassed-in malls, lived Lester and Amy Pickering.

Lester was a roofer. He'd started small and poor, working out of a garage in East Nashville. Now, he was halfway to being rich. Halfway exactly was how he thought of it, when he drove down Belle Meade Boulevard and past the Country Club and saw and understood what rich was. And at fifty-two, he'd begun to wonder whether he'd get there, or whether this was how he'd remain—stuck at the halfway point.

"Lester, you know, he's tiring," said Amy to her friends at the Green Hills Women's Yoga Group. "I see it plain as death. It's like he's up against a wall and he just don't have the go in him to climb it. It's like gettin' this far took all the vim he had."

"Well, Amy," the friends would reply, "let him tire, honey. You got a good house an' your kids both in college. What more d'you want?"

"Ain't a question of want," said Amy. "It's a question of dream. 'Cos one thing you can't stop Lester doing, you can stop him doing 'most anything 'cept having these dreams a' his. He's the type, he'll die dreaming. He's descended from a Viking, see? Got this conqueror still goin' round in his veins."

On that July morning at six, as more of Willa's regular customers stumbled into Mr Pie's and she wiped the counter for them, taking care not to look at her elbow's reflection, Lester Pickering climbed into his pick-up and drove south toward Franklin. He'd been asked to tender for a job on a Baptist church, to replace tin with slates. "Git out here early, Lester," the minister had advised, "'fore the ole tin git too hot to touch." And now he was doing sixty-five in the pick-up and his lightweight ladders were rattling like a hailstorm above his head. But his mind wasn't on his destination. He was driving fast to drive away the thoughts he was having, to jolt them out of his damn brain before they took hold and he did something stupid. Thoughts about Amy and the fruit seller. Thoughts about this guy who comes from nowhere and calls Amy up, knows her number an' all, and says meet me at such-and-such parking lot and I'll sell you raspberries from the mountains. And so she goes and she meets him and for two days she's bottling and freezing fruit and making jelly with a smile on her face.

"Who is he?" asks Lester.

"I dunno," says Amy. "Name of Tom. That's all I know."

"An' how's he got all them berries? Where they come from?"

"From the hills."

"What hills?"

"He said it's a secret where they precisely come from, Lester."

"Why's it a darn secret?"

"I dunno. That's it about a secret, uhn? You often don't know why it is one."

Lester was driving so fast, he missed the turn-off to the church. He braked and saw in the rear mirror a livestock truck come hissing up right behind him. Ready to ram me, thought Lester, because the thing of it is, people don't care any more. They don't care what they do.

While Willa worked at Mr Pie's, Vee slept on in the trailer. The sun got up high. Sweat ran down Vee's thighs and down his neck. He was on the verge of waking, it was so hot and airless in the trailer, but he kept himself asleep and dreaming. In his dreams, he was no longer Vee Easton, cleaner and dogsbody at Opryland; he was Vee La Rivière (he pronounced it 'Veeler Riveer'), songwriter to the stars of the whole darn world of country music. He was certain this future would come. He was so certain about it, he wasn't really dreaming it any more, he was thinking it up.

"What's the diffunce between dreamin' an' thinkin', Vee?" asked Willa.

"I'll tell ya, sweetheart. What the diffunce is, is between fairy tales and actuality. What them things are now is actual."

"You mean 'real', doncha? You mean re-ality, Vee. That's the word you were meanin'."

"If I'd've meant real, I'd've said real. What I mean is, things actually happening, or, like they say in the Bible, Coming to Pass. Vee La Rivière is gonna Come to Pass."

And when Vee woke, around eleven, he remembered what day it was. It was the day of the night of his meeting with Herman Berry. *The* Herman Berry, known nationwide, but with his heart and his house still in Nashville and a set of his fingernail clippings in a glass case in the Country Music Hall of Fame, right slap next to Jim Reeves's shoes.

Vee thumped his leg and sat up. He got out of his bunk and snatched up a towel and dried the sweat on him, then opened wide the four windows of the trailer and the daytime world of the trailer park came in, like homely music. He put on some stretch blue swimming trunks and made coffee. He didn't give one single thought to Willa or to anything in his life except this big meeting with Herman Berry, when he would play him three songs he'd written. "Keep it to three, boy," Herman had said. "Keep it to a trinity and I'll listen good. More 'an that and my mind starts walking away."

But which three would he offer? Veritably speaking, Vee admitted to himself, as he turned the pages of his music note book, there's only one of Herman's calibre and that's my new one.

He got his guitar and tuned it a bit. He felt suddenly chilly in his torso, so he put one of Willa's thin old counterpanes round his shoulders. Then he flipped the pages to his new song, called *Do Not Disturb*, and played the intro chords. Then he made like he was talking to Herman Berry and explaining the song to him:

". . . them ther's just the introductory bars, Herman. Key of C Minor. Little reprise here before the first verse. A moody reprise, I call it. Let every person know this is a sad song. Tragic song, in all absolute truth. Okay! So here we go with the first verse:

    'I went up to my hotel room
    And got some whiskey from the mini-bar,'

"In parenthetics, Herman, I didn't never stay in no hotel room with a mini-bar, but Willa put me straight on that detail. She said, you can't say 'got some whiskey from the bar' just, 'cos what hotel rooms have now is mini-bars, okay? Means adding coupla quavers to the line, but then I keep it scanning in the fourth, like this:

    'I set my pills out on the table,
    And wondered how it all had got this far.'

"You get 'it all', Herm? 'It all', that's his life and the way it's turning out.

"So now, another reprise of the opening chords. Still quietish. Still keepin' the tragic mood. Then we're into the second verse, like this:

'I thought of you in Ole Kentucky,
And the singing of the sweet blue grass.
For a year we'd been together,
Now you told me, Jim, all things must pass.'

"We could change Jim, right? It could be Chuck or Bill, right? Or Herm. It all depends on how you want to personalise it an' make it a true Herman Berry number.

"Anyway, it's the chorus now. Modulation. Big, swoopy modulation to C Major here. As we go into the big chorus that all America's gonna be singin' soon:

'Believe me, girl, my heart was breaking!
Breaking tho' I couldn't say a word,
It was my life I was intent on taking,
So then I hung the sign out,
The sign that stopped them finding out,
The little sign that said Do Not Disturb!'

"That's the thing I'm pleased with—the chorus. Whatcha say, Herm? You don't think they're gonna be humming that from Louisiana to Ohio? Before I go to the third verse, tell me how you feel about that big, sad chorus. You don't gotta speak. Just stick your thumbs up."

Amy Pickering knelt down on her yoga mat in her living room and folded her large-boned body into a small, coiled position called the Child Position. She shut her eyes. She tried to have vacant, childlike thoughts, but these didn't seem easy to come by, because what was in her mind was Lester.

Why did you lie to him, Amy Pickering? she asked herself. Why did you make out there was a secret about the raspberries? When all that guy was, was some friend of Betty Bushel's that likes to bypass retail and sell direct to housewives?

She didn't know the answer. All she knew was she had liked to do it. Lying about the raspberries had made her feel beautiful. It had. She had stood in her kitchen, smelling all that scented fruit, and feeling like Greta Garbo.

Amy lifted her head. She stretched her neck and smoothed her greying hair she wore in a French pleat. Beyond the sunlit sills of her room, she could hear the peaceful neighbourhood sounds—lawn mowers and birds and Betty Bushel's dog yapping at shadows.

Then, in her mind, she saw Lester, years ago, wearing his old hunting jacket, standing in his father's yard with his father's dog, Jackson, sniffing at his boots. He'd built the kennel for that dog. He'd put on a neat little shingled roof and that was what got him started on the idea of roofs. "It had a twenty-six year life, that kennel," Amy liked to boast fondly. "Two dogs, both named Jackson one after another, lived to thirteen in it. That's how good made it was. But then, Lester's dad, he said to me: 'Dogs is heartbreak, Amy. I jes' can't stick to have another Jackson leave me for the Lord!' So I dunno what he did with that kennel then. 'Less he kept it somewhere to remind him of his son . . .''

He was still alive, the old man. The idea of him dying seemed to hurt Lester in his chest. When he thought about his father dying, he'd knead the area of his heart. And this is what he'd done when Amy had told him her lie about the raspberry seller: he'd stood looking at her and kneading his heart through his Dralon shirt.

"Oh my . . ." sighed Amy. "Oh my, my . . ."

"Git through m' shift at two, be home at three," Willa had told Vee in the night. "Then what I'll do, darlin', I'll press your shirt and tie and steam out the fringes on your coat, so they fall good. And that way, Herman Berry's not solely gonna 'ppreciate your songs, he's gonna see yore an upright person."

"Upright?" Vee had burst out. "What's upright got to have to do with song writin'? You could be a mean, wastrelling bum, an' still make it big in this business, honey. You could be a orang-utan. It wouldn't matter. 'Cos no one's lookin' at ya. They only listening. They only sayin' to theirselves, is this gonna catch on? If I record this *Do Not Disturb*, will it make it to number one in Anusville, Milwaukee?"

Now, as Willa took off her lace cap and changed out of her gingham frock, she told her friend Ileene: "You could be an orang-utan an' still make it in Nashville, Ileene. 'Cos the point is, all anyone's got is their eyes closed."

"Oh yeh?" said Ileene. "What about here, then? I swear some pairs of eyes go up your ass, Willa, when yore wipin' tables."

"Well, that," said Willa, "but then I ain't singing."

Ileene shook her head and smiled as she pulled on her lace cap. "Darn cap!" she grinned. "Look like a friggin' French maid in that, don't I?"

"I dunno," said Willa dreamily. "Bein' as how I never saw no French maid in my whole existence."

As soon as she got off her bus at the trailer park, Willa knew that Vee wasn't there, because his car was gone.

"Drove off about half an hour ago with his guitar," Mr Zwebner said. On hot days, Mr Zwebner sat on a plastic chair in the narrow band of shade made by his trailer, reading some old, mutilated book. Willa could not imagine any mortal life so monotonous as his.

"Thank you, Mr Zwebner," she said. Then she added: "Got an appointment with Herman Berry tonight. 'Fore the Opry starts."

"He famous, then? He someone I should know of?"

"Who? Herman Berry?"

"Yeah."

"You never done heard of Herman Berry, Mr Zwebner?"

"No."

"You kiddin' me?"

"No."

"Shoot! I jes' don't believe what yore saying! I don't believe my eardrums, Mr Zwebner!"

"Okay. You don't believe."

"Herman Berry? Why, he's so darn famous, he can't go anywhere without people want to touch him and git bits of him."

"Why they want to do that, Willa?"

"*Why*? Well, 'cos that's what they wanna do. They wanna touch his fame and have it touch them."

Mr Zwebner smiled and closed his leatherbound book.

"Have it touch them, eh? Like it's catching?"

"It *is* catchin'. Fame is, I swear. Vee had this friend he used to visit with, who somehow stole a dry cleaning ticket offa Dolly Parton's manager or secretary or someone. One Pair Ladies Pants, Silver. Got it framed an' all in a silver frame. And then fame came to him in the form of he began his own dry cleanin' outlet in Hollywood, an' now he's doing shirts for Mel Gibson and so forth."

Mr Zwebner shook his head. Old folks like him, thought Willa, they never believe one word you tell 'em. Like as if reality ended 'fore you was borned. So she told him, have a nice afternoon, Mr Zwebner, and went into her trailer and stood in the dark of it, looking at the two bunks, hers and Vee's and deciding then and there she'd like Vee in her life for ever. She sat down on his bunk that was still damp from his sleep and smoothed his pillow.

Then, in her quiet voice that had this kind of crack in it, ever since she was a kid and sang *Jesus Loves Me, This I Know* with her head lying on her Grandma's lap, she began to sing Vee's new song:

"I thought of you in Ole Kentucky,
And the singing of the sweet blue grass,
For a year we'd been together,
Now you told me, Jim, all things must pass."

Out at the Lyleswood Baptist Church, Lester was up on his ladders, measuring the tin roof and the tin-capped belfry. The minister stood on the ground and stared up.

"Tin warped a bit, Lester?" he called.

"Yeh. It's warped, John."

"Gonna look a whole lot finer in grey slate!"

"Cost y'all a whole lot more 'an the tin did, too."

" 'S okay. We been fund raisin', like I tell you. Auctions.

That's the way to do it. Hog auctions. Needlework auctions. Jelly auctions, we even had."

"Little by little you did it, then?"

"You got it, Lester. Little by little."

"Same way as I built my business up."

He was about to smile down at the reverend, but then and there as he said these words, Lester felt himself falter, like old age had climbed up the ladder and put its awful hands on his shoulders. He held on to the guttering. Little by little, small contract by small contract, he'd made it to halfway. Halfway between East Nashville and Belle Meade. Halfway to the ante bellum-style house he dreamed of with white colonnades and a fruit garden in back, where he'd grow raspberries. But how in hell could he find the strength to make through the second half? I won't, was his thought. Amy knows I won't, which is why, I guess, she keeps going with that yoga of hers. Hoping, if she can stand on her head, her hope's gonna fall out.

"You okay up there, Lester?" called the minister.

"Yeh. Comin' down now, John."

Slowly, taking care to feel each rung of the ladder under his shoe before putting his weight on it, Lester descended. He could feel the sun burning down on his bald spot, but his belly was cold.

"Don't it scare you never, bein' up on a roof, Les?"

"No."

"Guess up there yore nearer to God."

"Day I'm scared, that's the day I'll quit."

"How much it's gonna be, then, for the slate roof?"

"I ain't worked it out yet."

" 'pproximately how much?"

"I ain't done the sums, John."

"We got four thousand raised. Keep it near to that, an' you'll get the tender. We don't want no big firm comin' in and takin' our money. That's the people's roof, Lester. That's a roof built of crochet and jelly and pies."

Lester nodded. "Amy makes a lotta jelly," he said, "outta all the summer fruit."

Willa sat on Vee's bunk a long time, singing. Then she lay down and pulled the damp sheet over her head and went right to sleep.

When she woke, she knew something had changed inside the trailer, so she sat up and stared around and then she got what it was: the hot sun had gone and at the open windows the little thin curtains were flapping about like crazy and the whole air was cold, not like the air of a summer storm, but like the air of winter.

Willa got up and put on one of Vee's sweaters, then closed the windows, snatching the curtains in. She took one look at the sky and swore she'd never seen anything made her more afraid, because the sky was cut in half, half hazy and bright and the other half pitch inky black, and the black half was coming nearer and nearer, like the end of the world was just sliding in over Tennessee.

She wanted to call someone. She would have even called to Mr Zwebner, but he wasn't outside on his chair. He'd taken his chair in and locked his door, and Willa had the feeling that in the whole darn trailer park no one was moving.

So she turned on the radio, hoping for some bulletins telling her if the end of the world was coming or not, but all she could get clear enough to hear through the static was the Grand Ole Opry, live, and who was up there singing, but Herman Berry. Hearing Herman, she thought, now, soon, I'm gonna feel less scared to my teeth, 'cos Vee's gonna drive home an' be with me.

She sat on her hands on Vee's bunk, listening to Herman Berry sing a Johnny Cash number and hoping Vee wasn't there, at the side of the stage where he liked to be, but in the car already, coming towards her. She didn't care one speck whether Herman Berry had liked *Do Not Disturb*; all she minded was whether Vee was going to get to her before the sky fell down on her head.

"Come on!" she called aloud. "Come on, Vee!"

She turned the radio down and started listening for a car. But all she could hear was the wind. The wind was getting so bad, she felt the trailer move. She felt it rock, or lean or something, like there was an earth tremor under it.

"Willa," she said to herself, "yore thirty years old and yore about to die!" And the weirdest thing was, old Herman Berry just went on singing the song and at the end of it the audience clapped and shouted, like the Opry was far away in another state, where the sky was normal and the sun was going down in a normal way.

"Herman," Willa said, "the world is ending, honey. Someone go out an' take a look!"

Lester and Amy Pickering were at supper when they first heard the wind. Then the room got dark and Amy said: "My! Whatever is happening, Lester?"

Lester had a mouthful of corn bread. Chewing, he went to the window and saw what Willa had seen—the slab of darkness moving over the sky.

"Uh-huh," he said.

"What is it, dear?"

"Boy oh boy . . ."

"Lester . . .?"

"Take a look, Amy."

Amy came and stood beside her husband and looked out. Then she took hold of his hand. "God Almighty, Lester! What the heavens is it?"

"Low pressure. Big low front movin' in."

"Jesus Christ! Looks like a building fallin' down on us!"

"Severe low. Knock out the power, maybe. Better get us some candles and a flashlight."

"Shoot! I never seen such a thing!"

"We got any candles?"

"I guess."

"Get 'em then, Amy."

"*God!* I never in my life saw that."

" 's only weather."

"Don't look like weather, do it? Look like *Apocalypse Now*."

"Get the candles, okay?"

"Come with me, Lester."

"Why?"

"I'm scared, that's why."

"Told you, Amy, it's only weather."

"Okay, so it is. That don't mean I don't have to be afraid."

" . . . afraid?" said Willa. "That ain't the word for what I felt that night. If I live to be sixty—which I won't, now my heart's got broke—I'll never be that terrorised. Bad enough it was, I guess, for folk in houses. But for us in the trailer park, well, you couldn't imagine how it was, because that wind, it came and lifted up our homes. It lifted them plumb off the earth, and one of 'em, the trailer of my neighbour, Mr Zwebner, it lifted so high, it came down on the Interstate and how Mr Zwebner didn't die was only because he wasn't *in* his trailer; he was in mine, tryin' to stop me screamin' . . ." The worst thing was, Vee didn't come home.

If Vee had come, Willa could have clung to him and maybe they would have sung songs or something to keep their fear from getting the better of them. But the hours passed and full night came on, and there wasn't a sign of him. No car arriving. No Vee in his cowboy boots, holding his guitar. Nothing. Just darkness and the screaming, tearing wind and the trailer creaking and moving and the sirens going and all the thin poplars that screened the park from the Interstate snapping in half, like matchwood.

What could Willa do but start screaming?

"Vee!" she screamed, "Help me, Vee! Vee! Come help me! Vee! Where are ya? Vee! VEE! *VEE!*"

And some time after all that hollering for Vee, there'd been a thumping on her door and she thought, Sweet Jesus, he's home, and she undid the latch and the chain and went to pull him in, to take him in her arms and not let go of him till she died or the wind ceased, whichever came soonest. But it wasn't Vee. It was Mr Zwebner in his thick night clothes that smelled of onion or something, and he began hollering back at her not to scream. "You make yourself sick with this screaming, Willa, I swear!" he shouted. And he put his smelly hand over her mouth and gripped her arm and shook her like you would shake a chicken, to wring its neck.

And after a moment of this shaking, she came out of her

screaming and broke down and sobbed with her head on Mr Zwebner's chest, through which she could hear his old heart still just about beating.

"Mr Zwebner," sobbed Willa, "where's Vee? Don't tell me he's gone?"

And then the gust came that picked Mr Zwebner's trailer onto its end and sent it spinning down onto the highway.

"Woulda killed him dead," said Willa, " 'cept he was with me, helpin' me in my hour a'need."

Though Amy had found some candles, she and Lester didn't need them, because, by some kind of miracle, the power lines in Green Hills stayed standing.

What came flying off were the roofs. On almost every house on every bit of the green hills, the wind tore in under the shingles and sent them hurtling down.

Lester heard this happen and saw it in his mind's eye—all the roofs just being blown away. And he stayed up all night, sitting in a chair, not afraid of the wind, but just thinking about it.

Near two o'clock, Amy said: "Maybe we should go to bed. Or at least lie down for a while?"

But Lester shook his head. "Can't lie down, Amy," he said. "Too much on my brain."

So they sat on in the living room. Amy picked up photos of their grown-up children and looked at them and thought back to how, when they were little and they had their rickety old house in East Nashville, they used to be afraid of it in a high wind, as if it planned to do them harm.

But Lester wasn't thinking about his children, or about the past. He was thinking about Belle Meade and the future. He was thinking about money.

"Amy," he said, after some hours, "know what?"

"What, Lester?"

"This storm ain't gonna hurt us none."

"I sure hope not," said Amy.

And then they were silent again. But Lester smiled as he sat there, because he saw what was coming. In a few months—if he stayed cool and cunning and didn't let the pressure get to him—he could make more money than he'd seen in years. Enough to get beyond this halfway point. Enough for the house with the fruit garden and the colonnades.

Only thing was, he wouldn't be able to do the Baptist church. There just wouldn't be any time for that. "I sure am sorry, John," he'd say to the minister, "but that night of the storm, it changed a lotta things."

It got light.

The wind mellowed down, and the people of the trailer park stood about, looking at the ruin all around them.

Half the roof was gone from Willa's home, but it was still standing, so she said to Mr Zwebner: "You have a nice rest, till the police an' all come, Mr Zwebner. You lie down right here, on Vee's bunk, okay, and cover yourself with the counterpane."

"What will you do, Willa?"

"Ain't nothin' for me to do, really, 'cept go to work. Take my mind offa things. Always supposin' Mr Pie's ain't blown away to Kansas."

So Willa washed her face and hands, wiped all the blotched shadow from her eyelids and put on fresh, and went to wait for the five-thirty a.m. bus, which never arrived.

She began to walk. The sky was a kind of dead white colour and there were no shadows anywhere on anything.

As she walked, she thought, I dunno, I jes' dunno what coulda happened that Vee never got home. It's like God said: "I'm gonna take one on them, Willa. Vee, or the trailer. I'm gonna puff one on them away." 'Cos what life is, it's *never* all the way you want it. More like half. Like you can have Vee, or you can have your home be one of the lucky ones not destroyed by the wind. But you can't have both.

Soon after Willa arrived at Mr Pie's, while she and Ileene were still setting up the relishes and sauces, Lester Pickering came in and sat down at the counter and ordered an Early Breakfast.

He knew Willa by name, for it was a thing he loved to do, to get up early, while Amy was still sleeping, and treat himself to sausage, biscuit, grits, hash browns and egg before he went to work.

"How yo're, Willa?" he asked, with a grin. "Survive the storm, did ya?"

"Just about, Mr Pickering. Trailer next to mine blew down. You want coffee, Sir?"

"Sure. Lotsa coffee. Sat in a damn chair all night."

"Me, my neighbour done come in to quieten me. I was screamin' so hard, I couldn't hear m'self."

"Where was Vee, then?" asked Ileene. "He didn't come back after his big success, then?"

"What 'big success'?"

"You didn't listen to the Opry, Willa?"

"Sure. Bits of it."

"You didn't hear Herman Berry?"

"Yeh. I heard him."

"Singin' Vee's song?"

"He weren't singin' no songa Vee's. He was singin' a Johnny Cash number."

"Before that, he sang Vee's song."

"You was hearin' things, Ileene."

"No, I wasn't. Tell you the title of the song, if you want: *Do Not Disturb*. Told the audience, 'I learned this just today, in one afternoon, 'cos I liked it so much I wanted to sing for y'all tonight. An' it's written by a new songwriter, resident here in Nashville, name of Vee La Rivière.' "

Willa put the coffee back on its burner. She rested her elbow on the chrome counter and gave Ileene one of the long, hard stares she was famous for in her childhood.

"You lyin' to me, Ileene?"

"No. I ain't lyin'. *Do Not Disturb*. He ain't written a song called that?"

"Yeh. That's his new one."

"Well then, there y'are. He's famous now. Vee La Rivière."

Willa said nothing more to Ileene. She went into the kitchen and waited there while Fat Pete cooked Lester Pickering's breakfast. Then she took the plate of sausage and grits and the side order of doughnuts and set them up on the counter.

"Everything okay for you here, Mr Pickering?"

"Yes, thank you, Willa."

"You gonna be busy, I guess, with all them roofs flyin' off?"

"Yeh. Busier than I ever been."

"What happens, then, to folk as lost their roof? Insurance pays, do they?"

"Yeh. Most everyone's got coverage."

"That's lucky." Then she smiled at Lester Pickering, whose mouth was stuffed with sausage. "Shame I couldn't of had somethin' like that on Vee," she said. "Some insurance, like. Know what I mean? So that when his good luck blew in, I was covered. Know what I'm sayin', Mr Pickering?"

margaret atwood

Weight

I am gaining weight. I'm not getting bigger, only heavier. This doesn't show up on the scales: technically I'm the same. My clothes still fit, so it isn't size, what they tell you about fat taking up more space than muscle. The heaviness I feel is in the energy I burn up getting myself around: along the sidewalk, up the stairs, through the day. It's the pressure on my feet. It's a density of the cells, as if I've been drinking heavy metals. Nothing you can measure, although there are the usual nubbins of flesh that must be firmed, roped in, worked off. *Worked*. It's all getting to be too much work.

Some days, I think, I'm not going to make it. I will have a hot flash, a car crash. I will have a heart attack. I will jump out the window.

This is what I'm thinking as I look at the man. He's a rich man, that goes without saying: if he weren't rich, neither of us would be here. He has excess money, and I'm trying to get some of it out of him. Not for myself; I'm doing nicely, thank you. For what we used to call charity and now call good causes. To be precise, a shelter for battered women. *Molly's Place*, it's called. It's named after a lawyer who was murdered by her husband, with a claw hammer. He was the kind of man who was good with tools He had a workbench in the cellar. The lathe, the vice, the buzz saw, the works.

I wonder if this other man, sitting so cautiously across the tablecloth from me, has a workbench in the cellar too. He doesn't have the hands for it. No callouses or little nicks. I don't tell him about the claw hammer, or about the arms and legs hidden here and there about the province, in culverts, in wooded glades, like Easter eggs or the clues in some grotesque treasure hunt. I know how easily frightened such men can be by such possibilities. Real blood, the kind that cries out to you from the ground.

We've been through the ordering, which involved the rueful production of the reading glasses, by both of us, for the scanning of the ornate menu. We have at least one thing in common: our eyes are going. Now I smile at him and twiddle the stem of my wine glass, and lie judiciously. This isn't even my thing, I tell him. I got sucked into it because I have a hard time saying no. I'm doing it for a friend. This is true enough: Molly was a friend.

He smiles and relaxes. *Good*, he's thinking. I am not one of those earnest women, the kind who lecture and scold and open their own car doors. He's right, it's not my style. But he could have figured that out from my shoes: women like that do not wear shoes like this. I am not, in a word, *strident*, and his instinct in asking me to lunch has been justified.

This man has a name, of course. His name is Charles. He's already said: *Call me Charles*. Who knows what further delights await me? *Chuck* may lie ahead, or *Charlie. Charlie is my darling. Chuck, you big hunk*. I think I'll stick with Charles.

The appetizers arrive, leek soup for him, a salad for me, endives with apples and walnuts, veiled with a light dressing, as the menu puts it. *Veiled*. So much for brides. The waiter is another out-of-work actor, but his grace and charm are lost on Charles, who does not reply when ordered to enjoy his meal.

"Cheers," says Charles, lifting his glass. He's already said this once, when the wine appeared. Heavy going. What are the odds I can get through this lunch without any mention of the bottom line?

Charles is about to tell a joke. The symptoms are all there: the slight reddening, the twitch of the jaw muscle, the crinkling around the eyes.

"What's brown and white and looks good on a lawyer?"

I've heard it. "I'll bite. What?"

"A pit bull."

"Oh, that's terrible. Oh, you are awful."

Charles allows his mouth a small semi-circular smile. Then apologetically: "I didn't mean women lawyers, of course."

"I don't practise any more. I'm in business, remember?" But maybe he meant Molly.

Would Molly have found this joke funny? Probably. Certainly at first. When we were in Law School working our little butts off because we knew we had to be twice as good as the men to end up less than the same, we used to go out for coffee breaks and kill ourselves laughing, making up silly meanings for the things we got called by the guys. Or women in general got called: but we knew they meant us.

"*Strident*. A brand of medicated toothpick used in the treatment of gum disease."

"Okay! *Shrill*. As in the Greater Shrill. A sharp-beaked shore bird native to the coasts of . . ."

"California? Yes. *Hysteria?*"

"A sickly-scented flowering vine that climbs all over Southern mansions. *Pushy?*"

"Pushy. That's a hard one. Rude word pertaining to female anatomy, uttered by drunk while making a pass?"

"Too obvious. How about a large soft velvet cushion . . ."

"Pink or mauve . . ."

"Used for reclining on the floor, while . . ."

"While watching afternoon soaps," I finished, not satisfied. There should be something better for *pushy*.

Molly was pushy. Or you could call it determined. She had to be, she was so short. She was like a scrappy little urchin, big eyes, bangs over the forehead, tough little chin she'd stick out when she got mad. She was not from a good home. She'd made it on brains. Neither was I, so did I; but it affected us differently. I for instance was tidy and had a dirt phobia. Molly had a cat named Catty, a stray of course. They lived in cheerful squalor. Or not squalor: disorder. I couldn't have stood it myself, but M liked it in her. She made the messes I wouldn't allow myself to make. Chaos by proxy.

Molly and I had big ideas, then. We were going to change

things. We were going to break the code, circumvent the old boys' network, show that women could do it, whatever it might be. We were going to take on the system, get better divorce settlements, root for equal pay. We wanted justice and fair play. We thought that was what the law was for.

We were brave, but we had it backwards. We didn't know you had to begin with the judges.

But Molly didn't hate men. With men, Molly was a toad-kisser. She thought any toad could be turned into a prince if he was only kissed enough, by her. I was different. I knew a toad was a toad and would remain so. The thing was to find the most congenial among the toads and learn to appreciate their finer points. You had to develop an eye for warts.

I called this compromise. Molly called it cynicism.

Across the table, Charles is having another glass of wine. I think he's deciding that I am a good sport. So necessary in a woman with whom you're considering what used to be called an illicit affair; because that's what this lunch is really about. It's a mutual interview, for positions vacant. I could have made my charity plea in Charles' office, and been turned down shortly and sweetly. We could have kept it formal.

Charles is good looking, in the way such men are, though if you saw him on a street corner, lacking a shave and with his hand out, you might not think so. Such men always seem the same age. They were longing to be this age when they were twenty-five, and so they imitated it; and after they pass this age they will try to imitate it again. The weightiness of authority is what they want, and enough youth left to enjoy it. It's the age called *prime*, like beef. They all have that beefy thing about them. A meaty firmness. They all play something: they begin with squash, progress through tennis, end with golf. It keeps them in trim. Two hundred pounds of hot steak. I should know.

All of it swathed in expensive dark-blue suiting, with a thin stripe. A conservative tie down the front, maroon with a little design. This one has horses.

"Are you fond of horses, Charles?"

"What?"

"Your tie."

"Oh. No. Not particularly. Gift from my wife."

I'm putting off any renewed mention of *Molly's Place* until dessert—never make the heavy pitch till then, says business etiquette, let the guy suck up a little protein first—though if my guess is right and Charles too is concerned with his weight, we'll both skip dessert and settle for double espresso. Meanwhile I listen to Charles, as I dole out the leading questions. The ground rules are being quietly set forth: two mentions of the wife already, one of the son at college, one of the teenage daughter. Stable family is the message. It goes with the horse tie.

It's the wife who interests me most, of course. If men like Charles did not have wives they would have to invent them. So useful for fending off the other women, when they get too close. If I were a man, that's what I'd do: invent a wife, put one together from bits and pieces—a ring from a pawn shop, a photo or two snuck out of someone else's album, a three-minute sentimental drone about the kids. You could fake phone calls to yourself, you could send postcards to yourself, from Bermuda, or better, Tortuga. But men like Charles are not thorough in their deceptions. Their killer instincts are directed elsewhere. They get snarled up in their own lies, or give themselves away by shifty eye movements. At heart they are too sincere.

I on the other hand have a devious mind and little sense of guilt. My guilt is about other things.

I already suspect what this wife will look like: over-tanned, over-exercised, with alert, leathery eyes and too many tendons in her neck. I see these wives, packs of them, or pairs or teams, loping around in their tennis whites, over at the Club. Smug, but jumpy. They know this is a polygamous country in all but name. I make them nervous.

But they should be grateful to me for helping them out. Who else has the time and expertise to smooth the egos of men like Charles, listen to their jokes, lie to them about their sexual prowess? The tending of such men is a fading art, like scrimshaw or the making of woollen-rose mantelpiece decorations. The wives are too busy for it, and the younger women don't know how. I know how. I learned in the old school, which was not the same as the one that gave out the ties.

Sometimes, when I have amassed yet another ugly wristwatch or brooch (they never give rings; if I want one of those I buy it myself), when I've been left stranded on a weekend in favour of the kids and the Georgian Bay cottage, I think about what I could tell and I feel powerful. I think about dropping an acerbic, vengeful little note through the mailbox of the wife in question, citing moles strategically placed, nicknames, the perverse habits of the family dog. Proofs of knowledge.

But then I would lose power. Knowledge is power only as long as you keep your mouth shut.

Here's one for you, Molly: *menopause*. A pause while you reconsider men.

At long last here come the entrées, with a flashing of teeth and a winsome glance from the waiter. Veal scallopini for Charles, who has evidently not seen those sordid pictures of calves being bleached in the dark, seafood *en brochette* for me. I think: now he'll say *Cheers* again, and then he'll make some comment about seafood being good for the sex drive. He's had enough wine for that by now. After that he'll ask me why I'm not married.

"Cheers," says Charles. "Any oysters in there?"

"No," I say. "Not a one."

"Too bad. Good for what ails you."

Speak for yourself, I think. He gives a meditative chew or two. "How is it that you never got married—an attractive woman like you?"

I shrug my shoulder pads. What should I tell him? The dead fiancé story, lifted from the great-aunt of a friend? No. Too World War One. Should I say, "I was too choosy?" That might scare him: if I'm hard to please, how will he manage to please me?

I don't really know why. Maybe I was waiting for the big romance. Maybe I wanted True Love, with the armpits airbrushed out and no bitter aftertaste. Maybe I wanted to keep my options open. In those days I felt that anything could happen.

"I was married once," I say, sadly, regretfully. I hope to convey that I did the right thing but it didn't work out. Some jerk let me down, in a way too horrible to go into. Charles is free to think he could have done better.

There's something final about saying you were married once. It's like saying you were dead once. It shuts them up.

It's funny to think that Molly was the one who got married. You'd think it would have been me. I was the one who wanted the two children, the two-car garage, the antique dining table with the rose bowl in the centre. Well, at least I've got the table. Other women's husbands sit at it and I feed them omelettes, while they surreptitiously consult their watches. But if they even hint at divorcing the wife, I heave them out the door so fast they can't even remember where they left their boxer shorts. I've never wanted to make the commitment. Or I've never wanted to take the risk. It amounts to the same thing.

There was a time when my married friends envied me my singleness, or said they did. I was having fun, ran the line, and they were not. Recently though they're revising this view. They tell me I ought to travel, since I have the freedom for it. They give me travel brochures with palm trees on them. What they have in mind is a sunshine cruise, a shipboard romance, an adventure. I can think of nothing worse: stuck on an overheated boat with a lot of wrinkly women, all bent on adventure too. So I stuff the brochures in behind the toaster oven, so convenient for solo dinners, where one of these days they will no doubt burst into flames.

I get enough adventure right around here. It's wearing me out.

Twenty years ago I was just out of Law School, in another twenty I'll be retired and it will be the twenty-first century, for whoever's counting. Once a month I wake in the night, slippery with terror. I'm afraid, not because there's someone in the room, in the dark, in the bed, but because there isn't. I'm afraid of the emptiness, which lies beside me like a corpse.

I think: what will become of me? I will be alone. Who will visit me in the old age home? I think of the next man as an aging horse must think of a jump. Will I lose my nerve? Can I still pull it off? Should I get married? Do I have the choice?

In the daytime I am fine. I lead a rich full life. There is of course my career. I shine away at it like an antique brass. I add on to it like a stamp collection. It props me up: a career like an underwired brassiere. Some days I hate it.

"Dessert?" says Charles.

"Will you?"

Charles pats his midriff. "Trying to cut down," he says.

"Let's just have a double espresso," I say. I make it sound like a delicious conspiracy.

Double espresso. A diabolical torture devised by the Spanish Inquisition, involving a sack of tacks, a silver boot jack, and two three-hundred-pound priests.

Molly. I let you down. I burnt out early. I couldn't take the pressure. I wanted security. Maybe I decided that the fastest way to improve the lot of women was to improve my own.

Molly kept on. She lost that baby-fat roundness, she developed a raw edge to her voice and took to chain smoking. Her hair got dull and her skin looked abraded and she paid no attention. She began to lecture me about my lack of seriousness, and also about my wardrobe, for which I overspent in her opinion. She began to use words like *patriarchy*. I began to find her strident.

"Molly," I said. "Why don't you give it up? You're slamming your head against a big brick wall." I felt like a traitor saying it. But I'd have felt like a traitor if I hadn't said it, because Molly was knocking herself out, and for peanuts. The kind of women she represented never had any money.

"We're making progress," she'd say. Her face was getting that ropey look, like a missionary's. "We're accomplishing something."

"Who is this *we*?" I'd say. "I don't see a lot of people helping you out."

"Oh, they do," she said vaguely. "Some of them do. They do what they can, in their own way. It's sort of like the widow's mite, you know?"

"What widow?" I said. I knew, but I was exasperated. She was trying to make me feel guilty. "Quit trying for sainthood, Molly. Enough is enough."

That was before she married Curtis.

"Now," says Charles. "Cards on the table, eh?"

"Right," I say. "Well, I've explained the basic position to you already. In your office."

"Yes," he says. "As I told you, the company has already allocated its charitable-donations budget for this year."

"But you can make an exception," I say. "You could draw down on next year's budget."

"We could, if—well, the bottom line is that we like to think we're getting something back for what we put in. Nothing blatant, just what you might call good associations. With hearts and kidneys, for instance, there's no problem at all."

"What's wrong with battered women?"

"Well, there would be our company logo, and then right beside it these battered women. The public might get the wrong idea."

"You mean they might think the company was doing the battering itself?"

"In a word, yes," says Charles.

It's like any negotiation. Always agree, then come at them from a different angle. "You have a point," I say.

Battered women. I can see it in lights, like a roadside fast-food joint. *Get some fresh.* Sort of like onion rings and deep-fried chicken. A terrible pun. Would Molly have laughed? Yes. No. Yes.

Battered. Covered in slime, then dipped into hell. Not so inappropriate, after all.

Molly was thirty when she married Curtis. He wasn't the first man she'd lived with. I've often wondered why she did it. Why him? Possibly she just got tired.

Still, it was a strange choice. He was so dependent. He could hardly let her out of his sight. Was that the appeal? Probably not. Molly was a fixer. She thought she could fix things that were broken. Sometimes she could. Though Curtis was too broken even for her. He was so broken he thought the normal state of the world was broken. Maybe that's why he tried to break Molly: to make her normal. When he couldn't do it one way he did it another.

He was plausible enough at first. He was a lawyer, he had the proper suits. I could say I knew right away that he wasn't totally glued together, but it wouldn't be true. I didn't know. I didn't like him very much, but I didn't know.

For a while after the wedding I didn't see that much of Molly. She was always busy doing something or other with Curtis, and then there were the children. A boy and a girl, just what I'd always expected, for myself. Sometimes it seemed that Molly was leading the life I might have led, if it hadn't been for caution and a certain fastidiousness. When it comes to the crunch, I have a dislike of other people's bathtub rings. That's the virtue in married men: someone else does the maintenance.

"Is everything all right?" says the waiter, for the fourth time. Charles doesn't answer. Perhaps he doesn't hear. He's the sort of man for whom waiters are a kind of warm-blooded tea-trolley.

"Wonderful," I say.

"Why don't these battered women just get a good lawyer?" says Charles. He's genuinely baffled. No use telling him they can't afford it. For him that's not a concept.

"Charles," I say. "Some of these guys *are* good lawyers."

"Nobody I know," says Charles.

"You'd be surprised," I say. "Of course, we take personal donations too."

"What?" says Charles, who has not followed me.

"Not just corporate ones, Bill Henry over at ConFrax gave

two thousand dollars." Bill Henry had to. I know all about his useful right-buttock birthmark, the one shaped like a rabbit. I know his snore pattern.

"Ah," says Charles, caught unawares. But he will not be hooked without a struggle. "You know I like to put my money where it's doing some real good. These women. You get them out, but I've been told they just go right back and get battered again."

I've heard it before. They're addicted. They can't get enough of having their eyes punched in. "Give it to the Heart Foundation," I say, "and those ungrateful triple bypasses will just croak anyway, sooner or later. It's like they're asking for it."

"Touché," says Charles. Oh good. He knows some French. Not a complete oaf, unlike some. "How about I take you out for dinner on, say—" he consults his little book, the one they all carry around in the breast pocket—"Wednesday? Then you can convince me."

"Charles," I say, "that's not fair. I would adore to have dinner with you, but not as the price of your donation. Give first, and then we can have dinner with a clear conscience."

Charles like the idea of a clear conscience. He grins and reaches for his chequebook. He's not going to look cheaper than Bill Henry. Not at this stage of the game.

Molly came to see me at my office. She didn't phone first. It was right after I'd left my last high-class flunky company position and set up on my own. I had my own flunkies now, and I was wrestling with the coffee problem. If you're a woman, women don't like bringing you coffee. Neither do men.

"Molly, what's wrong?" I said. "Do you want coffee?"

"I'm so wired already I couldn't stand it," she said. She looked it. There were half-circles under her eyes the size of lemon wedges.

"It's Curtis," she said. "Could I sleep over at your place tonight? If I have to?"

"What's he done?" I said.

"Nothing," she said. "Not yet. It isn't what he's done, it's how he is. He's heading straight for the edge."

"In what way?"

"A while ago he started saying I was having affairs at work. He thought I was having an affair with Maurice, across the hall."

"Maurice!" I said. We'd both gone to Law School with Maurice. "But Maurice is gay!"

"We aren't talking rational here. Then he started saying I was going to leave him."

"And were you?"

"I wasn't. But now, I don't know. Now I think I am. He's driving me to it."

"He's paranoid," I said.

"*Paranoid*", said Molly. "A wide-angle camera for taking snapshots of maniacs." She put her head down on her arms and laughed and laughed.

"Come over tonight," I said. "Don't even think about it. Just do it."

"I don't want to rush it," said Molly. "Maybe things will work out. Maybe I can talk him into getting some help. He's been under a lot of strain. I have to think about the kids. He's a good father."

Victim, they said in the papers. Molly was no victim. She wasn't helpless, she wasn't hopeless. She was full of hope. It was hope that killed her.

I called her the next evening. I thought she would have come over, but she hadn't. She hadn't phoned either.

Curtis answered. He said Molly had gone on a trip.

I asked him when she'd be back. He said he had no idea. Then he started to cry. "She's left me," he said.

Good for her, I thought. She's done it after all.

It was a week later that the arms and legs started turning up.

He killed her in her sleep, I'll give him that much credit. She never knew. Or so he said, after he got around to remembering. He claimed amnesia, at first.

Dismemberment. The act of conscious forgetting.

I try not to think of Molly like that. I try to remember her whole.

Charles is walking me to the door, past white tablecloth after white tablecloth, each one held in place by at least four pinstriped elbows. It's like the Titanic just before the iceberg: power and influence disporting themselves, not a care in the world. What do they know about the serfs down in Steerage? Piss all and pass the port.

I smile to the right, I smile to the left. There are some familiar faces here, some familiar birthmarks. Charles takes my elbow, in a proprietary though discreet way. A light touch, a heavy hand.

I no longer think that anything can happen. I no longer want to think that way. *Happen* is what you wait for, not what you do; and *anything* is a large category. I am unlikely to get murdered by this man, for instance; I am unlikely to get married to him either. Right now I don't even know whether I'll go as far as dinner on Wednesday. It occurs to me that I don't really have to, not if I don't want to. Some options at least remain open. Just thinking about it makes my feet hurt less.

Today is Friday. Tomorrow morning I'll go power walking in the cemetery, for the inner and outer thighs. It's one of the few places you can do it in this city without getting run over. It isn't the cemetery Molly's buried in, whatever of her they could put together. But that doesn't matter. I'll pick out a tombstone where I can do my leg stretches, and I'll pretend it's hers.

Molly, I'll say. We don't see eye to eye on some things and you wouldn't approve of my methods, but I do what I can. The bottom line is that cash is cash, and it puts food on the table.

Bottom line, she will answer. What you hit when you get as far down as you're going. After that you stay there. Or else you go up.

I will bend, I will touch the ground, or as close to it as I can get without rupture. I will lay a wreath of invisible money on her grave.

lucy ellmann

Love: the world's oldest profession

. . . loveable, desirable, likeable, congenial, after one's heart, winsome, amiable, sweet, angelic, divine, adorable, beautiful, intriguing, seductive, appealing, prepossessing, cuddly . . .

Christ! Give me a break, muttered Maisy in exasperation. She reached for her note-pad and crossed off "Reading the Thesaurus" from her list of Things To Do In London For Free. She was preparing a shortish book on the subject, getting ever shorter. All her pleasures seemed to be transitory or increasingly expensive, and her free-thinking was becoming distinctly uninspired. She suggested, for instance, that you could go to the Barbican and various other theatres and watch the play on the latecomers' TV set. You could sit around hospital waiting-rooms and see injured people. You could go on long walks with eyes to the ground in search of pound coins, buttons and the occasional aubergine. You could count the number of playgrounds that have turned into carparks during Thatcher's rule. To alleviate loneliness, you could phone Free-Phone numbers or pretend to be a house-buyer or lie around reading the thesaurus, but that was now ruled out.

Frank woke early, as usual of late. The sun was just peeping under the blind, giving a weird glow to the vase of dried flowers that adorned his windowsill. He tiptoed round to Annabelle's side of the bed, trying not to disturb her as he collected his clothes. A light sleeper, Annabelle was now lightly sleeping off back pain, mild conjunctivitis and menstrual trouble, either pre or post or concurrent—he wasn't sure what stage they were at with it. Annabelle had amassed a number of physical ailments that made her life of leisure, security and solitary confinement a cause for concern and frequent, if inexpert, back rubs administered by Frank.

Strange, this early morning race for the train and traipse across London for rough sex with Maisy, followed by the torment of her nosing around in his balls while he tried to rid himself of raunchy smells with the soap and shampoo they'd romantically bought together in obscene but perfect imitation of the brands he used at home. And other suchlike sensual experiences.

But Maisy was irresistible. A woman without back trouble, who admired his gentles as she called them. He couldn't remember when Annabelle had last found him acceptable in any way. His body was too hairy, his penis too big, his hand wobbled when pouring wine, TV documentaries put him to sleep, and he had an inaccurate understanding of the right night to put out the rubbish.

His mother had liked him. He'd been the one exception to her belief that men were not to be trusted (his father had once had a brief affair and had spent all his time growing turnips ever since). She'd fed Frank sardine sarnies as a sign of their confederacy, while he leant back against the kitchen cupboards in his customary pose—one ungainly knee thrust forward and the foot somewhere underneath propping him up—and related the events, sorry though they might be, of his schooldays.

From the bedroom Annabelle listened to Frank moving about the house, collecting his briefcase and the lunch money she'd carefully allocated from the Food Expense Jar the night before. She didn't move for fear the bed might creak and she would be called upon to make early morning chit-chat. Obscuring herself under the covers, she clung to vestiges of oblivion, the unadult world of blankets and half-light in which mussed hair and bad breath and the sad intimacy of the warmed bed could not yet trouble her. She needed to collect herself at a dignified pace, feeling dishevelled by her dreams. In one, tube train doors had opened to emit a surge of giant Heinz spaghetti. After which, she had ridden up a number of escalators in search, apparently, of chamois leather camiknickers.

When she heard the quiet implosion of the front door shutting behind Frank, Annabelle lugged her body to the bathroom where she began to engage in the power and glory of existence by dealing with excreta and a pain in her lower spine. She rose as quickly as possible from the loo and went downstairs to drink herbal tea and to hoover. The house was in perfect shape.

Annabelle then wandered around, desultorily dusting. She was compiling a compendium of compassion for suffering throughout the world. It was her Christian faith, she felt, that led her to take a particular interest in such matters. There was no limit to her indignation, outrage and despair on behalf of the meek, the poor and the ugly. The radio gently fed her capacious sensibility.

A call-in programme had just begun on the question of women priests, yes or no. A woman phoned to say that God had created Man and Woman in His Own Image. She repeated this a number of times, but the studio guest was unimpressed. The role of priest, he said, was based on that of the twelve apostles, and they had all been male. Genesis was passé.

It didn't take him long to convince Annabelle. The female body was too heathen, too prone to mess, to be a messenger of God. Into her mind came images of white-robed choristers spattered with menstrual blood, Carefree panty-pads let loose amongst the Communion wafers, and the church lit by Tampax candles.

Annabelle proceeded to the loo again to check that she herself wasn't leaking any unseemly substances at the moment, and found that she wasn't. She then lay down on the pristine-clean, still-wrapped-in-polythene sofa-bed they'd bought for the front room, where she could watch TV in relative calm while awaiting 10.30, the time when she always called Frank at the office.

Why were sheets and blankets and pillows and pillowcases and mattresses suspended somewhere above the floor, so common worldwide as a mean of sleeping? mused Maisy (forgetting all about Japanese bedtime arrangements). Rather whimsically, she added "Musing" to her list of urban freedoms. Eventually she would assemble them all according to the mood one might wish to accommodate or generate: what to do on a good/bad/indifferent day.

Maisy's own day was improving. Frank had a meeting in the afternoon so she was planning to skive off to a film with Tim, who still pined for her. The trouble, she found, with married men is all the gaps they leave in your life. She was counter-attacking by creating, and filling, free time where there wasn't supposed to be any.

When the phone rang, Maisy put it through with her customary efficiency, using an American drawl. "Fra-ank, Hollywood calling. Your chance to break into the movies!"

It was of course Annabelle. Frank thought Maisy was admirably patient about Annabelle's daily interruptions of their smooth-running office life. This time Annabelle wanted him to buy soured cream and pork chops at Sainsbury's on his way home. She'd seen a recipe whereby you fry the pork chops, flambé them in brandy and then plop a spoonful of soured cream on each one and simmer a few more minutes.

Frank wished Annabelle didn't read so many women's magazines—all about how if you slop this on your face or hair or your pork chops, exercise those abdominal muscles, keep abreast of cultural events in which you have no intention of participating, and get your perverser impulses under control by reading some romantic fiction, your Partner has got to love you more.

Then there was Maisie, so pleasingly indifferent to pleasing anyone but herself. She didn't even shave her legs. She'd achieved a quality of autonomy that made him want to spend the whole day in her arms.

Of course, she was a bit cynical. Within days of arriving at his office she had filled Frank in on many of the astounding inadequacies of the dozens of men to whom she had at some point given the benefit of the doubt. Frank had felt no inclination at all to join this discredited crowd. Not only fearful of competition, he didn't even fancy Maisy at first. She was too tall, too stocky, too loud-mouthed and uncouth. He'd never before heard a woman talk so unguardedly, so unendingly, and so off-puttingly about sex.

So it had been something of a revelation when she waylaid him at the annual booze-up and fucked him and sucked him as if he were a frog who'd just turned into a prince and was long overdue for a good time. He'd never been quite sure his existence was one of his unhappy parents' happiest accidents. But now he walked tall in the knowledge that whatever antipathy Annabelle had felt for him since they'd met as virgin undergraduates, he was in fact, according to Maisy, a godsend to womankind.

Frank forgot all about the pork chops.

At the pub at lunchtime, he paid for their drinks with the Maisy Fund, a clandestine accumulation of lunch money from Annabelle that he'd managed to piece together over the months—it wasn't fair to expect Maisy to pay all the time. She had enough to put up with already. Maisy was presently going on and on about free things to do in London, a subject of conversation surely geared to elicit sympathy for her poverty. But if she was so poor, how was she able to afford those new boots? Frank had to admit he was a little afraid of Maisy's new stiletto-heeled cowboy boots. It wasn't their pointedness that depressed him, but their cocksure air. For some reason they made him uncomfortably aware of her other lovers, the ones she saw in the evenings. In restaurants, In pubs, In clubs, IN SOHO. His only consolation was: those guys had to endure the boots too.

Annabelle made herself a toasted cheese sandwich with their sandwich maker, and served it up on an old blue paper plate. She didn't feel she deserved a brand new one, much less a plate made from some more durable substance. Through little acts of self-denial followed by self-pity, Annabelle got through her days.

After lunch, her eye caught a magazine which said that there were approximately 5,000 million people in the world. The thought that over half of these must be *women* made Annabelle feel faint. She took to her bed for most of the afternoon.

Maisy lay on her front with legs apart on Tim's posh carpet, enjoying its thick white springiness beneath her. She was reading old Sunday papers and feeling seriously annoyed with Frank, who'd confessed at lunchtime that he was still reluctantly carrying on his monthly endeavours to impregnate his infantile and self-indulgent wife.

"She probably doesn't even buy coloured toilet paper," Maisy mumbled to herself. "Trying to save the whale all day or something." Maisy had lately taken against ecology.

On and on Frank had gone about how much Annabelle needed him, how she wasn't strong like Maisy. Maisy was familiar with this notion that mistresses are automatically strong. What Frank didn't seem to realise was that what most women NEED is two men per day, and two new ones the next.

Maisy felt a sudden wave of despondency at the prospect of going home to her monastically empty bed, preserved these days for her initiate, Frank. I'll never find a man who can give me enough. They like depriving us, she summarised, and reached for the magazine section.

Tim came into the room and said she looked like she was making snow fairies. He explained the child's game of lying in the snow and waving one's arms and legs about in order to make indentations like the wings and gown of a fairy. In fact, he lay on top of her to show her how.

A Sunday. Frank is doing the ironing as Annabelle, who usually does it, has morning sickness and pain in her knees. Frank is feeling overwhelmed. The loneliness of weekends, stuck in the outskirts of London performing rituals of various kinds which he once fully endorsed. The shopping and gardening and home-making, the bickering and punitive sulking, the massages and embarrassments and silences and indignity of lovelessness that seem to stretch into eternity as he waits anxiously for his release on Monday morning: Married Life.

As for the baby-making, Frank has for some time been treasuring the realisation that he no longer fancies Annabelle. So small and pretty and unattainable, her sexual unwillingness had formerly given structure to his life. He can still remember the poignancy of those rare encounters, when his desires and her surrender briefly united in a shared shame. Her endurance of the pain of it for his sake—the only moments of certainty for him that she cared. He'd grown accustomed to the cycle of forgiveness, which took forever, and reward, which could be momentary. Annabelle had eroticised her own sullenness for him.

But since Maisy enlightened him as to his own considerable charms, Annabelle's spell had been broken. It was only at Annabelle's insistence (she wanted a child) that their sex life has continued at all. And has now borne fruit.

Feeling increasingly alienated toward the house and its contents, toward Annabelle and her contents, Frank burns a shirt.

Annabelle, gloomy, made her way to a hospital where she was booked to see a skin specialist. There was a mole on her head that Frank had commented on once in a tone of distaste. She wanted to please him. She was willing to risk a local anaesthetic and minor surgery to please him. There was a row of six medical students in the consulting room, being steered towards omnipotence by a doctor who never looked up from his desk. Annabelle's heart sank. She had hoped for an anonymous meeting, with a minimum of interrogation and deliberation— not all these youngsters tentatively rubbing her nodule, her excrescence, her embossed carbuncle, her deformity and wondering how a pregnant woman could be so vain. The doctor kept referring to it ominously as a lump, and the students couldn't decide whether it was part of her dermis or her epidermis. They were still puzzling over it when she was dismissed from the room. Epidermis or otherwise, she would never know.

Annabelle's nodule was removed in a comparatively private ceremony. She bought a woolly hat afterwards on her way to

Frank's office, to cover the unsightly spot where the unsightly lump had been. A tuft of royal blue stitches encrusted with blood had taken its place.

It wasn't pleasant for Frank when Annabelle, still jittery from surgery, turned up at his office a little later. Annabelle didn't immediately seem to understand why Frank's secretary was leaning over his desk with her hand inside his belt and her mouth on his mouth. Maisy unruffled, turned to Annabelle and said, "Loosen up, babe. Breathe some air now and then— there's plenty to go around."

"I just came to tell Frank I got the mole cut off my head he didn't like," Annabelle replied.

"Frank," said Maisy. "Am I to take it that this hatted figure, with an evident bun in the oven, is your WIFE?"

It seemed to Frank in the days that followed that his delicacy and discretion toward both ladies had badly misfired. They began to complain, at their different times of the day, about his lack of Frankness. In desperation he renewed his pledges to both parties, assuring Annabelle that he would sack Maisy, have nothing more to do with her, not even by telephone, and that he would try to prove to Annabelle his loyalty and devotion in the physically and emotionally arduous days to come; and telling Maisy that he had to see Annabelle through the pregnancy and stay with her for three months afterwards in order to avert post-natal depression, but after that he would move in with Maisykins, pretty please, and get a divorce.

From now on the two women took Frank with a pinch of salt: Annabelle made him do the hoovering before he left for work, and Maisy objected to the name "Maisykins".

The Marriage Guidance Counsellor, for whom Frank's parents were paying, shook Annabelle's hand with a grip capable of fracturing bones. Trying to prove he was confident about something or other, she supposed. Which was more than she felt, what with all the energy sucked out of her by the fluttering foetus and the philandering fandangoing fellatio-prone (for all she knew) Frank.

She was getting a lot of sympathy these days, but underneath it all she felt blamed for everything. Frank's waywardness, as well as his previous uxoriousness, Frank's father's waywardness thirty years before, their ten years of childlessness and their present fecundity, Frank's discontent, Annabelle's discontent, Annabelle's suicidal tendencies and frigidity—it was all her fault.

What wasn't she wondered. Hurricanes in Eastern Japan perhaps? Coups d'état in the Maldive Islands? Great mishaps of the world were suddenly a comfort. Frank droned on beside her with illustrations of his own blamelessness while Annabelle thought with satisfaction of the negligible chance that she had played any part in the deaths of 56,000 men in an hour during the First World War, or had in any way encouraged the bee disease spreading across Europe, or the incidence of AIDS amongst New York heterosexual women. But then it occurred to her that Frank had probably contracted AIDS and given it to her, and she would no doubt be blamed for passing it on to their unborn child.

"You seem, Annabelle, to have a very regular sleeping pattern," suggested the counsellor, with an uncalled-for amount of eyebrow movement. Frank too looked at her piercingly, as if her difficulties with sleep, which he had just been describing to the counsellor, might indeed be the root of all their problems.

"I think I sleep as well as most women who've just found out their husband's screwing his secretary," said Annabelle, and two tears dripped simultaneously down her cheeks.

The counsellor, having previously considered Annabelle radiant, now began to find her repellent. Obviously a self-pitier who hid from marital responsibilities behind moral righteousness and ill-health. This mother-to-be had to grow up.

It was a difficult birth. Despite every available drug being administered, it was clear that the frail and spiritual Annabelle was not well-designed to bear a baby engendered by Frank. It was nobody's fault—God had made her pelvis too small. She called for forceps, a Caesarian, any unnatural method of birth she could think of. The midwife kept checking Annabelle's genitals and making philosophical remarks about Mother Nature.

"FUCK mother-fucking Nature!" spat Annabelle, at the height of her agony.

A little shocked, Frank wiped her forehead with a sweaty cloth and reflected spitefully that Annabelle seemed to find giving birth about as enjoyable as conception, before the bleating bloody baby was suddenly thrust into his stiff grasp.

It was a moving, tender moment.

When Frank left her for Maisy a few weeks after Isabel's birth, Annabelle wrote him pathetic, pleading letters which he wept over and hid at the office. Leaving the baby to cry in her cot, Annabelle wrote about all the wonderful times they'd had together at university and the Christian Summer Camp and their honeymoon in Malta where she'd refused to swim at the Blue Grotto but did get lasciviously drunk once. She told him how the roses and turnips were doing, and that if he came home now she would forgive him. She reminded him of how well, how patiently and uncomplainingly, how *nobly* she had ironed his shirts. "Does this woman iron them or what? You see, I worry about you," she scrawled. She told him how lovely the wailing baby looked in pink. Annabelle had never been so communicative, so loving, in the whole of their life together.

His parents wrote to him too, saying that they would never speak to him again. But he now felt committed to Maisy. They'd finally mentioned love to each other. He was the Man for her, she the Woman for him.

Maisy and Frank drove down to his house on the fringes of Essex one night when he knew Annabelle and the baby would be out. Frank thought this would be the most diplomatic time to rescue some of his belongings since Annabelle tended to weep all through his visits to Isabel and searching for his camera and climbing boots had therefore proved tricky.

Appalled by the semi-detached brick number from which her otherwise well-endowed lover had emanated, Maisy sat uncomfortably in the car. A goofy rose-bush grew from a grassless circle in the middle of the patioed front garden. Where the vegetables could be she had no idea. As Frank scoured the house, one room lit up after another, revealing a tiny bunch of dried flowers at every single window.

Maisy wasn't convinced by this cohabitation lark. As the poor fellow didn't know how to live alone, she said she'd give it a try. But she didn't like all the housework. Frank squeamishly removed her dirty knickers from every corner and crevice, and did the washing-up at all hours. The question of Supper had taken on a newfound significance. And he now wanted to regulate all this with a rota system. She could see he was aching to dust her collection of peacock feathers.

He was around a lot more, but spent most of the time talking about Annabelle and how much alimony he ought to give her (about 90 per cent of his income, as far as Maisy could work out). She liked him best, as before, in the early morning, although he still hadn't quite mastered the mature ejaculation.

Maisy took to going out at night on her own to the Kitsch & Chintz Club, where she danced with Tim for whom she still pined. On her return, the domesticated Frank would be fast asleep. Maisy masturbated noisily beside him—another free thing to do in London.

jeanette winterson

The World and Other Places

When I was a boy I made model aeroplanes. We didn't have the money to go anywhere, sometimes we didn't have the money to go to the shop. There were six of us at night in the living room, six people and six carpet tiles. Usually the tiles were laid two by three in a dismal rectangle, but on Saturdays, Aeroplane Night, we took one each and sat cross-legged with all the expectation of an Arabian prince.

We were going to fly away and we held on to the greasy underside of our mats waiting for the magic word to lift us. Bombay. Cairo. Paris. Chicago. We took it in turns to say the word and the one whose word it was took my model aeroplane and spun it where it hung from the ceiling, round and round our huge blow-up globe. We'd saved cereal tokens for the globe and it had been punctured twice. Iceland was covered in Sellotape and Great Britain was only a rubber bicycle patch on the panoply of the world.

I had memorised all the flight times from London Heathrow to anywhere you could mention. It was my job to announce them and to wish the passengers a pleasant flight. Sometimes I pointed out landmarks on the way and we would lean over into the fire-place and have a look at Mont Blanc or crane our necks round the back of the sofa just to get a glimpse of The Rockies.

About halfway through our trip, Mum, who was Chief Steward, swayed down the aisle with cups of tea and toast and Marmite. After that, Dad came forward with next week's jobs around the house written on bits of paper and put in a hat. We took out our share and somebody, the lucky one, would just get Duty Free on theirs and they didn't have to do a thing.

When we reached our destination, we were glad to get up and stretch our legs and then my sister gave us each a blindfold. We put it on and sat quietly while one of us started talking about this strange place we were visiting . . .

How hot it is getting off the plane. Hot and stale like opening the door of a tumble drier. There are no lights to show us where to go. Death will be this way. A rough passage with people we have never met and a hasty run across the tarmac to the terminal building. Inside, in the day for night illumination, a group of Indians are playing the cello. Where are they from, these orchestral refugees? Can it be part of the service? Beyond them, urchins in bare feet leap up and down with ragged cardboard signs, each bearing the name of someone more important than us. These are the people who will be whisked away in closed cars to comfortable beds. The rest of us will get on the bus.

Luggage. Heaven or Hell in the afterlife will be luggage or the lack of it. The virtuous ones, the ones who knew that love is enough and that possessions are only pastimes, will float free through the exit sign, their arms ready to hug their friends, their toothbrush in their pocket. The greedy ones, who stayed up late, gathering and gathering like demented bees, will find that you can take it with you. The joke is that you have to carry it yourself.

Here's the bus. It has three maybe four wheels and the only part noisier than the engine is the horn. All human life is here. There is something to be said for not being in a closed car. I am travelling between a crate of chickens and a fortune teller. The chickens peck at my leg and the fortune teller suddenly grabs my palm. She laughs in my face.

"When you grow up you'll learn to fly."

For the rest of the journey I am bitten by midges.

At last we have reached The Hotel Cockroach. Dusty mats

cover the mud floor and the clerk on reception has an open wound in his cheek. He tells me he was stabbed but I am not to worry. Then he gives me some lukewarm tea and shows me my room. It has a view over the incinerator and is farthest from the bathroom. At least I will not learn to think highly of myself. In the darkness and the silence, I can hear far below, the matter of life going on without me. The night shift. What are they doing, the people who come and go? What are their lives? Whom do they love and why? What will they eat? Where will they sleep? How many of them will see the morning? Will I?

Dreams. The smell of incense and frangipani. The moon sailing on her back makes white passages on a dun-coloured floor. The moon and the clouds white at the window. How many times have I seen it? How many times do I stop and look as though I've never seen it before? Perhaps it's true that every day is the world made new again but for our habits of mind. Frozen in thought, fossilised in what we have built. How dark is the tundra of our soul? During the night a mouse gives birth behind the skirting board.

At the end of the story my family and I swopped anecdotes and exchanged souvenirs. Later we retired to bed with all the weariness of a traveller's reunion. We had done what the astronauts do: belted the world in a few hours and still found breath to talk about it.

I knew I would get away, better myself. Not because I despised who I was but because I didn't know who I was. I was waiting to be invented.

We went up in an aeroplane, the pilot and I. It was a Cessna, modern and beautiful, off-white with a blue stripe right round it and a nose as finely balanced as a pedigree muzzle. I wanted to cup it in boths hands and say, "Well done boy."

In spite of the air-conditioned cockpit, overwarm and muzzy, in an unexpected economy classy way, the pilot had a battered flying jacket stuffed behind his seat. It was a real one, grubby sheepskin and a steel zip. I asked him why he bothered. "Romance," he said. "Flying is romantic. Even now. Even so." We were under a 747 at the time and I thought of its orange seats crammed three abreast on either side and all the odds and ends of families struggling with their beach mats and headphones. "Is that romantic?" I said pointing upwards.

He glanced out of the window. "That's not flying. That's following the road."

For a while we continued in silence. He didn't look at me but sometimes I looked at him; strong jaw with a bit of stubble, brown eyes that never left the sky. He was pretending to be the only man in the air. His dream was the first dream when men in plus fours and motorcycle goggles pedalled with all the single-mindedness of a circus chimp to get their wooden frames and canvas wings upwards and upwards and upwards. It was a solo experience even when there were two of you. What did Amy Johnson say? "If the whole world were flying beside me, I would still be flying alone." Rhetoric, you think. Frontier talk. Then you reach your own frontier and it's not rhetoric any more.

My parents were so proud of me when I joined the airforce. I stood in our cluttered living room in my new uniform and I felt like an angel on a visit. I felt like Gabriel coming to tell the shepherds the Good News.

"Soon you'll have your wings," said my mother and my father got out the Guinness.

In my bedroom, the model aeroplanes had been dusted. Sopwith Camel, Spitfires, Tiger Moth. I picked them up one by one and turned over their balsa wood frames and rice paper wings. I never used a kit. What hopes they carried. More than the altar at church, more than a good school report. In the secret places: under the fuselage, stuck to the tail-fin, I had hidden my hopes.

My mother came in. "You won't be taking them with you?"

I shook my head. I'd be laughed at, made fun of. And yet each of us in our silent bunks at lights out would be thinking of model aeroplanes and the things at home we couldn't talk about any more.

She said, "I gave them a wipe anyway."

Bombay. Cairo. Paris. Chicago. I've been to those places now. I've been almost everywhere and the curious thing is that after a while they begin to look the same. I don't mean the buildings or the scenery, I mean the people. We're all preoccupied with the same things; how to live, who to love and where we go when it's over. Pressing needs, the need to eat, the need to make money, both forcing the same hungry expression into the face, sometimes distract us from our mortality. Those needs met, however temporarily, we can't stop ourselves reviewing again and again how short is the space between day and night.

I saw three things that made this clear to me: The first was a beggar in New York. He was sitting, feet apart, head in hands, on a low wall outside an all-night garage. As I went past him he whispered, "Do you have $2?" I got out the change and gave it to him. He said, "Will you sit with me a minute?"

His name was Bill and he was a compulsive gambler trying to go straight. He thought he might get a job on Monday morning if only he could have two nights in a hostel to sleep well and keep clean. For a week he had been sleeping by the steam duct of the garage. I gave him the hostel money and some extra for food and the clenched fist of his body unfolded. He was talkative, gentle. Already in his mind, he had got the job and was making a success of it and had met a sweet woman in a snack bar. He got up to hurry over to the hostel before it closed. He shook my hand. "You know, the worst thing about being on the street, it's not that you're hungry and cold, it's that nobody sees you. They don't look at you or they look through you. It's like being a ghost. If you're already dead what's the point of trying to live?"

The second was a dress designer I met in Milan. She was at the very top of her profession and she worked long after the others had gone home. Anyone passing could see the light in her window. It was the only one. I never had time to talk to her over a meal or even a cup of coffee. She had food brought into her studio and she ate like an urchin, pencil in one hand, the other a palm-full of olives. She spat the stones at her models.

"I never take holidays," she said. "My models, they are always taking holidays. They don't care."

"Perhaps you should rest," I said. "Go to one of your houses." She had five houses but she lived in a rented flat above her studio.

"And what would I do all day, Mr Pilot? Stare at the sky?" She went to her work table and picked up a pair of shears. "You start thinking, you cut your own throat. What is there to think about? I've tried it and it ends up the same way. In your mind there is a bolted door. You spend your life trying to avoid that door. You go to parties, work hard, have babies, have lovers, it doesn't make any difference what way you choose. But when you are on your own, quiet, nothing to do, or sometimes just walking up the stairs, you see the door again, waiting for you. Then you have to hurry, you have to stop yourself pulling the bolt and turning the handle. On the other side of the door is a mirror and you will see yourself for the first time. You will see what you are and worse than that, what you are not."

The third was a woman in the park with her dog. The dog was young, the woman was old. She carried a shopping bag and every so often took out a bottle and a bowl and gave the dog a drink of water.

"Come on Sandy," she'd say when he'd finished.

Then she'd disappear into the bushes, the dog's tail bobbing behind.

She fascinated me because she was everything I'm not. Put us together side by side and what do we look like? I'm six feet tall in an airman's uniform and I have a strong grip and steady eyes. She's about five feet high and threadbare. I could lift her with one hand.

But if she met my gaze, I'd drop my eyes and blush like a teenager. She's got the edge on me. She's not waiting to be invented. She's done it herself.

How do I know? I don't know, but increasingly I'm looking at people to see who's a fake and who's genuine. Most of us are fakes, surrounded by gilded toys and fat address books and important offices, anything to keep away from that bolted door.

For some years, the early years of my airforce days, I stopped worrying about such questions. I was happy and adventurous and it was obvious that I was a man because I was doing a man's job. That's how we define ourselves isn't it? Then one day I woke up with the curious sensation that I wasn't myself. I hadn't turned into a beetle or a werewolf. My friends treated me as they usually did. I put on my favourite well-worn clothes, bought newspapers, eggs, walked in the park. At last I went to see a doctor. I said, "Doctor, I'm not myself these days." He asked me about my sex life and gave me a course of anti-depressants.

I went to the library and took out books from the philosophy and psychology sections. I read R D Laing who urged me to make myself whole. Then Lacan who wants me to accept that I'm not.

And all the time I thought, "If this isn't me then I must be somewhere." That's when I started travelling so much, left the airforce and bought my own plane. Mostly I teach, sometimes I take out families who've won the first prize in a soup-packet competition. It doesn't matter, I have plenty of free time and I do what I need to do, which is look for myself. I know that if I fly for long enough, for wide enough and far enough, I'll get a signal that tells me there's another aircraft on my wing. I'll glance out of my window and it won't be a friendly Red Devil. It'll be me I see in the cockpit of that other plane.

I went home to see my mother and father. I flew over their village, taxied down their road and left the nose of my plane pushed up against their front door. The tail was just a little on the pavement and I was worried that some traffic warden might give me a ticket for causing an obstruction. I hung a sign on the back saying, "Flying Doctor".

I'm always nervous about going home just as I'm nervous about re-reading books that have meant a lot to me. My parents want me to tell them about the places I've been and what I've seen. Their eyes are eager and full of love. Bombay. Cairo. Paris. Chicago. We've invented them so many times that to tell the truth can only be a disappointment. The blow-up globe still hangs over the mantelpiece, its faded plastic crinkly and torn. The countries of the Common Market are held together by red tape.

We go through my postcards one by one and I give them presents. A sari for my mother, a stetson for my father. They are the children now. We have a cup of tea and in the evening they come outside to wave me off.

"It's a lovely plane," says my mother. "Does it give you much trouble?"

I rev the engine and the neighbours stand astonished in their doorways as the plane gathers speed down on our quiet road. A moment before the muzzle breaks through the apostles window in our little church, I take off, rising higher and higher and disappearing into a bank of cloud.

alison lurie

Ilse's House

Sure, I'm aware that people still theorise why I never married Gregor Spiegelman. I can understand that; Greg was a madly eligible man: good looking, successful, charming, sexy. He reminded me of those European film stars of the Thirties you see on TV reruns; he had that same low-key sophisticated style. And then not only was he chairman of his department, he was important in his field. Everyone agreed that there were only two people in the world who knew as much as he did about Balkan economic history—some said only one.

Whereas I was just a fairly attractive young woman with a good job as a market-research analyst. It seemed kind of a fluke that I should have caught Greg, when so many had tried and failed. Women had been after him for four years, ever since his marriage ended and his wife went back to Europe. I was rather pleased myself. Though I didn't let on, privately I thought Dinah Kieran was about the luckiest girl in upstate New York.

Of course some of my friends thought Greg was too old for me, by more than twenty years. But he didn't look anywhere near fifty-four. His springy light brown hair was scarcely grey at all, and he was really fit: he played squash, and ran two miles every day. I didn't see why his chronological age should bother me. Back in the past it used to be regarded as a coup to marry a man who was already established, instead of taking a chance on some untried boy like my poor old Ma did, to her lifelong regret.

A couple of people I knew said Greg was a bit of a male chauvinist, but I couldn't see it. I wasn't exactly a feminist then anyhow. Sure, I was for equal rights and equal pay; I was making as much as any man in my department, though I'd had to fight for it. But when one of my girlfriends started complaining about how having a chair pulled out for her in a restaurant was insulting, I got really bored. Holy God, why shouldn't a guy treat women with old-fashioned courtesy and consideration if he felt like it?

I rather liked being Greg's little darling, if you want to know the truth. I liked it when he helped me into my coat and gave me a secret squeeze as he settled it round me. I liked having him bring me old-fashioned presents at the least excuse: expensive perfume and flowers and sexy lingerie in the anemone colours that go best with my black-Irish looks: red and lavender and hot pink. I suppose he spoiled me, really, but after the kind of childhood I had there was a lot to make up for.

The only thing I didn't care for from the beginning was the way Greg used to refer to me as "the little woman", even though I'm five seven. I once pointed this out to him; I said it might have been true of his ex-wife, but it didn't make sense for someone practically his own height. But he only laughed and said it was just a conventional phrase, and I mustn't be so literal.

When we split up some people blamed it on the age difference, and others said I wasn't intellectual enough for Gregor, or mature enough. Or they said our backgrounds were too different; what that meant was that I grew up in a trailer camp and didn't attend the right schools and had never been to Europe. Well, it ended so suddenly, that always makes talk. The date had been announced, the wedding invitations sent out, the caterer hired, the University chapel reserved . . . And then, two weeks before the ceremony, kaflooey, the whole thing was off.

In fact I was the one who broke it off. Everybody knew that, we didn't make a secret of it, and the reason we gave was the real one in a way; that I didn't want to live in Gregor's house. Of course people thought that was completely nuts, since I'd been more or less living there for months.

Greg didn't usually let on that I claimed his kitchen was

haunted, because in his view that was just a crazy excuse. After all, I might not be an academic, as he said once, but I wasn't an ignorant uneducated person. I had a Masters in statistics and ought to be more rational than most women, not less. He never believed I'd really seen anything. Nobody else had had any funny experiences there, not even his hippie cleaning lady, who believed in astrology and past lives.

You've got to understand, there was nothing intrinsically spooky about Gregor's house. It was the kind of place you see in ads for paint and lawn care; a big white modern Colonial, on a broad tree-lined street in Corinth Heights. Ma would have died for it. Gregor bought it when he got married, and the kitchen had been totally redone the year before his wife left. It was a big room with lots of cupboards and all the top-of-the-line equipment anyone could want: two ovens, microwave, disposal, dishwasher, you name it. It had avocado-green striped-and-flowered wallpaper, and the stove and fridge and cupboards and counters were that same pale sick green. Not my favourite colour, and it was kind of dark in the daytime, because of the low ceiling and the pine trees growing so close. Still, it was just about the last place you'd expect to meet a ghost.

But I did see something. At least I thought I saw something. What I thought I saw was Ilse Spiegelman, Greg's ex-wife. Of course that didn't make any sense, because how could Ilse be a ghost if she wasn't dead? And as far as I know she still isn't: she's alive and well back in Czechoslovakia, or as well as you can be under the present regime, and teaching at her university again.

She was probably much happier there, Greg said. She'd liked his house, but she never cared much for the rest of America. Even after eight years she hadn't really adjusted.

"I blame myself," he told me once. "I didn't think enough about what I was doing, taking a woman away from her country, her family, her career. I only thought of how narrow and restricted Ilse's life there was. I thought of the cold cramped two-room apartment she had to share with her sister and her parents, and how she couldn't afford a warm winter coat or the books and journals she needed for her research. I imagined how happy and grateful she would be here, but I was wrong."

Greg said that naturally he'd expected Ilse would soon learn English. He was born in Europe himself and only came to America when he was ten, but you'd never know it. But Ilse wasn't good at languages, and she never got to the point where she was really comfortable in English, which made a real problem when she started looking for work. Eventually she found a couple of temporary research jobs, and she did some part-time cataloguing for the library; but it wasn't what she wanted or was used to, or what she'd thought she could expect when she married Greg.

After a while Ilse didn't even try to find a job, he said, and she didn't make many friends. She wasn't as adaptable as he'd thought. In fact she turned out to be a very tense, stubborn, high-strung person, and rather selfish. When things didn't go exactly as she liked she became touchy and withdrawn. She started imagining things: slights and insults and intrigues.

For instance, Greg said, Ilse got so she didn't want to go places with him. A concert was possible, or a film, especially if it was in some language she knew. But she didn't like parties. She claimed that people talked fast so she couldn't understand them, and that they didn't want to speak to her anyhow: she was only invited because she was Gregor's wife. Everyone would be happier if she didn't go, she insisted.

But when Ilse stayed home she wasn't happy either, because she imagined Greg was flirting with other women at the party. I could sort of understand how she got that idea. Greg liked women and was comfortable with them. He had a way of standing close to someone attractive and lowering his voice and speaking to her with this little quiet smile. Sometimes he would raise just his left eyebrow. It wasn't deliberate; he couldn't actually move the right one, because of a bicycle accident he'd had years ago; but it was devastating.

The way he talked to women even bothered me a bit at first, though I told myself it didn't mean anything. But it always made Ilse really tense and touchy. Though she must have

known what a gregarious person Greg naturally was, she
started trying to get him to decline invitations. And when he
did persuade her to go to some party, he told me, she followed
him around, with her narrow white hand pinching tight on to
his coat sleeve like a big plastic paper clip. If they got separated
she watched him all the time. And she always wanted to leave
before he did. Well, of course that wasn't much fun for either of
them, so it's no wonder if after a while Greg stopped trying to
persuade her to come along.

When he went out alone, he said, Ilse would always wait up
for him, even though he'd asked her over and over again not to.
Then while she was waiting she'd open a bottle of liqueur,
Amaretto or crème de menthe or something like that, and start
sipping, and by the time he came home she'd be woozy and
argumentative. If Greg told her it worried him to think of her
drinking alone, Ilse got hysterical. "You have drink, at your
party, why should I not have drink?" she shouted. And when
Greg pointed out to her that she had finished nearly a whole
bottle of Kahlua that had been his Christmas present from his
graduate students, she screamed at him and called him a tight-
wad, or whatever the Czech word for that is.

Finally one evening Greg came home at about one-thirty
a.m. It was completely innocent, he told me: he'd been
involved in a discussion about politics and forgotten the time.
At first he thought Ilse had gone to sleep, but she wasn't in the
bedroom, and didn't answer when he called. He was worried,
and went all round the house looking for her. Finally he went
into the kitchen and turned on the light and saw her sitting on
the floor, wedged into the space between the refrigerator and
the wall where the brooms and mops were kept.

Greg said he asked her what she was doing there. I could
hear just how his voice would have sounded: part anxious, part
irritated, part jokey. But Ilse wouldn't answer.

"So what did you do?" I said.

"Nothing," Greg shrugged.

"Nothing?" I repeated. I didn't think he would have lost his
temper, because he never did; only sometimes when he was
disappointed in someone or something he'd give them this kind

of cold tight look. I expected he would have looked at Ilse like that, and then hauled her out of there and helped her upstairs.

"What could I do, darling? I knew she'd been drinking and wanted to make a scene, even though she knew how much I dislike scenes. I went upstairs and got ready for bed, and after I was almost asleep I heard her come in and fall into the other bed. Next morning she didn't apologise or say anything about what had happened, and I thought it would be kinder not to bring it up. But that was when it became clear to me that it wasn't going to work out for Ilse here."

The next time I was alone in Gregor's house I went into the kitchen and looked at the space between the fridge and the wall. It didn't seem wide enough for anyone to sit in. But when I pushed the brooms and mops and vacuum back and tried it myself I discovered that there was just barely enough room. I felt weird in there, like a kid playing hide-and-seek who's been forgotten by the other kids. All I could see was a section of avocado-green cupboard opposite, and a strip of vinyl floor in the yellowish-green swirly seasick pattern that I'd never liked too much. The cleaning rags and the dustpan brushed against my head and neck. I wouldn't have wanted to sit there for any length of time, even if I was a kid. And I thought that anybody who did must have been in a bad way.

I think that was a mistake, trying it out, because now I had a kind of idea of how Ilse Spiegelman must have felt. But then for a while I forgot the whole thing, because Greg asked me to marry him. Up till then he had never even mentioned marriage, and neither had I. I certainly wasn't going to hint around the way he'd said his last live-in girlfriend had, or pressure him like the one before that.

That was the year there was so much excitement in the media about a survey which claimed to prove that college-educated women over thirty had just about no chance of getting married. A couple of times people said to me, Dinah, you're a statistician, aren't you worried? Well, Jesus, of course I was worried, because I was nearly twenty-nine, but I just smiled and said that everybody in my field knew that study was really badly flawed, technically speaking.

By Christmas of that year, though, I'd begun to sense a rising curve of possibility in the relationship. But I waited and kept my cool. Then Greg told me he'd been invited to the Rockefeller Foundation Study Center on Lake Como for a month the next summer. He said he wished I could come with him, but you weren't allowed to bring anyone but a spouse. I didn't make any suggestions. When he told me how luxurious and scenic Bellagio was, I just said Oh really and That's great.

Three days later he brought it up again, and asked me what I'd think of our getting married before he went, because he knew I'd enjoy seeing Italy and he really didn't like the idea of leaving me behind. I didn't shriek with joy and rush into his arms, though that was what I wanted to do; I just smiled and said it sounded like a fairly good idea, as long as he didn't want us to be divorced as soon as we got back, because my poor old Ma couldn't take it.

It was after that that I saw Ilse for the first time. I still had my apartment downtown, but I was spending a lot of time at Greg's, and sleeping over most nights. I got up early one Sunday to make sausages and waffles with maple syrup, because we'd been talking about American country breakfasts a couple of days before, and it turned out he'd never had a good one.

It was a wet dark late-winter morning, and the kitchen windows were streaked with half-frozen rain like transparent glue. When I went into the room the first thing I noticed was what looked like somebody's legs and feet in grey tights and worn black low-heel pumps sticking out between the refrigerator and the wall. I kind of screamed, but nothing came out except a sort of gurgle. Then I took another step and I saw a pale woman in a dark dress sitting wedged in there.

I didn't think of Ilse. If I thought anything, I thought we must have left the back door unlocked and some miserable homeless person or schizo graduate student had got in. I gasped, "Jesus Christ, what the hell!" and backed away and turned on the light.

And then I looked again and nobody was there. All I saw was Greg's black rubber galoshes, left to drip when we'd come in from a film the night before, and his long grey wool scarf hanging from a hook by the dusters. I couldn't see how my brain had assembled these variables into the figure of a woman, but the brain does funny things sometimes.

Later, after I got my breath back, I thought of Greg's story and realised that what I'd seen or imagined was Ilse Spiegelman. I didn't like that because it meant that Greg's ex-wife was on my mind to an extent I hadn't suspected.

I didn't say anything about it. I damn sure wasn't going to tell Greg, who said sometimes that one of the things he loved most about me, besides my naturally pointed breasts, was my well-organised mind. "You're a wonder, Dinah," he used to tell me. "Under those wild black curls, you're as clear-headed as any man I ever met." Like a lot of guys his age, he believed that no matter how much education they got most women never became rational beings and their heads were essentially full of unconnected lightweight ideas, like those little white styrofoam bubbles they pack hi-fi equipment in.

So I didn't say anything to anybody. What I did was, I tried to find out what Ilse had looked like. My idea was that if she was really different from the thing I thought I'd seen, it would prove it was a hallucination. That wouldn't be so great, but it would be better than a ghost.

Greg didn't have any photos of Ilse as far as I knew; at least I couldn't find any around the house. When I asked him what she was like he only said she was a blonde and shorter than me. Then I asked if she was pretty. He looked at me and laughed out loud and said, "Not anywhere near as pretty as you, my lovely little cabbage."

After that I did a sample among his friends. I didn't take it too far; I didn't want people to think I was going into some type of retrospective jealous fit. So I didn't have a significant data base, and when I averaged their statements out all I got was the profile of a medium-sized woman in her early forties, with dirty-blonde hair. Some said it was wavy and others said it was straight. They all said she didn't seem to have much to say, and her accent was hard to understand, but she was attractive, at least to start with. Later on, some of them said, she seemed to kind of let herself go, and towards the end she looked ill a lot of the time.

Greg's department secretary told me Ilse was slim but a little broad in the beam; but that information wasn't much use if you were trying to identify somebody sitting on the floor behind a refrigerator. A couple of people said she looked "foreign", whatever that meant; and a colleague of Greg's said she had a "small sulky hot-looking mouth", but I had to discount that because he was always on the make. It was really aggravating, but that's what you get when you do interviews after a time-lapse, with informants to whom your focus of interest never meant much.

Well, I decided that it could just possibly have been Ilse, but most likely, it was my imagination. That was bad enough, because I'd never been the imaginative type, and I didn't like the idea that I was starting to see things, like one of Ma's superstitious old-lady neighbours.

The thing was, though, I began to feel funny about Greg's kitchen. I didn't like going in there much any more; and I always made sure to switch on the overhead light first, even if it was a bright day. I had the theory that if the light was on I wouldn't think I saw Ilse Spiegelman, and in fact I didn't.

Weeks went by, and my funny feeling about the kitchen should have gone away, but somehow it hung on. So one day I asked Greg casually what he thought of our moving after we were married. We'd been to a cocktail party at my boss's new house up the lake. It had a big fieldstone fireplace and sliding glass doors onto a deck and a really super view. I said I'd love to live in a place like that. I think it was the first time I ever asked Greg to do anything more for me than stop at the store for a bottle of Chardonnay on his way home. Up to then he'd more or less anticipated my every wish.

Well, Greg didn't see the point of it, and from a practical view there was no point. His house was in good condition, and its location was ideal: less than a mile from the University, so that on most days he could walk to his office. He said that for one thing it would be a real drag for both of us driving to town in the kind of weather they have here from December through March. Then he reminded me how much work he'd done on his garden and grounds over the years. Next year his asparagus bed would be bearing for the first time. I wouldn't want to miss that, he said, and laughed and kissed me.

So I let it pass. By that time I'd just about convinced myself that I hadn't seen anything.

Then one day in March I came in after work with two bags of groceries and dropped them on the counter and turned, and Holy Mother of God, there she was again, squeezed in by the refrigerator. It was nearly dark out, and darker inside, but I knew it was the same woman: the hair like frayed rope, the shapeless dress and shiny grey tights and black clunky pumps, scuffed at the toes, sticking out into the room.

She didn't seem to see me. She wasn't looking in my direction anyhow, but down at the seasick-green floor, just sitting there, not moving, as if she were drunk or stunned. It was much worse than the first time. Then I was just surprised and uneasy, the way anyone would be if they found a strange woman in their kitchen, but now I was like really terrified.

I almost couldn't breathe, but somehow I stumbled back and put on the light, and when I looked round she'd disappeared again. But I was sure I'd seen someone, and I was practically sure it had been Ilse. And what was worse, I got the idea that she'd been sitting there on the floor for a long time. Or maybe she was always sitting there, only mostly I couldn't see her.

I can tell you I was in a bad state. I figured I'd seen a ghost, or I was losing my mind. But I didn't feel crazy, I felt normal, except whenever I had to go into the kitchen I panicked. The main idea I had was that I had to get out of that house.

Next day at breakfast I brought up the idea of moving again, but I didn't get anywhere. Greg made all the points he'd made before, and also he mentioned the financial aspects for the first time. It turned out he had no savings to speak of and not much equity in the house. But he had a nine per cent mortgage; he couldn't possibly get that kind of rate again, he said. I was a little surprised that Greg didn't have more net worth, but it made sense when I thought about it. He liked to live well: trips to New York and to conferences all over the world, expensive food and liquor, and a new Volvo every five years.

He assumed the issue was settled, but I didn't want to let it drop. I said I was making enough money to help out, and I had some savings besides; and I knew I'd be happier in a new place. Greg lowered his newspaper for a moment and glanced at me, and for the first time I saw, just for a second, that thin cold look he gave people and things he didn't like.

But then Greg smiled slowly and folded the newspaper and put it down and came over and kissed me and said I mustn't ever worry about money. He wouldn't think of touching my little savings, he said; he had plenty for both of us.

I kissed him back, of course, and felt all warm and loved again, but at the same time just for a moment I remembered something a friend of mine at work had said when I first started going out with Gregor. "He's really a sweet guy until you cross him," she said. "Then, watch out."

In a couple of days I'd more or less forgotten about that look Gregor had flashed at me; but also I realised I'd stuck myself with Ilse's kitchen, and my morale slid way down the chart. I didn't know what the hell to do. If I said anything to anybody they'd think I was nuts, and maybe they'd be right. Maybe I ought to just drive up to the state hospital and turn myself in. I thought of telling Ma; she believed in ghosts, and a couple of her friends had seen them; but those were always ghosts of the dead.

Then I remembered something I read in an anthropology book in college. There were sorcerers in Mexico and Central America, it said, that could project an image of themselves to anywhere they chose. The author hadn't seen it done herself, but all the locals were convinced it could happen. Well, I thought, it could be. There were some weird things in the world. Maybe Ilse Spiegelman was some kind of Czechoslovakian witch, and if she wanted to keep me from marrying Greg and moving into her house and her kitchen she might do it that way. The distance wouldn't faze her—for that kind of project two thousand miles was the same as two yards.

If I told Ma, she'd probably say I should go to a priest and ask for an exorcism. But I knew if I did that he'd give me a lot of grief for not having been to confession for three years, and living in sin with Greg. And besides, how the hell could I ask Greg to have his kitchen exorcised? I considered trying to sneak a priest into the house when Greg was at the University, but I decided it was too risky.

So I told myself okay, let's assume it was Ilse, trying to scare me off. Well, I wouldn't let her. The next time she appeared I'd make the sign of the cross and tell her to get the hell out and leave me alone. I'd tell her, Listen, sister, you had your chance with Greg, now it's my turn.

After that, instead of praying I wouldn't see Ilse I actually tried to catch her at it. For a couple of weeks, whenever Greg went out, I set my jaw and said a Hail Mary and marched into the room. I never saw a damn thing. Then, late one evening after I'd rinsed our coffee mugs in the sink and turned out the light and was leaving the kitchen, I saw her again, sitting shadowy by the refrigerator. I wasn't expecting her, so I screamed out, "Jesus Christ!"

Greg had gone up to bed already, and he heard me and called out. "What's the matter, darling?" I was frightened and confused, and I called back, "Nothing, I just cut my hand on the breadknife." Then I switched on the light, and of course nobody was there.

I thought, oh Holy God. That's what she wanted. She's never going to appear when I'm ready for her; she wants to surprise me, and hurt me. And now she had, because of course I had to get out the breadknife then and saw a hole in my hand to show Greg.

By that time I was kind of desperate. I didn't want to see Ilse when I wasn't expecting her, but I couldn't remember her the whole time, and I was developing a full-blown phobia about the kitchen. So I came right out and told Greg that there were things I didn't like about his house.

He was very sweet and sympathetic. He put his arms round

me and kissed one of his favourite places—the back of my neck just above the left shoulder, where I have a circle of freckles. Then he asked me to tell him what it was I didn't like, and maybe it could be fixed. "I want you to be perfectly happy here, Dinah, my love," he said.

Well, I told him there were three things. I said I'd like the downstairs bathroom repapered, because I'd never cared for goldfish, they had such stupid expressions; and I'd like a deck by the dining room so that we could eat outdoors in the summer. "All right, little woman; if it's what you want, why not?" Greg said, holding me and stroking me.

Then I said I'd also like a new cabinet built in the kitchen, between the refrigerator and the wall. That was the only thing I really cared about, because I thought if there weren't any space there Ilse couldn't come and sit in it; and that was the only thing Greg made any objection to. If we put a cabinet there, he said, where would I keep my cleaning equipment? Well, I told him I'd move it out to the back entry. No, I didn't think that would be inconvenient, I said; anyhow I'd always thought a kitchen looked messy when there were old brooms and rags hanging around. I was terrified that he'd suggest building a broom cupboard, which would have been worse that nothing, but luckily it didn't occur to him.

"You want your kitchen just like your graphs, all squared away," Greg said. "All right, darling." And he laughed. He used to tease me sometimes about my passion for order.

Greg promised to have the improvements made before the wedding, and he carried through. The day the new cabinet was installed I went in the kitchen the minute I got home, Just as I'd planned, it completely filled the space where Ilse had sat. There was a drawer under the counter, and a shelf under that; nobody could possibly get in there. I stooped down and looked to make sure, and then I put in a couple of baking tins and some bags of paper cups and plates.

Blessed Mother of God, I've done it, I thought, and I was really happy. I thought how generous and brilliant and goodlooking Greg was, and how smart I was, and how we were going to Montreal for our honeymoon and then in July to

Europe. I'd bought a beautiful wedding dress: heavy ecru silk with a sexy low square neck and yards of lace.

Well, it got to be two weeks before the wedding. I was so high I was even beginning to be a little sorry for Ilse. I thought how she was probably back in those two nasty little rooms again with her family. I knew what that was like, from the years I spent with my mother and sisters in the trailer camp, with cold sour air leaking through the window frames and the kitchen faucet spitting rust and the neighbours playing the radio or screaming at each other all night. No wonder she was jealous.

Then the term was nearly over, and Gregor's department was giving a reception. He called me that Friday afternoon from his office to say they were short of paper plates and could I drop some by after work? So when I got home I went into the kitchen and opened the new cabinet by the refrigerator.

It was a good thing I was alone, because I let out a real burglar-alarm screech. There was Ilse Spiegelman, just like before, only now she was shrunken down into some kind of horrible little dwarf about two and a half feet high. I didn't even try the light, I just howled and stumbled out into the hall.

It took me nearly thirty-five minutes to get up my nerve to go back into the kitchen—where of course Ilse wasn't anymore, or at least I couldn't see her—and put my hand into the cabinet, maybe right through her, and take out those paper plates that Gregor was waiting for.

After that I knew I was beaten. If Ilse could shrink herself like that she could appear any size, and anywhere she goddamn wanted to. Maybe she'd get into the shelves of my bedroom closet next, or maybe some day when I took the lid off the top of my sugar bowl she'd be in there, all squnched up.

I was really depressed and sort of desperate. But then I thought that maybe Ilse wouldn't mind my living with Gregor as long as we weren't married. After all, she hadn't even appeared until after we got engaged. So that evening I told Gregor I didn't think I could go through with it. I said I was terrified of the responsibility of marriage. At first he was wonderful. He held me and kissed me and petted me and said that was perfectly natural: marriage *was* frightening. And of course, he added, I was probably apprehensive about becoming a department chairman's wife.

"Yeah, that's right," I said, though it hadn't occurred to me.

He understood, Greg said. I might not think I was up to the job, but he would help me; and if anybody tried to make me feel incompetent or not worthy of him, he would give them hell.

When I kept on insisting that I didn't want to get married, Greg asked what had changed my mind. I was still afraid to tell him about Ilse; I didn't want him to think I'd gone off the deep end. So I came up with the kind of stuff you read everywhere these days about marriage being an outmoded patriarchal contract, and how the idea of owning another human being was fascist. I probably didn't make a very good presentation, because I didn't believe in what I was saying. Anyhow, Greg didn't buy it.

"You surprise me, Dinah," he said, raising his left eyebrow. "I've never heard you talk like this before. Who's been brain-washing you, I wonder?"

Well, I swore nobody had. I babbled on, saying I loved him so much, but I was frightened, and why couldn't we just go on the way we were? After all, I said, he'd been with other women and he hadn't wanted to marry them. That was a mistake. Greg's face changed, and he gave me that bad look again. Then he dropped his arm and sort of pushed me aside.

"What is this?" he said, laughing in an unfriendly way. "The revenge of the bimbos?"

"Huh?" I was completely at a loss; but finally I got what he meant. There were maybe four or five women in town who had wanted to marry Greg, and some of them were still pretty hurt and angry, according to rumour. He meant, was I doing it for them?

"Jesus no, I don't owe these woman anything," I said. "They're none of them my friends." Then he seemed convinced and quieted down some.

But I still said I didn't want to get married. Greg tried to reassure me some more, but I could see he was getting impatient. Then he asked if I realised that if I broke off our engagement it would embarrass him in front of everyone and make him a local joke. He'd already had to take some kidding from friends because he'd sworn so often that he was never going to marry again. And there were quite a few people on campus who weren't Greg's friends: people who envied his success and would have loved for him to mess up somehow.

I felt awful about that, and I said he could blame it all on me: he could tell everybody I was being silly and neurotic. But Greg explained that this would be almost as bad, because people would think less of him for having a relationship with someone like that.

Then he sat back and looked at me in that hard considering way, as if I was a student who'd plagiarised a paper or some article he didn't approve of, and finally he said slowly, "There's something else behind this, Dinah. And I can take a guess at what it is."

What it turned out to be was, Gregor thought I must have got involved with somebody else, probably some scruffy guy nearer my own age, only I was afraid to admit it. I swore there wasn't anybody. I kept saying I loved him, that he was the only person I loved but he didn't seem to hear me any more. He pushed his face close up to mine so it filled my whole visual field and looked all distorted, like something you see in the previews of a horror film for a split second: not long enough to be sure what it is, but long enough to know it's something terrible.

"All right, who is it, you bitch? Who?" he said, and when I kept saying "Nobody," he took hold of me and shook me as if I were a bottle of ketchup and he could shake out some man's name, only there wasn't any name.

When Greg let go, and I could stop trembling and crying, I told him the truth, only he didn't believe me. Instead, he started going over all the other explanations he'd thought up. Gradually things got really strange and scary. Greg was cursing in this tight hard voice and saying that if I really thought I'd seen Ilse sitting in the kitchen cabinet I must be crazy; and I was weeping. I said that if I were going crazy it would be wicked of me to marry him and ruin his life, and he said I had already done that.

It went on like that all weekend. We hardly slept, and finally I got so miserable and mixed-up and exhausted that I started agreeing with everything Greg said. That I had probably been brainwashed by feminists, and that I was sometimes attracted to other men; and that I was basically irrational, deceptive, cowardly, neurotic, and unconsciously envious of Greg because he was a superior person and I was nobody to speak of. The weird thing was that I didn't just agree to all this; in the state I was in by then, I believed whatever he said.

Then on Monday morning we were in the kitchen pretending to have breakfast. I was really in bad shape; I hadn't had a bath or done anything about my hair for two days, and over my nightgown I had on an old red terrycloth bathrobe with coffee stains. I had got to the point where I didn't care any more if I was crazy or not. I thought that if Ilse Spiegelman meant to haunt me for the rest of my life it couldn't be worse than this.

So when Greg came downstairs I told him I wanted to forget the whole thing and go ahead with the wedding. I put two pieces of Pepperidge Farm raisin toast on his plate, and he looked at them. And then he looked at me, and I thought that he didn't want to marry me any more, and also he didn't want to live with me.

I was right, too. Later that morning Greg called my office and said that he thought it would be best if we didn't see each other or speak to each other again. So he was putting all my "debris" out in the back entry, and would I please collect it before six p.m.?

Well, after work I went round. I could tell how upset and furious Greg still was by the way he'd pitched everything out the kitchen door. My lavender nightgown looked as if it had been strangled, and there was raisin granola spilled everywhere; and a bottle of conditioner that he hadn't bothered to close had leaked over everything. It was a total mess. All the time I was picking it up I was crying and carrying on, because I still thought I was in love with Greg and that everything that had happened was my fault. And I couldn't help it, I didn't want to, but I looked through the glass of the kitchen door to see if Ilse was there. Maybe she would be smiling now, I thought, or even laughing. The cabinet door was hanging open, but it was empty.

I piled everything into the car and drove to my apartment; thank God, the lease still had three weeks to run. But the place looked awful. I'd hardly been there for weeks, and there was dust everywhere and the windows were grimed over with soot. I managed to unload the car and carry everything upstairs, and dumped a heap of clothes sticky with conditioner and granola into the bathtub, and knelt down to turn on the water.

But then it really hit me. I felt so defeated and exhausted and crazy and miserable that I slid down onto the dirty yellow vinyl and sat there in a heap between the tub and the toilet. I felt like killing myself, but I didn't have enough energy to move. But I thought maybe in a little while I could crawl across the floor and put my head in the gas oven.

Then all of a sudden I thought that I was sitting on the floor in a cramped space, just like Ilse. She's finally reduced me to her own miserable condition.

But maybe she wasn't the only one who had done that, I thought. And for the first time I wondered if Greg had ever said the kind of things to Ilse he'd been saying to me all weekend, till she blamed herself for everything and was totally wiped out and beaten down. I remembered how his face had turned into a horror-film preview, and suddenly I felt kind of lucky to have got out of his house. I thought that even if he changed his mind now and took me back, and was as charming and affectionate as before, I would always remember this weekend and wonder if it would happen again, and I would have to sort of tiptoe round him the rest of my life.

Maybe I was wrong to believe Ilse had been trying to stop me marrying Greg, I thought. Maybe she had been trying to warn me.

I still don't know for sure if that's right. I'd like to go to

Czechoslovakia and look her up and ask her. But I don't see how I can, now I've got a husband and a baby.

Gregor's never married again; but he's been with a lot of different women since we separated. I wonder sometimes if any of them have seen Ilse. But maybe she hasn't had to appear, because none of his relationships seem to last very long.

tobias wolff

Sanity

It isn't easy to get from San Diego to Portola State Hospital unless you have a car, or a breakdown. That's what hapened to April's father and they got him out there in no time at all. The trip took longer for April and her stepmother; they had to catch three different buses, walk up a long road from Pendleton Boulevard to the hospital grounds, then walk back again when the visit was over. There were plenty of cars on the road, but nobody stopped to offer a lift. April didn't blame them. They probably figured she and Claire were patients—fruitcakes, her dad called them—out for a stroll. That's what she would have thought, coming upon the two of them out here, on foot and unaccountable. she would have taken one look and kept going.

Claire was tall and erect. She was wearing her grey business suit and high heels and a wide-brimmed black hat. She carried herself a little stiffly because of the heels but kept up a purposeful, dignified pace. "Ship of State"—that was what April's father called Claire when she felt summoned to a demonstration of steadiness and resolve. April followed along in loose order. She stopped now and then to catch her breath and let some distance open up between herself and Claire, then hurried to close that distance. April was a short muscular girl with a mannish stride. She was scowling in the hazy August light. Her hands were rough. She had on a sleeveless dress, yellow with black flowers, that she knew to be ugly and wore anyway because it made Claire intensely aware of her.

Cars kept going by, the tyres making a wet sound on the hot asphalt. April's father had sold the Buick for almost nothing a few days before he went into the hospital, and Claire hadn't even looked at anything else. She was saving her money for a trip to Boston before April's father came home.

Claire had been quiet through most of the visit, quiet and edgy, and now that it was over she did not try to hide her relief. She wanted to talk. She said that the doctor they'd spoken with reminded her of Walt Darsh, her husband during the last ice age. That was how she located whatever had happened to her in the past—"during the last ice age". April knew she wanted to be told that she still looked good, and it wouldn't have been a lie to say so, but April never did.

April had heard about Walt Darsh before, his faithlessness and cruelty. The stories Claire told were interesting, but they left April troubled and quickened; strange to herself. As soon as Claire got started, April said, "If he was so bad, how come you married him?"

Claire didn't answer right away. She walked more slowly, and inclined her long neck at a meditative angle. She gave every sign of being occupied with a new and demanding question. After a time she turned her head and looked at April, then looked away again. "Sex," she said.

April could see the glitter of windshields in the distance. There was a bench at the bus stop; when they got there she was going to lie down and close her eyes and pretend to sleep.

"It's hard to explain," Claire said, cautiously, as if April had pressed her. "It wasn't his looks, Darsh isn't really what you'd call handsome. He has a sly, pointy kind of face . . . like a fox. You know what I mean? It isn't just the shape, it's the way he watches you, always grinning a little, like he's got the goods on you." Claire stopped in the shade of a tree. She took off her hat, smoothed back her hair, curled some loose strands behind her ears, then put her hat back on and set it just so across her forehead. She found a Kleenex in her purse and dabbed the corner of one eye where a thin line of mascara had run. Claire had the gift, mysterious to April, of knowing what she looked like even without a mirror. April's face was always a surprise to her, always somehow different than she'd imagined it.

"Of course, that can be attractive, too," Claire said, "being looked at in that way. Most of the time it's annoying, but not always. With Darsh it was attractive. So I suppose you could say that it *was* his looks, in the literal sense of looks. If you see the distinction."

April saw the distinction, also Claire's pleasure in having made it. She was unhappy with this line of talk. But she couldn't do anything about it, because it was her own fault that Claire believed she was ripe for unrestrained discussion of these matters. Over the last few months Claire had decided that April was sleeping with Stuart, the boy she went out with. This was not the case. Stuart dropped hints now and then in his polite, witty, hopeless way, but he wasn't serious and April wasn't interested. She hadn't told Claire the truth because in the beginning it gave her satisfaction to be seen as a woman of experience. Claire was a snob about knowing the ways of the world; it pleased April to crowd her turf a little. Claire never asked anything anyway, she just assumed, and once the assumption took hold there was no way to straighten things out.

The brim of Claire's hat waved up and down. She seemed to be having an idea she agreed with. "Looks are part of it," she said, "definitely part of it. But not the whole story. It never is, with sex, is it? Just one thing. Like technique, for instance." Claire turned and started down the road again, head still pensively bent. April could feel a lecture coming. Claire taught sociology at the same junior college where April's father used to teach history, and like him she was quick to mount the podium.

"People write about technique," she said, "as if it's the whole ball game, which is a complete joke. You know who's really getting off on technique? Book publishers, that's who. Because they can turn it into a commodity. They can merchandise it as know-how, like travelling in Mexico or building a redwood deck. The only problem is, it doesn't work. You know why? It turns sex into a literary experience."

April laughed.

"I'm serious," Claire said. "You can tell right away that it's coming out of some book. You start seeing yourself in one of those little squiggly drawings, with your zones all marked out and some earnest little cartoon guy working his way through them, being really considerate."

Claire stopped again and gazed out over the fields that lined the road, one hand resting in a friendly way on top of a fence post. Back in the old days, according to April's father, the fruitcakes used to raise things in these fields. Now they were overgrown with scrub pine and tall yellow grass. Insects shrilled loudly. April felt a strong hidden rhythm in the sound.

"That's another reason those books are worthless," Claire said. "They're all about sharing, being tender, anticipating your partner's needs, etcetera etcetera. It's like Sunday school in bed. I'm not kidding, April, that's what it's all about, all this technique stuff. It's Victorian. It's trying to put clothes on monkeys. You know what I mean?"

"I guess," April said. Her voice came out dry, almost a croak.

"We're talking about a very basic transaction," Claire said. "A lot more basic than lending money to a friend. Think about it. Lending is a highly evolved activity. Other species don't do it, only us. Just look at all the things that go into lending money. Trust. Generosity. Imagining yourself in the other person's place. It's incredibly advanced, incredibly civilised. I'm all for it. My point is, sex comes from another place. Sex isn't civilised. It isn't about giving. It's about taking."

A pick-up truck went past. April looked after it, then back at Claire, who was still staring out over the field. April saw the line of her profile in the shadow of the hat, saw how dry and cool her skin was, the composure of her smile. April saw these things and felt her own sticky, worried, incomplete condition. "We ought to get going," she said.

"To tell the truth," Claire said, "that was one of the things that attracted me to Darsh. He was a taker. Totally selfish, totally out to please himself. That gave him a certain heat. A certain power. The libbers would kill me for saying this, but it's true. Did I ever tell you about our honeymoon?"

"No." April made her voice flat and grudging, though she was curious.

"Or the maid thing? Did I ever tell you about Darsh's maid thing?"

"No," April said again. "What about the honeymoon?"

Claire said. "That's a long story. I'll tell you about the maid thing."

"You don't have to tell me anything," April said.

Claire went on smiling to herself. "Back when Darsh was a kid his mother took him on a trip to Europe. The grand tour. He was 13, 14 at the time—that age. By the time they got to Amsterdam he was sick of museums, he never wanted to see another painting in his life. That's the trouble with pushing culture at children, they end up hating it. It's better to let them come to it on their own, don't you think?"

April shrugged.

"Take Jane Austen, for example. They were throwing Jane Austen at me when I was in the eighth grade. *Pride and Prejudice*. Of course I absolutely loathed it, because I couldn't see what was really going on, all the sexual energy behind the manners. I hadn't *lived*. You have to have some life under your belt before you can make any sense of a book like that.

"Anyway, when they got to Amsterdam, Darsh dug in his heels. He wouldn't budge. He stayed in the hotel room all day, reading mysteries and ordering stuff from room service, while his mother went out and looked at paintings. One afternoon a maid came up to the room to polish the chandelier. She had a stepladder, and from where Darsh was sitting he couldn't help seeing up her dress. All the way up, okay? And she knew it. He knew she knew, because after a while he didn't even try to hide it, he just stared. She didn't say a word. Not one. She took her sweet time up there, polishing every pendant, cool as a cucumber. Darsh said it went on for a couple of hours, which probably means an hour, which is a pretty long time, if you think about it."

"Then what happened?"

"Nothing. Nothing happened. That's the whole point, April. If something had happened it would have broken the spell. It would have let all that incredible energy out. But it stayed locked in. It's always there, boiling away at this insane

14-year old level, just waiting to explode. It's one of Darsh's real hot spots. He bought me the whole outfit, in fact he probably still has it—you know, frilly white blouse, black nylons with all the little snaps."

"He made you wear that? And stand on things?"

April saw Claire freeze at her words, as if she had said something hurtful and low. Claire straightened up and slowly started walking again. April hung back, then followed a few steps behind until Claire waited for her to catch up. After a time Claire said, "No, dear. He didn't make me do anything. It's exciting when somebody wants something that much, it turns you to butter. You should have seen the way he looked at me. Pure hunger, like he wanted to eat me alive. But innocent too.

"Maybe it sounds cheap, but I liked it. It's hard to describe."

Claire was quiet then, and so was April. She did not feel any need for description. She thought she could imagine the look Darsh had given Claire, in fact she could see it perfectly, though no one had ever looked at her that way. Definitely not Stuart. He never would, either, he was too respectful and refined. She felt safe with him. Safe and sleepy. Nobody like Stuart would ever make her careless and willing as Darsh did through the stories Claire told about him, even the worst stories. It seemed to April that she already knew Darsh, and that he knew her—as if he had sensed her at the margin of the stories, and was conscious of her interest. She understood that she would be at risk if she ever met anyone like him, as one day she knew she must.

They were almost at the road. April stopped and looked back but the hospital buildings were out of sight now, behind the brow of the hill. She turned and walked on. She had one more of these trips to make, one more Sunday. The weekend after that her father would be coming home. He had the doctors eating out of his hand with that amused, I-don't-know-what-came-over-me act. It worked because he believed it himself. He'd been theatrically calm all through their visit. He sat by the window in an easy chair, feet propped up on the ottoman, a newspaper across his lap. He was wearing slippers and a cardigan sweater. All he needed was a pipe. He seemed fine, the very picture of health, but that was all it was: a picture. At home he never read the paper. He didn't sit down much, either. The last time April saw him, six days earlier, he was under restraint in their landlord's apartment, where he had gone to complain about the shower. He'd been kicking and yelling. His glasses were hanging from one ear. He was shouting at her to call the police, and one of the policemen holding him down was laughing helplessly.

He hadn't crashed yet. He was still flying, April had seen it in his eyes behind the lithium or whatever they were giving him, and she was sure that Claire had seen it too. Claire didn't actually say anything, but April had been through this with Ellen, her first stepmother, and she'd developed an instinct. She was afraid that Claire had had enough, that she wasn't going to come back from Boston, or that if she did come back it wouldn't be to live with them. Not that Claire was planning any of this. It wouldn't happen that way, it would just happen. April didn't want it to, especially not now. She needed another year. Not even a year—10 months, until she finished school and got into college somewhere. If she could cross that line she was sure she could handle whatever came after.

She didn't want Claire to go. Claire had her ways, but she had been good to April, especially in the beginning, when April was always finding fault with her. She'd put up with it. She'd been patient, and let April come to her in her own time. April used to lean against her when they were sitting on the couch, and Claire would give and press back at the same time. They could sit for hours like that, reading. Claire thought about things. She had talked to April, honestly but with a certain decorum. Now the decorum was gone. Ever since she got the idea that April had lost her virginity, Claire had withdrawn the protections of ceremony and tact, as she would soon withdraw the protection of her own self.

There was no way to change things back. And even if there were, even if by saying, "I'm a virgin," she could turn Claire into some kind of perfect mother, April wouldn't do it. It would sound ridiculous, untrue. And it wasn't true, except as a fact about her body. But April did not see virginity as residing in the body. To her it was a quality of the spirit, and something you could only surrender in the spirit. She had done this; she didn't know exactly when or how, but she knew she had done this and she did not regret it. She did not want to be a virgin and she would not pretend to be one, not for anything. When she thought of a virgin she saw somone half-naked, with dumb trusting eyes and flowers woven into her hair, a clearing in the jungle, and in the clearing an altar.

They'd missed their bus. Because it was Sunday they had a long wait until the next one. Claire settled on the bench and started reading a book. April had forgotten hers. She sat with Claire for a while, then got up and paced the street when Claire's serenity became intolerable. She walked with her arms crossed and her head bent forward, frowning, scuffing her shoes. Cars rushed past, each in its own blare of music, a big sailboat on a trailer, a long slow convoy of military trucks, soldiers swaying in the back. The air was blue with exhaust. April, passing a tyre store, looked at the window and saw herself. She squared her shoulders and dropped her arms to her sides, and kept them there by an effort of will as she walked further up the boulevard to where a line of plastic pennants fluttered over a car lot. A man in a creamy suit was standing in the showroom window, watching the traffic. He had high cheekbones, black hair combed straight back from his forehead, a big clean blade of a nose. He looked like a gambler, or maybe a hit man. April knew he was aware of her but he never bothered to look in her direction. She wandered among the cars, all Toyotas, then went back to the bus stop and slumped down on the bench.

"I'm bored," she said.

Claire didn't answer.

"Aren't you bored?"

"Not especially," Claire said. "The bus should be here pretty soon."

"Sure, in about two weeks." April stuck her legs out and

knocked the sides of her shoes together. "Let's take a walk," she said.

"I'm all walked out. But you go ahead. Just don't get too far away."

"Not *alone*, Claire, I didn't mean alone. Come on, this is boring." April hated that sound of her voice and she could see that Claire didn't like it either. Claire closed her book. She sat without moving, then said, coldly, "I guess I don't have any choice."

April rocked to her feet. She moved a little way up the sidewalk and waited as Claire put the book in her purse, stood, ran her hands down the front of her skirt, then came slowly toward her.

"We'll just stretch our legs," April said. She kept chattering until they reached the car lot, where she left the sidewalk and began circling a red Celica convertible.

"I thought you wanted to walk," Claire said.

"Right, just a minute," April said. Then the side door of the showroom swung open and the man in the suit came out. At first he seemed not to know they were there. He knelt beside a station wagon and wrote something down on a clipboard. He got up and peered at the sticker on the windshield and wrote something else down. Only then did he take any notice of them. He looked their way and after he'd had a good long look he told them to let him know if they needed anything. His voice had a studied, almost insolent lack of concern.

"We're just waiting for a bus," Claire said.

"How does this car stack up against the RX-7?" April asked.

"You surely jest." He made his way toward them through the cars. "I could sell against Mazda any day of the week. If I were selling."

April said. "You're not a salesman?"

He stopped in front of the Celica. "We don't have salesmen here. We just collect money and try to keep the crowds friendly."

Claire laughed. She said, "April."

"That's a year old," he said. "Got it in this morning on a

repossession. It'll be gone this time tomorrow. Look at the odometer, sweet pea. What does the odometer say?"

April opened the door and leaned inside. "Four thousand," she said. She sat in the driver's seat and worked the gearshift.

"Exactly. Four K. Still on its first tank of gas."

"Little old lady owned it, right?" Claire said.

He looked at her for a time before answering. "Little old Marine. Got shipped out and didn't keep up his payments. I'll get the keys."

"We're just—"

"I know you're waiting for a bus. So kill some time."

April got out of the car but left the door open. "Claire, you have to try this seat," she said.

"We should go," Claire said.

"Claire, you just have to. Come on," April said. "Come on, Claire."

The man walked over to the open door and held out his hand. "Madame," he said. Claire stood her ground. "Claire, *get in*," April said. She had never spoken to Claire in this way, and did not know what she would do.

Claire walked up to the car. "We really should go," she said. She sat sideways on the seat, then swung her legs inside, all in one motion. She nodded at the man and he closed the door. "Yes," he said, "just as I thought." He walked to the front of the car. "Exactly as I thought. The designer was a close friend of yours. This car was obviously built with you in mind."

"You look great," April said. It was true, and she could see that Claire was in possession of that truth. The knowledge was in the set of her mouth, the way her hands came to rest on the wheel.

"There's something missing," the man said. He studied her. "Sunglasses," he said. "A beautiful woman in a convertible has to be wearing sunglasses."

"Put on your sunglasses," April said.

janice galloway

Frostbite

Christ it was cold.

And only one glove as usual. The bare hand in the pocket, sweaty against the change counted out for the fare; the other inside the remaining glove, cramped stiff round the handle of the fiddle case. Freezing. Her feet were solid too, just a oneness of dead cold inside her boots in place of anything five-toed or familiar. She stamped them hard for spite, waiting and watching for the fingers of light smudging through the dark, the bus feeling its way up the other side of the hill. The last two had been full and driven straight on. No point getting angry. That was just the way of it.

Nothing yet.

Cloud came out of her mouth and she looked up. There on the other side of the road was a spire. Frame of royal blue, frazzled through with sodium orange, and the spire in the middle, lit from beneath by a dozen calendar windows: people working late. There was a hollow triangle of light above the tip; a clear opening in the sky where she could see the snow flurry and settle on the stone like white ivy. The University.

This was the best of the place now—the look of it. Still able to catch her out. As for the rest, it had not been what she had hoped. Her own fault, of course, expecting too much as usual. They said as much beforehand, over and over: it's no a job though, music willny keep you, it's no for the likes of you—cursing the teacher who had put the daft idea into her head in the first place. Still, she went, and she found they were right and they were not right. It wasn't her *likes* that bothered them, not that at all. Something much simpler. It was her excitement; all that gauche intensity about the thing. Total strangers wondered loudly who she was trying to impress. There was more than the music to learn: a whole series of bitter little lessons she never expected. It was hard, but she managed. She learned to keep her ideas in check and her mouth shut, to carry her stifled love without whining much. But on nights like this, after compulsory practice that was all promise and no joy, cold and tired and waiting for a hypothetical bus, it was heavy and hard to bear. Even with her face to the sentimental spire, she wondered who it was she was trying to fool.

Low-geared growling turned her to the hill again. This time the effort paid off. Not one but two—Jesus wasn't it always the way—sets of headlamps were dipping over the brow, coming on through the fuzzy evening smirr. She bounced the coins in her ungloved hand and watched as they nosed cautiously down through the slush. Then there was something else. A shape. A man lumping up and over the top of the hill, flapping after the buses. One was away already, had overtaken and gone ahead to let the other make the pick-up. She stood while it braked and sat shivering at the top, one foot on the platform to keep the driver and let the wee man catch up. The windows were yellow behind the steam. She looked to see if he was nearer and he stumbled, slittered to the gutter, fell. The driver revved the engine. The man lay on, not moving in the gutter like an old newspaper. The driver drew her a look. She shrugged, embarrassed. The bus began sliding out from under her foot. Too late already. There was nothing else for it. She settled the case in a drift at the side of the pole and turned and made a start, picking carefully up the hill towards the ragged shape still lying near the gutter. An arm flicked out. She came nearer as he struggled onto his hands and knees, trying to stand. Then he crashed down again on the thin projections of his backside and groaned, knees angled up, fingers clutching at his brow in a pantomime of despair. By the time she reached him he was bawling like a wean. She could see blood congealed, red jam squeezing between the fingers. The line of his jaw was grey.

OK?
The man said nothing. Just kept sobbing away. He was a fair age too.
OK eh? What happened to you, grandad?

She had never called anybody grandad in her life. And that voice. Like a primary teacher or something. She started to blush. Maybe she should get him onto his feet instead. Touch would calm him down and he might stop greeting to concentrate. She looked about first to check if there was another witness, hoping for a man. A man would be shamed by her struggling on her own and come and do the thing for her, leave her clucking on the sidelines while he took over. But there was no one and she knew she had called the thing upon herself anyway. Fools rushed in right enough.
An acrid smell of drink, wool and clogged skin rose as she bent towards him, and she saw the knuckles scraped raw, the silted nails. Closing her eyes, she linked his arm and started pulling, hoping for the best. They must look ridiculous.
C'mon then, lets get you up. Need to get up. Catch your death sitting in the wet like this. Come on, up.

He acquiesced, child-like, letting himself be hauled inelegantly straight before he finished the rest for himself. He backed onto a low wall and waited while he caught his breath. O thanks hen, between wheezes, words vapourising in the cold. Am that ashamed, all no be a minute but am that ashamed. All be fine in a minute. Am OK hen.

He didn't look OK. He looked lilac and the sodium glare didn't do him any favours. He puffed on about being fine and ashamed while she foraged in her pocket for a paper hanky to pat at the bloody jelly on his temple, the sticky threads stringing across to his nose. She thought better of it and gave it to him instead—something to do, shut him up for a minute, maybe. But neither the idea nor the mopping up worked too well. His hand stopped at his brow only as long as she held it there. When he saw what it produced the whine started again. O my god hen, o hen see, o look at that, as he dabbed and looked, dabbed and looked.

You're fine, fine. Just a wee bit surprised, that's all. Take your time and just relax OK? Relax. Where is it you're going anyway? He kept patting and looked at her. Very pale eyes, coated like a crocodiles, the sockets over-big.

O he'll be that angry hen. He will and am that ashamed. Am a stupit old fool a am. Nothing but a stupit old man. The pale eyes threatened to leak. Who? Who'll be angry? The trick was to keep him talking and standing up. Every time he stumbled, he repeated what he'd just said. Between repetitions, she found he had been due at his son's house, due at a particular time and he was late. They were supposed to be going somewhere. It sounded like a pub. They were to set off from the son's house and he was chasing the bus because he was already late did she see? She tried to.

Och he'll not be mad. Just tell him you were running for the bus and you fell. How will that get him angry? You'll be fine. He wasn't content yet. The specs but. A broke the specs hen.

There was a lull. She looked about the tarmac and the pavement. There weren't any specs. Then his hand was into his pocket, fumbling out three pieces of plastic and glass: See? She broke ma specs.

She. He said *she*; *she* broke the specs. Right enough, that couldn't have happened just now. There had to be more to it, and she knew already she didn't want to hear it. All she had wanted was to make sure he was all right, get him on his feet and back on his way. But this was what she was getting and it was difficult to get out of now. It was her that had started it, her choice to come up that hill. This was part of it now.

Who broke your specs?

She knew it had to happen and it did. He started to cry. He howled for a good minute or so while she cursed silently and patted clumsily at his sleeve, shooshing. He caught enough breath to hiccup out some more: It's ma own fault hen. It was a bad woman, a bad woman. She hit me hen, o she killed me. She had to smile. The exaggeration wasn't just daft, it was reassuring too. He couldn't see her anyway.

Still, even as she told him he was fine, she knew there was more coming she wasn't going to like. The story. A man's story about what he would call a *bad woman*, and he would tell it as though she wasn't a woman herself, as if she shared his terms. As though his were the only terms. And she wouldn't be expected to argue—just stand and listen. The smiling didn't last long. He told her about a pub, having a drink, then a bad woman, something about a bad woman but he hadn't known it at the time, and as they were leaving the pub together, going out the door, she hit him. Knocked him down in the street, hard, so it broke his specs. When he reached that part he gazed down at the bits he held in his hand, taking in the fact with a deep sigh that exhaled as cursing and swearing. He whooered and bitched till he was unsteady on his legs again then started whining. He was a stupit old fool and a silly old man, should never have had anything to do with the bad woman. Bad bad bitchahell. Then there were more tears.

She hadn't reacted once. And maybe it was worth it. He seemed steadier ready to make off again for the stop. She let him walk, moving slowly alongside to keep him straight while he muttered and sobbed about himself. She knew better than to ask but she wondered, step by step, steering him downhill. She wanted to know about the woman. What had he said to make her do that? Was that when he had been cut—where the blood had come from? It must have happened right enough: he would hardly make a thing like that up. But it was hard to imagine this sorry, snivelling wee man provoking it, being pushy or lewd-mouthed. It was in another place though, with another woman altogether. He could have been different. And he must have done something. Unless of course there really were such bad women that went about hitting old men for nothing. What the hell was a *bad woman* anyhow—was it a prostitute he meant? The corner of her eye caught his face, the mottle purple skin under grey veins and a big dreep at the end of his nose. The very idea turned her stomach. Yet she couldn't stop her chest being sore for the stranger: he seemed so beaten, so genuinely surprised by what had hit him not just once but twice that day. He was still muttering when they reached the stop: broke ma specs, cow. She felt her jaw sore with remembering to be quiet. Shhh.

Shhh, forget about her eh? She's away now, forget about it. Let's just get you to your boy's place. Get you on the bus. What else could she do?

Canny be up to them hen. She realised this was a confidence. Advice. Canny be up to them. A bad lot.

Aye, a lot of it about. What bus is it you get?

Aye, don't you worry. Get the bus. All be fine in a minute, get the bus.

There was no point in keeping asking, best just to wait with him. The right bus would come and he would recognise it instinctively. Fair enough. Holding some of the weight, she kept her arm under his: the wet frosting on his sleeve burned the fingers of her gloveless hand. He was looking down at something, staring as though to work out what it was.

Violin hen. Eh—violin? Nice, a violin. A like that stuff, classical music and that. She shook her head thinking about it. Victorian melodrama as they chittered in the twilight under the university spire—Hearts and Flowers. But she said nothing. Knew enough by this time not to respond to remarks, even harmless ones, about being *on the fiddle* or *doing requests*, or any of the other fatuous to obscene things some men assumed a lassie carrying a violin case was asking for. Anyway, the bus was coming now: she could hear it. Good timing. She turned for the pleasure of watching it approach: twin haloes of deliverance.

This one do you? A 59?

She couldn't hear his answer for the searing of brakes. He seemed ready enough to get on, though his hands stretching out full, paddling towards the pole to prepare for the assault on the platform. She shunted the case to one side with her foot and moved with him. The conductress hauled while she pushed till he was inside, clutching the pole. Then he swivelled suddenly to face her.

Cheerio hen and A have to thank you very much, very much indeed. Yiv been kind to me yi have that. He was leaning out dangerously and shaking her hand uncomfortably tightly in both of his, the pole propping his chest. She nodded in what she hoped was a reassuring way, weary. She hadn't the heart left to explain she had meant to get on too, this was her bus as well. She just kept patting and shaking at his hand; giving up to it. He felt daft enough already and it would take forever to pantomime through. She wasn't in any hurry, could easily wait for the next one. Parting shot then. What's the name? What do they call you eh?

The conductress and driver looked but the engine continued to purr neutrally. Her smile was as much for them: indulge it a wee bit longer?

Me? He was pleased. Pat, am Pat Gallagher hen. Pat.

Cheerio then Pat. See you and look after yourself a wee bit better in future eh?

His face changed then, remembering. He hesitated for a second, baring his teeth, then he spat, suddenly vicious.

Aye. Keep away from bastart women, that's what yi do. Filth. Dirty whooers and filth the lot a them, the whole bloody lot. Get away fi me bitchahell—and he lunged a fist. It wasn't well-aimed and she had enough of a glimpse to see it come. It didn't connect: just made her totter back a few steps; enough for the driver to seize this as his moment and drive off, chasing an already sliding schedule.

She stood on the pavement and watched till it went round the corner, then stood on watching the space where it had been. After a moment, she shut her mouth again and pulled up her coat collar. Warm enough now just as well there was no one about, though she looked round to check and shrugged to be casual just in case. The spire was still there across the road; still beautiful, still peaceful. Snow feathered about and nothing moved behind the gates. No difference. Thankful, she leaned back against the stop: it would be a while yet. Then she remembered the case and stooped to lift it out of the snow, leaving a free-standing drift where it had been. Didn't want it to get too cold, go out of tune. Not as though it was her own. Then, unexpectedly, she felt angry; violently, bitterly angry. The money in her pocket cut into her hand. Who did he think he was, lashing out at people like that? And what sort of bloody fool was she, letting him? What right had he? What right had any of them? She'd show him. She'd show the whole bloody lot of them. Shaking, she snatched up the fiddle case and glared at the hill. To hell with this waiting. There were other ways, other things to do. Take the underground; walk, dammit. Walk.

She crossed the road, defying the slush underfoot, making a start up the other side of the hill.